Vicariously

Me

A NOVEL

DP Fletcher

Vicariously Me is a work of fiction. Names, characters, businesses, places, events and incidents are either the products of the author's imagination or used in a fictitious manner. Any resemblance to actual persons, living or dead, events, or locales is entirely coincidental.

Published in the United States by Six Gun Publishing, Arkansas.

Originally published by Amazon KDPublishing, in 2013.

ISBN-13:
978-1494258405

ISBN-10:
1494258404

PRINTED IN THE UNITED STATES OF AMERICA

www.amazon.com

LIBRARY OF CONGRESS CATALOGING-IN-PUBLICATION DATA
Coming Soon

For Granddad

He's a walking contradiction… partly truth… and partly fiction.

Kristofferson

DP Fletcher

Forward

Now in my late forties, I am looking back more and more often. I want to remember the friends I had as a boy, the dances we went to, high speed bicycle ramps over tin garbage cans, the hunting trips with my grandfather, the rodeos I competed in, the motorcycle races in dust or mud, riding my Harley on mountain roads… becoming part of a rock and roll band. I am running out of fantasies.

I am living the ultimate dream. I have no schedule to live by, other than mother-nature's. My wife is beautiful, and she will always be twenty years younger than me. Our kids are intelligent, athletic, and brave. Yep, life is good.

So how did all this happen? I ask myself this question as I ride around our property on my John Deere tractor, the grasshoppers flittering around my head. It's been a long road really, although in a relatively short amount of time.

I hear people say I'm rich, with implications I was born lucky. To them I say a resounding Fuck You. To them I say, I dared to dream, and I took the risks. I also did the work necessary to be successful, usually a substantial amount more work than the competition was willing to put in. I bared the criticism, and took the blame for things even when I wasn't guilty. I paid my debt when I was, by God. I paid the price, many times. In my mind, all the world's a stage, and I am the main character. In other words, I don't just listen to the music, I live the songs.

When I was a boy, my paternal grandmother, herself a home economics teacher, always encouraged me to write. I figured out long ago that everyone has a story to tell. I wanted mine to be an exciting and adventurous one. Enjoy.

Vicariously Me,

D.P. Fletcher

Vicariously Me

Chapter One

Crazy Bitch!

I tried to open them, but my eyelids weighed a ton each, and all I could manage was the slightest opening of the left eye. My right one didn't seem to be working at all. I lay there, wondering where I might be this time. Not that I cared a whole lot. *By the way, what day is this? And why does my back feel like it's on fire?*

My head spinning like a drunken saucer, I heard and felt the moaning. Then I felt my cock enlarging and something warm and wet surrounding it. Holding up my head with my hands, I finally cranked my eyelids open and looked down to see the top of her head, bobbing up and down and taking me in her mouth. I wondered and tried to recall where I was and what I was doing there. I could recall I was going to a party. *This must be it.*

It was a party to be held at Bobby Ritchie's house. Bobby to his friends, was actually white Detroit rapper turned southern rocker, Kid Rock. Rock and I met backstage at one of his concerts in L.A. a few years back. We've been like brothers ever since. He and I both had father issues and anger management problems. And we were pimps. Together, we were like gasoline and fire. Fortunately, we chose careers that made being bad a commodity.

The girl, whoever she was, had long bleach-blonde hair, and it flowed all over my thighs and stomach. She smelled cheap I thought… the usual party mix of Chanel and Marlboro Lights. I was nauseous, and though my organ was only half erect, she got me hard enough to think she would mount me. I realized that she thought I was still unconscious , and was trying to molest me without any concern for whether I was awake to enjoy it or not.

"Get off me you crazy bitch!" as I grabbed her by the arms and slung her to the side between the mattress on the floor and the set of steal barbells. "Jesus! What the fuck are you trying to do?" Yeah, even I was shocked at my response. I don't know why. I just got pissed that's all. Hey, don't judge me until you've been there.

"I want your baby Johnny", she whispered, way too calmly, except that she was still trying to catch her breath, and saliva dangled from her chin. "I want to have your baby" she repeated as if I might change my mind due to her sincerity. But, man, she had those crazy eyes. You know, like she didn't blink, and her eyes were wide open, like a crazed vampire.

"Get the fuck out! NOW! Get out you crazy fucking Bitch!" And before I knew it I was upright, buttoning my jeans and pushing her out the door. My heart was pounding out of my chest from the sudden tension… my eyes now wide open and beaming with surprise. *What a way to wake up. And why is my back burning?*

I couldn't help but laugh out loud at the situation. *I'll probably write about this someday.*

She picked her white blouse up from the floor where she had apparently laid it prior to her attempt to rape me, and repeated again, "Johnny… I'll take care of our baby, and you can ride..."

"You're crazy!" I thought for a moment I might fuck her anyway, for she was very sultry and sexy, standing there in the hallway, her black lace bra in direct contrast to the plaid school girl skirt hanging flirtatiously on her hips, and I tried hard to remember if I knew this crazy female… but only for a moment. Her mind was obviously a little tilted to one side, and so, if I did know her, this was a damn good time to end the relationship.

"Johnny… I think you're the sexiest man in the whole world. I love the way you talk. I love the way you walk. I love everything about you."

As I was laughing at her, with spit still hanging from her lip, and mascara smeared on her pink cheeks. "You are sooo scaring me right now!"

And she just stood there in the hallway, looking like some freaky chick in a horror movie… quietly, deliberately giving me her pitiful look.

"You don't know me!" I yelled, uncharacteristically. And with that I pushed the door shut, leaving her standing there in all her glory. She banged her fists on the heavy wooden door a few times, simultaneously shouting belittling slurs for a few seconds. "You're a faggot!" "You can't handle this!" "You're scared!" And I'm thinking, *Wow, that was a close one!*

I waited until I heard her say "Mother Fucker" and walk away.

I sat on the edge of the mattress, sheets tangled and damp in a wad in the center of the bed, and long, narrow, faded streaks of blood on the mattress cover… a pair of pink lace panties on the floor between my legs, and a black bikini top twirling above my head from the mahogany ceiling fan. I checked to see if I had my wallet, and remembered I stopped carrying one because I kept losing it at parties.

I had visions of three women all doing at me once. One had pink underwear on, another had a black string bikini, and the other nothing at all.

My boots were on, but they were wet. I gazed out the open window to the ocean below. I was at Bobby's house in Carmel. Bobby called a few friends over… a couple of days ago, I figured, and I had come over last night for a little jam session with Bobby's band and the party grew from there, as usual. *I don't know who that crazy bitch was*, still putting the pieces together, smirking as I considered it.

Judging by the aftertaste in my mouth, I got drunk on straight Kentucky Bourbon, and smoked way too many cigars and cigarettes.

I made my way to the bedroom door to make sure SHE was gone, and saw the other rooms down the hallway all had closed doors, each with some… thing… hanging from their door knobs…. One bedroom door knob had burgundy colored panties hanging from it. Another had a man's white crew sock hanging from it, and one door knob even had a condom over it. There were clothes strewn down the hall and onto the stairway leading down to the marble tile below. I navigated the dark wooden stairs slowly, surveying the bodies that lie just beyond. There were people sleeping everywhere. I remembered a movie I saw one late night, or more probably early morning, while an English major at LSU. *Caligula.*

I went to the game room, where I slowly remembered being for some time the night before. There was a nude blonde sleeping on the pool table, and some guy eating a slice of cold pizza and licking her between the thighs as she slept. I paused as if about to step in and save the girl, then she seemed to moan with some half-asleep, half-awake prompt for the strange man to keep licking and eating, and pulled his face into her. I could hear music playing, faintly in the background. *Rock Star by Nickelback.*

Smoke drifted in and out of the interior spaces. I slumbered through the living area, stepping over bodies, some clothed, some not. I got to the kitchen where I saw Slash, the Rock and Roll Hall of Fame guitarist from Guns, and two Russian models smoking a joint and laughing at a Shitzu poodle doing flips on the slick tile floor. Apparently the little dust mop was stoned too. One of the girls spoke to me, pointing to her backside, and then pointing at me. I couldn't understand her broken English in my current state, and it hurt too much to try very hard. In this case, however, it was obvious we either already did it, or we probably would. I waved politely, and kept on toward the interior door that led to what used to be a four car garage.

Bobby had another garage built around the rear of the house. The old garage had been turned into a jam room, complete with acoustical tiles on the walls and ceiling, Marshalls and surround sound Peaveys. There were guitars galore! I used to just walk around looking and fondling all the fucking guitars. Collector stuff. Classic Fenders, vintage Martins, antique Gibsons. Bobby liked to hang here and play music with his buddies. Which worked out well because I liked hanging out with musicians. I'd always wanted to be one, but didn't have the patience to learn.

Willie Nelson, Kris Kristofferson, Johnny Cash, Hank, Jr.... and Kid Rock... were my singing heroes. For neither one had any singing ability by conventional standards, and yet they sang anyway. They expressed themselves from places deep in their souls, shot the bird at their critics and just sang anyway!

The jam room, labeled "My Sanctuary" in reddish brown blood on a white door, I thought had been preserved. Not a soul in sight at first, but I heard someone moan. It came from behind the Baby Grand... there two translucent bone-skinny people with most of their clothes off, sat leaning against the wall, rubber bands on their arms and shooting heroin. I walked over to check it out... it was Courtney Love and Scott Weiland of STP and Velvet Pistols fame. Slash invited Scott, but when we saw Courtney and Scott together, we knew he'd fallen off the train again. I remembered the two last night looking to score China White. I, was curious about the drug that seemed to nurture creativity among the rock world, but not stupid enough to stick needles in my arm. I just stood there gazing upon the two wretches. Courtney was passed out, mascara running down her face and bright red lipstick smeared around her mouth. Scott looked at me, and didn't know or care who I was. *Doesn't look fun to me.*

"Only way to turn up the quiet", he said to me before his eyes rolled back into his head.

As Scott went on his magical mystery tour, I turned and found my way to the back patio, where the pool side guests had started to stir and come back to life, against a purple sky over a violet sea... subtle tones that pleased hung-over eyeballs. I could hear laughter and conversation coming from behind the concrete water fountain, which I now remembered as the centerpiece for the foam party. *The foam party… that's why my boots are wet.*

Someone got the great idea of pouring an entire bottle of banana colada foam bath into the concrete water fountain last night, which turned the laid-back affair into what may have been the party of the year. Men and models doffed their clothes and frolicked in the bubbles that at the highest point were about nipple level. Remembering the scene brought an instant smile to my face. I walked closer and could tell it was Bobby talking to a rather short, skinny brunette, with seven inch stilettoes.

"Hey, Johnny. You survived it I see. Hey Man, this is… ahhhhh..." Bobby couldn't fill in the blank, and I knew the sign. Bobby and I were always bailing each other out.

"Hi," I quickly stepped toward the girl with no name and reached for her hand. "I'm Johnny."

"Hi, Johnny. I'm Juliet. Akshully, we met last nat," she stated with a thick southern accent, holding her slender tanned hand out to grip mine.

"Nice to meet you… again", I said back to her timidly.

"So", said Bobby with a grin, in his favorite maroon and white checkered fedora, his long stringy sandy blonde hair hanging down to his shoulders and smoking a big fat illegal Cuban.

"How was she?" Bobby had one of those sheepish grins that just always made you think he was up to something.

"WHO was she?" I asked quickly, scratching my head. I don't think either one of us knew what the other one was talking about, and it didn't matter. No one else knew either.

Bobby broke out in to a loud uproar that startled Juliet, shattered the morning silence and echoed through the Carmel mansion.

"Who? Well ain't that just like you, Man." Bobby, Kid Rock to the outside world, had a scruffy voice made by years of yelling into a mic, drinking straight whiskey and smoking joints, cigarettes and cigars. "I introduce you to one of the hottest chicks in Europe and you can't fuckin' remember the favor. Fuck me, Johnny!" He was doing his impression of the Godfather.

I stood there, leaning against one of the many teak tables at poolside, and thinking *I will never, never, never, drink again.* With a blank look in my eyes, I said, "I honestly don't remember Bobby. Who?"

"Ta-she-ann-a!" Bobby emphasizing each syllable so I could read his lips. Bobby knew a hangover when he saw one. "She's the Russian model I told you about. You two started talkin' last night, and, shit. You don't remember?"

"Yeah, I'm starting to… the Ukraine."

"What?" asked Bobby quickly.

You said she was from Russia… Where is she?"

"Hell if I know, Man." Bobby had an unmistakable Michigan accent. No matter how hard he tried, he could never get away from the wealthy gated community lifestyle in which he was raised. His father was the owner of several automobile dealerships in suburban Detroit, around the Romeo area, back when the economy was booming under trickle-down economics. But Dad and Son simply never found that common ground… time together just for the sake of it. Bobby was resentful of it, and also because when Bobby went all rebel by dressing, acting and talking ghetto, his father gave him the ultimatum to shape up or move out. Not quite the kind of attention he was aiming for. So, Bobby left the comforts of his dad's golf course lifestyle, and went to the ghetto. Nowadays, he was a man of varied tastes and style. But he made the style his own, when no one else would have had the balls. Now kids dress like him, men emulate him, parents complain about his lyrics, and then buy the CDs and the concert tickets and the tee shirts.

I related to Bobby on many levels. We both had bad relationships with our fathers, and our anger issues played perfectly with our bad boy images. We both were pussy hounds. And we were both single fathers.

Now, the Ukrainian girl… I could recall meeting her. I recalled she had good teeth, unlike so many Russian and Ukraine women. I could even remember talking most of the night. But I couldn't recall anything else yet. *Too many concussions… too much alcohol… too many pain pills.*

Just then, Juliet reached out to my shoulder and turned my back to them. "Why is your back bleeding?" she asked with a sense of horror.

"What? I thought that burnin' feeling was odd."

"Dude, your back is covered in scratches!" Bobby proclaimed with his cigar clinched between his teeth.

"Yeah, like you have skin missing! You poor thang", Juliet said, the concern showing on her face.

I smiled all of a sudden. *Oh yeah, NOW I remember.*

"Look at 'im smilin'! You kinky whore!" Bobby shouted and punched me in the chest.

"What day is it?" I asked the girl. I knew not to ask Bobby.

"Sun-day", Juliet said with a Georgia twang, who was now hanging on to Bobby's arm and tugging at him to walk inside the house with her.

"Bobby", turning my head away from her gaze, "… I'm gonna crash out for a while… sleep off my drunk. You goin' anywhere?"

"No Man. I've gotcha back…" to which he began laughing loudly and bragging to Juliet about his play on words. "Sleep in my room so I can know which room to protect, you know what I mean? And don't sleep under the fuckin' covers. I fuck in that bed!"

†

The next day, Monday, mid-morning… I crawled off the covered mattress and into the bathroom. The bedroom was very formal, as if Bobby had bought it furnished or the interior decorator got it all wrong… totally unlike Bobby, but had a really cool walk-in shower, with all sorts of nozzles coming out of the walls. It took me ten minutes just to figure out how to turn everything on. The steam was incredible.

I couldn't find any clean looking towels or wash cloths… or soap. There was a half full bottle of Suave 2-n-1 shampoo, which I used to lather up. The whole scene reminded me of college, only a much fancier bathroom. The shower was exactly what I needed to get back in operation. The body I'd been blessed with had been so abused over the years, and the healing process was impeded more and more by my own reckless behavior as much as it was my age.

My age, by the way, was kind of a secret. That is to say, years prior, while filling out my PBR Member card, I added a few years to my birth year. Besides family, only my manager knew my real age, which was, then, thirty-four. No one ever cared enough to look it up in public records. I'd always looked ten years younger, so Ari thought it would lengthen my career if everyone believed I was really in my twenties. Or, better yet, he said, "Don't give 'em reason to wonder." Worst case would be that folks would get downright confused by the conflicting reports of my age.

"Your viewing public is entertained by seeing a twenty-something year old man do the things they wished they had the balls to do. Your career'll last longer, too. Mark my words." And by career, he meant more than just bull riding… he had bigger plans for me. My profile was in all the rodeo programs… my false name, my false age, my false hometown… You could Google me, and the bio had been written by a publicist whom Ari hired. Due to the "secret", I tried to avoid talking to the press, for fear I'd give it away somehow, which, as it turned out, made me the "strong silent type" as I was described by a female reporter for Yahoo Sports. Here is an excerpt from the article.

After seeing last night's performance, it would be difficult for anyone to deny that Johnny Outlaw is truly a man among men, both in the arena and out.

On the night this interview took place, he went on to win the Atlanta Invitational just two short hours later. He did so even after suffering a concussion last weekend in St. Louis, and dislocating his shoulder in the process. But that was last week. On this night, you couldn't have scripted it any better.

After two rounds it was Outlaw, against the 'Brazilian Mafia' of Jose "Quervo" Martinez and former world champ Adrianro Morias. Outlaw drew the 'rankest' of the three bulls, named 666, increasing his chances for a higher score, if he could stay on. Four points separated the three men. In the end, Johnny Outlaw would be king. And the crowd roared!

But that isn't all. Afterward, he was arrested outside a well-known gentleman's club on the west end of town, and taken to jail for assault and battery. According to the police report, numerous eyewitnesses came forward and gave similar accounts… that the cowboy was defending the honor of one of the female employees of the club, and though Mr. Outlaw did not throw the first punch, he did throw the last one.

The next day it was reported by the Memphis Herald that Johnny Outlaw donated his entire winnings from the Atlanta Invitational, one hundred thousand dollars, to St. Jude Children's Hospital.

So let's look at this again. Johnny Outlaw rides three two-thousand pound man-stomping bulls to victory… shortly after suffering a concussion and separated shoulder the week before. To celebrate, he beats up a bully while defending a stripper, signs autographs for guards at the county 'pokie', and the next morning flies to Memphis to give his award money away to sick kids.

Boy, if only football players were still that way.

It was a flattering article, and caused my name, Johnny Outlaw, to trend on Yahoo for a week.

†

The hot shower and steam provided lubrication for my aching joints. I tried to clear my mind, to get focused, on where I was actually supposed to be, almost regretting coming to the party at all. I would need to get to my car, get my cell and wallet, then call my agent. Ari would know.

Ari Pei was sort of a babysitter to the bad boy stars. And why not? At a cool fifteen percent of the gross take, Ari was one of the wealthiest managers in Hollywood. At the time, he represented the Kid, Slash, and Charlie Sheen of Two and a Half Men. Ari profited taking care of, and propagating, bad boys like us. Slash was born Saul Hudson in Hampstead, London to a black mother who was a costume designer for rock stars like David Bowie and Elton John. His English father was an artist who designed album covers for artists like Neil Young and Joni Mitchell. So he was always around crazy, drugged out rockers as a child. In his teens, Saul told me he was a problem child, mostly due to his mother's abandonment of him to pursue her career, and his father, who was a mean drunk. Like me, Saul ended up with is grandparents. Charlie was just a spoiled rich kid, born and raised in the Hollywood façade, and knew how to exploit the entire business. I had nothing in common with him, except women, drugs, and booze… which was enough.

I sat on a granite bench that was built into the wall, where one of the jet nozzles could be focused on my ruptured disk. The scar on my back, where the skin had been torn and shredded by the Black Plague's jagged-edged horns, and skillfully sewn back, was tightening at the edges. The nerves were cut too, which gave a weird sensation when the water jets hit it. I sat rubbing my knees, moving my feet back and forth to limber up the ankles and toes that had been broken in the chutes so many times.

My God, I considered more thoughtfully than ever before… *What the hell am I doing this for?* And then, like a dream sequence in some movie, I closed my eyes and recalled images from my past, one by one… The boys being born… cutting the chords… Marshall holding up his tiny fist and holding his breath until his little face turned beet red, showing his frustration that the bottle wasn't getting to his mouth fast enough… young Matthew always smiling and laughing so hard he could rarely finish a wrestling match… my mom talking on the phone to her female friends about injustices they encountered at work, and smoking her cigarettes while she stirred the hamburger helper in the green skillet… my dad's face as he walked away with his stripper girlfriend… my first Golden Retriever running through the fields of amber tipped sedge, his ears and tail flopping in the wind…. Gran-Gran, cooking and smiling in her kitchen, food always present on the countertop that separated the kitchen from the den…. My granddaddy with his Busch beer and flat top hair-cut, sitting on the front porch in his Red Wing ranch boots and khaki pants and shirt, swatting flies and complaining about the blue-jays… fishing on Lake Vernon in an aluminum flat-bottom boat for the first time by myself… gigging frogs in the middle of the night with Uncle David.

I was in the shower for what seemed like an hour, until the hot water began to run warm, and I snapped out of my euphoric state, reversing my prior start-up operation, and turning everything off… except the heat lamp in the ceiling… the heat felt great against what was otherwise a cold and bare tile floor. I dried off by pushing the water beads off my body with my hands while standing under the huge heat lamp, and did my best to brush my teeth with my finger, using a tiny dab of 2-n-1 shampoo for toothpaste, and the wet tip of my shirt… ran my fingers through what was now long sandy brown hair, and I noticed in the mirror, I was starting to grey. Grey in my receding hair, and on my chin. It was a gradual enough change that, even though I'd always noticed, it was never enough to warrant a whole lot of attention. I was in the sun a lot, which streaked my hair anyway. Most of the glam shots and paparazzi photos showed me in a hat and sunglasses at night, these days. But now, all of a sudden, it seemed very pronounced, and there were wrinkles in my forehead and around my eyes from squinting all the time.

Why I squinted all the time was because from the age of twelve I needed glasses. I told my mom that the reason I made a bad grade was because I couldn't see the blackboard. I figured this would at the very least, excuse the bad grade and at worst get me moved up to the front row. But Mom brought me to Sears for an eye exam, where I learned I would be "wearing glasses for the rest of your life." Huge backfire! My ego was devastated. I tried contacts but they were too hard to get on my eyeballs at seven a.m., so they just dried up in their case under the bathroom sink. Lasik worked well, but "the squint", as it was referred to in the press, looked very James Dean-like I was told once by Rebecca.

“Ahhh… that’s why I don’t look in mirrors”, I said out loud with disgust. I checked my shoulders and face for any renegade hairs that might have slipped through a prior inspection, which I had become more conscious of lately.

After donning my jeans and plaid pearl snap, western style shirt, with my trademark tightly rolled up sleeves, for which Bolo was willing to pay a cool million to get my endorsement, I strolled out to the pool one last time to say bye to Bobby.

But the whole place looked deserted. Just bottles, cans and food scattered everywhere… empty pizza boxes. I didn’t work very hard at finding any signs of life, grabbed my custom made black beaver felt cowboy hat with the bull rider’s crease, and just walked out the front door… huge glass and gold trimmed doors that made me feel small. At least that’s how I was feeling as I saw daylight for the first time in a week… small.

Oddly enough, there were no vehicles out front of the Kid Rock party mansion in Carmel. Only my almost all original 1977 Special Edition Pontiac Trans-Am, L78 four hundred big-block, black with gold trim, Hurst T-tops, gold honeycomb rims and the big gold metal-flake firebird on the scooped hood. Only 748 of these hot rods were ever built.

Space tape trimmed the dash, and the car was equipped with a 384 four speed manual shift tranny. I could burn rubber in all four gears. It was my dream car, and the first thing I bought for myself after my first PBR World Championship, three years before. I'd recently had the vinyl seats redone in tan deer skin, and the fresh smell of leather permeated my nostrils and pleased the senses.

It was a sunny but cool morning in Carmel, and I, Johnny Outlaw, had come an awful long way since leaving home an angry but determined and driven individual… all those years ago.

By the time in my career when I was the champion of the world, and famous people from LA and New York began asking ME to join THEM for fancy dinner parties and late night binges… I was like… *Hey motherfuckers, I'm supposed to be here. I'm the one ya'll keep singin about and makin movies about. I've done it. Hollywood ain't got nothing on me. I'm what ya'll try to be.*

I didn't say it with words. Well, maybe I did once or twice. But, mostly, I said it by saying nothing, like Clint would have. I said it with the way I entered the room, as James Bond might. I said it with the way I looked at the biggest guy in the bar like I could kick his ass any at any moment… and I could back it up, because I was never afraid to bleed. I said it with the way I returned their stares, as women in their designer gowns, married or not, gazed at me from across large rooms.

By now I knew, that people are just people. Everyone seemed to have an angle, a gimmick. No one was really who or what they seemed to be. It doesn't matter where they came from, or where they ended up, rich and famous or dirt poor and forgotten, we all shit the same. Everyone… and I mean everybody… has a story. I told myself that, before ever entering an arena, a stage, or a set.

I drove down Pacific Coast Highway, thinking first of Burt Reynolds in Smokey and The Bandit, pushing my black cowboy hat back on my head where it was comfortable, and then considered I should call my mother and let her know I was alright. I picked up my cell, and looked at the contact list. I studied the tricked-out touch screen pad in the dash, and on the FM tuner began to play Kristofferson's "Sunday Morning Coming Down". It was a song I often considered trying to record on my own, at some pay-as-you-go private recording studio out in some country town where no one would know. That way I'd be covered if it sucked. I would do so ten years later.

I always sang to myself when I was hung over, as a way to keep my mind off the nausea and headache. And so I set down my cell in the passenger seat, and turned up the volume... the road wind now blowing the cobwebs away through the tee tops above, my boggled mind clearing against the seashore, smiling involuntarily, smoking a spliff and just… being.

Chapter Two

The Stripper and the Old Black Lady

When I was a boy, we moved a lot, but never ventured far from the southeastern Louisiana region. The first time I saw snow was when we were living on the grounds of the Louisiana State Penitentiary, in Angola. It's in the Tunica Hills, the only hill country in the bayou state. My Great-Uncle Wingate, on my mother's side, was the warden of the prison, and hired my dad to be the athletic director, who went on to found the now famous Angola Prison Rodeo, which, to this day, draws an annual crowd in the thousands to watch convicts give their all against the meanest bulls and broncos anywhere. The convicts' reward… injuries that might get them a week in the infirmary, or if they win, a roar from the cheering fans who've traveled from all over a three state area to witness the craziness. Their goal, I was told by Uncle Wingate, was to "get to go to da hospital wuhd so they don't have to stay in de-uh cell".

The three of us lived in a small red brick two bedroom, one bath house outside the prison fences. I can remember seeing the prisoners, mostly black, wearing vintage black and white stripes, working in the fields, chained together at the ankles, pulling weeds in the crops of mustard greens, cabbages, potatoes, tomatoes, corn… you name it, if they cooked it in the prison, "it was grown ratch heuh". Uncle Wingate, his pants pulled high over his oversized belly to his belly button, would brag with a sloppy wet cigar in his mouth, chin up high and proud like a big shot "Looziana Politission". Granddad, my mom's father, would say that describing his brother-in-law, "Wingate", as just a "wanna-be Governor". Louisiana governors were always critical characters with lots of unbridled and often corrupt power… and the warden was the governor inside the razor wire fences of the Angola prison.

The guards, in blue uniforms, were on horseback carrying shot-guns and wearing dark sun-glasses when a big black car drove by, which was Uncle Wingate "goin' to an impotent meetin'". I don't recall ever seeing my dad while we lived there…just the snow, the prisoners, the guards, Uncle Wingate, and my aunt Helen.

Aunt Helen, actually my maternal grandfather's sister, died suspiciously in her mansion on the grounds, and most folks on momma's side of the family believed whole-heartedly that Uncle Wingate arranged for poor Aunt Helen to be murdered, and was able to cleverly cover up the crime due to his God-like power at the prison. The official determination of Aunt Helen's death, by the prison coroner, was suicide. The irony of this story will show itself later.

At one time, we lived in Waggoman, Louisiana, in a small ranch style rent house. My "Uncle" Roy and his wife and kids lived next door. I was around four years old, and had a wart on the corner of my thumb that was pretty big. Dad came home one night, said he was "tired of looking at that thing", and brought me to the bathroom. He pulled out a pair of pliers, grabbed my hand, and yanked that wart out by the roots. I stood there, never defying him, knees weakening, body trembling, crying at the sight of the blood streaming down the sink, trying to figure out just exactly what a man was supposed to be. I think the vision of the blood pouring out of my thumb, Dad holding my hand over the sink, against my will, though I never did anything about it… the pliers in his hand… that's the reason I still feel it. I have dreams about it to this day.

My next most powerful memories are when I was about six. I remember my mom and dad arguing a lot. I remember dad yelling louder than mom could. I remember mom picking up the phone to call the sheriff, whose name was simply "Fontenot" (Pronounced Fontenoe in Cajun) and Dad pulling the phone off the wall. I ran to the closet to hide. In fact, I did that every time they argued. I went into my closet, which had no light, and closed the door, shutting my eyes and ears to the outside world… and praying that God would send me a little brother and make everything better. I would later learn that Mom had two miscarriages after I was born, and that I had a baby brother, who was born premature, and died in the hospital due to insufficient lung capacity. I suppose if he were born that way today, he would survive, what with today's technologies and all.

Many, many, many times I wondered what he would have been like if he had lived. Would he be at all like me… or the opposite? Would I be the black sheep and he the good son?

When I was around seven years old, Dad had a manager's job at a Yamaha motorcycle dealership in Metairie, Louisiana, which was a good 60 miles across the Mississippi River from Belle Chasse, where we lived in a small duplex, next door to the Ostranders, and just down the road from the Porters. Ron Ostrander, Jr. (Ronnie) was a friend of mine, though a couple of years older than me. He was red-headed with lots of freckles, but had a big, strong, tough dad who was a deep sea diver, gone for weeks at a time.

Ronnie's mom, Roxanne, was beautiful, and I had a huge crush on her. She was a tan, California girl with beautiful straight blonde hair and a great smile, and didn't fit in Belle Chasse at all. She looked like a girl in a James Bond film. I used to sneak over and spy on her, using a bucket to stand on and looking over the wooden fence, while she lay out on her lounge chair in her back yard, tanning in the sun. Her favorite bikini… my favorite bikini… was lemon yellow.

One day little Ronnie and I were playing around in a sewer ditch, barefooted, after a rain storm. I stepped on an old rusty hoe, cutting my foot deeply between my toes. Ronnie picked me up, put me in the little green wagon, and pulled me home, running the entire way. It must have been a Sunday, because Dad and Mom were both home. Dad scooped me up. I was crying. Momma was screaming to bring me to the hospital. Dad just put me in the tub, turned on the tap, and grabbed the bottle of alcohol.

"Use the peroxide, damn it!" she yelled at him as he opened the bottle of alcohol.

And, wow, I know that hurt… 'cause I still dream about that, too. I remember it like it was yesterday, just like that wart on my thumb… but I lived. To this day, I get off on pain.

We, like most folks during those days, had a console TV set, the kind you had to get up to turn the channel dial… and three stations, not counting the under-powered, hard to get public broadcasting station. The bigger the antennae the better! Big gas guzzling automobiles were cool, but Mom drove an embarrassing two door six cylinder Ford Maverick, that I swear, sounded like a long chain of farts going off in succession as we puttered to the grocery store, or worse yet... football practice.

The Chevy Luv Van was the "in" thing. Dad had one… Yamaha yellow with a welded chrome chain for a steering wheel and bright metallic gas and brake pedals actually shaped like bare feet. It had a state-of-the-art eight track stereo, and bucket seats. The back windows were round. I remember that well.

It was Christmas and I was two months shy of my eighth birthday. My parents had been living apart for about a year I guess. Temperatures were most probably in the 70s. It was raining, which to me was almost like having it snow on Christmas Eve… although rain was a regular event, well… it was just all we could hope for in the form of any precipitation at all 'cause it sure wasn't going to snow.

It was around 8 pm when Mom and I got home from the Porter's in her little Maverick. I was childishly, stupidly embarrassed about a vehicle that was dependable, economical, showroom clean and worth lots of money in mint condition today.

From the driveway I could see through the windshield that there was a large black garbage bag sitting on the step between the screen door and the hollow, wooden entrance door… I know it was hollow because Dad punched a hole in it one night when Mom was trying to keep him from coming in to get me. It was a Friday night about midnight, and he was supposed to pick me up at 7 pm… five hours I had been waiting… sitting on the couch or laying on the floor in front of the TV, hoping and praying he would pull up any minute in his Corvette. The minutes went by into hours, yet I still wanted to go with him for the weekend, whenever I could get one, and wasn't going to worry about why he was late. He was there, and I wanted out… I wanted to go where the action was. Cool cars, motorcycles, and girls.

Mom and I dragged the big black garbage bag inside out of the rain. I tore it open, to find it was full of toys! A football, a basketball, a baseball glove, lots of little trucks and cars and jeeps… green plastic army men. In hind sight, it was if someone had just gone down the toy aisle at TG&Y and scooped a bunch of stuff up and put it all in the bag, without any consideration for who would receive the gifts. A few minutes later, there was a knock at the door. I heard my mom say "shit", put her cigarette on the ash tray, and open the door. It was him! It was Daddy! I didn't care that it had been months since I last saw him. I didn't care that he didn't send child support payments. I didn't care that he hadn't thought enough to call. He was here now, and that was all I cared about.

His hair was longer now. And he had new glasses that looked more like sunglasses than the black square ones I recalled. His jeans were pressed, creased, flared out at the bottom, overlapping his black leather ankle high boots with zippers on the sides. He wore a fancy paisley shirt with a wide collar and the buttons were undone enough to reveal he had a silver chain around his neck, with a zodiac emblem dangling from it. I remember it was the first time I saw a digital watch. It was silver with a red face, and the time came up whenever you pushed the button on the side. It was as if he had gone away to some other planet and came back looking so different. Mom was not happy to see him, claiming he had "shown up unannounced", and reminding him she still hadn't seen the child support check that was supposedly in the mail.

"And how dare you buy all these toys when I barely have enough money to buy his school clothes!"

Here we go again, I thought, and grabbed Daddy's arm and walked him outside. Mom yelling "you can't go out there in the rain, you'll catch pneumonia!"… Dad saying to her that we would sit in the van for a while and talk. And we did.

When he opened the door the interior light came on, and I could see her.

"Son, this is Maria", he said.

"Maria, this is my son."

"Nice to meet you… I've heard so much about you. Climb on in here, and sit in the bean bag chair." Words poured out of her moist, gloss covered lips.

So I did.

I didn't know quite what to think. I saw him so differently now. He looked more like Peter Fonda than the cowboy I remembered. I saw the Easy Rider poster right next to Farah Fawcett's poster in the Ben Franklin dime store. And Maria was different, too. She looked like the make-up counter ladies at DH Holmes in the mall. She wore make-up, and perfume, and dressed like no woman I'd ever known personally, except maybe Mrs. Ostrander… her blouse button undone revealing her cleavage, high heel shoes, painted toe nails. And her hair… was what I'd heard my mom refer to as "peroxide blonde" when we saw Miss Bush at the Ben Franklin. My head was spinning; I didn't know what to say to the stranger. My heart was hurting that my dad seemed to have found a new friend to take my mom's place… and where would that leave me?

All of a sudden I felt something cold and wet on my arm as I was sitting on the floor of the van in the bean-bag chair. It was a puppy… a cute little beagle-looking puppy. I would later find out this was a beagle mixed with Heinz 57, and picked up for free at the SPCA. But I loved the puppy immediately. She would be the answer to all my lonely nights and no one to play with all day. Maria? I later found out she was a stripper at a club in downtown New Orleans. And she did have fake blonde hair.

I can hear Mom now, "We can't afford a dog! Who's going to take care of that thing? How am I going to afford to feed it?" Of course she was totally justified in her anger and frustration at my father, but, being a kid, I just didn't want to see it.

Then Dad said they had to be getting back across the big bridge, which was the Greater New Orleans Mississippi River Bridge. And just like that, they drove away as I walked back to the old screen door in the rain, with my new dog… not a brother… and my dad drove away to his new life without me.

It didn't take long for Mom to get used to the puppy. Like she said, though, she was the one who ended up taking care of the potty training, the feeding, and the vet bills. It was the fact that Dad didn't consider the burden it put on an already tough situation that made her so angry. Somehow, the dog got the name "Wendy", which to this day I don't know how. Perhaps it was named Wendy at the SPCA, or maybe Mom made it up… though I have no idea why she would have called it Wendy for Christ's sake. I mean, it was after all a boy's dog. I think I would have named it something like Wonder dog, or Jake, or something… anything other than Wendy!

Eventually my parents were divorced, and I would not see my dad again for months and even then for only short weekends. I did, however, see him one night, unexpectedly. I was riding my bicycle through the White Oaks Estates, where the glamorous young Monica Bush lived, hoping to see her sitting out on her driveway. Instead, I saw a silver-blue Corvette Stingray, with t-tops off and windows down, driving away from the Bush home. The car drove right passed me. In it, my father and the glamorous Miss Bush, Monica's mother from the Ben Franklin Five and Dime. I hadn't seen or heard from him in several months, and there he was, just a mile from where I lived, and more than 60 miles away from where he called home, which broke my heart as they drove by, not even recognizing me.

From the ages of 7 until I was 12, I might have seen him three times.

My mother had a nervous breakdown after losing a prematurely born son, and after her husband left her for "the stripper". I, at eight years of age, was living with my mother only part time, and more and more with my grandparents, who themselves had already raised a daughter and four sons.

My grandparents were of the Greatest Generation. They suffered through dust bowls, world wars and the Great Depression. I still remember the plain black and white labels of generic food packages I grew up on in their home. Cheese that looked like it had been dropped from a cargo plane in Africa. I once explained to Granddaddy, "I want the good stuff. I want soft toilet paper!" I had, in fact, everything a boy growing up with my grandparents could ever need. Love. Care. A big and roomy, red brick house on a slope overlooking the canal that led to Vernon Lake. "Nothing fancy", Granddaddy would remind his grandchildren… "But it's always here for you." I can close my eyes and smell the pine floors, along with every meal ever cooked there… and the faint hint of moth balls on warm wool blankets.

†

As the only son of a divorced and abandoned mother, one of the original "latch-key" kids, growing up in a place I considered the arm-pit of the world, escapism was all I had. And escape I did.

My escape was through the movies. Reruns, primetime shows, cinemas. My favorites were James Bond films, Clint Eastwood spaghetti westerns, Steve McQueen in anything, and black and white Elvis movies. Sean Connery was the coolest James Bond ever. Tough but sophisticated, and could talk any woman out of her panties. Clint had his dirty wind-swept hair, the eyes always squinting, smoking a roll-your-own cigarette, never in a hurry, and fast with his pistols. This cowboy had no creases, and his boots were always dusty. McQueen… quiet and mysterious, a daredevil on a motorcycle, and always grinning… made others think he was up to something. Elvis, in King Creole or Jailhouse Rock… The sinister smirk represented rebellion, and the pelvic thrust moves were straight from the devil himself.

The similarities were apparent even then. I knew as a boy growing up in the bayous of Belle Chasse, on the Mississippi River, that tuxedoes and cowboy hats were in my future. I learned from James Bond that women were to be treated as lovers. Merely tell them the things they need to hear, touch them at the right times and in the right places, and they are putty in your hands. Clint taught me that silence could be damn intimidating, especially if your opponents see that you're not afraid to bleed. McQueen showed me that there was dignity in being humble, and to let my actions speak for themselves. Elvis, well… he had the perfect looks, all the right moves, the smile, the personality… his own style. And to top it all off he could sing. He also taught me that even the best looking, singing, dancing, acting, womanizing men in the world get old, lose their hair, get fat and die.

One day, my mother had come home from work, only to be greeted by me with the horrible news that Elvis was dead. She slapped me across the face, pointed her nervous finger between my eyes, and told me never to joke like that again.

"Look Mom, it's on TV", I said. She cried and called in sick to work for the next three days. So did most of her female friends.

I knew from that moment, that some people, even strangers, can have the most personal impact on others. Absent a father figure, I drew my examples of what a man was supposed to be by watching them do it on the movie screen. I was the leading man in my own mind, sang like a rock star, always won the fights, and the prettiest girl in town cried when I rode away.

Life, for me, was an imitation of art. And I was the leading man. Only, in my script, the actor really does his own stunts. He flies without a net.

Parented by a divorced, stubborn, high-school diploma toting beautiful young secretary to the administrator of the state school for retarded children, I must have been the perfect example of premature delinquency. She spent her week days working a mundane servitude existence, often the subject of peer worker criticism centered on rumors of an affair. She worked eight to five, with plenty of overtime, drove thirty miles home each week day to stir up the hamburger helper, while talking on the phone and chain smoking cigarettes. When I was twelve she even married a man she didn't love, Ed Murphy, just so I could have a nicer home with a big back yard and a father figure in my life. Two years later they divorced amid scandal, and I forced him from the home he paid for with the four-ten shotgun he bought me.

I remember coming home one afternoon from playing football with the neighborhood kids, and seeing Ed visibly angry, and Mom crying. This was a first for me. I had never seen Ed so much as raise his voice to my mother. In fact, I always had a lack of respect for the man, for letting Momma boss him around all the time. But I knew right away something was terribly wrong. I walked in, and Ed immediately looked at me and held up to my face a receipt that he said was a motel bill where Mom and her boss slept together on a business trip. The whole world began to spin again, just like that time when I met Maria.

Momma was yelling at Ed, "Don't do that to him!"

I ran into my room, but wasn't going to hide in the closet anymore… I was thirteen now. I grabbed my four-ten shotgun… the one Ed gave me for Christmas… loaded it with a slug, and ran back to the living room. I pointed at Ed's head, and told him to leave. It was a tense moment, my knees rattling, my hands shaking, lips quivering… neither of us knowing if I had the guts to pull the trigger or not. But a few seconds later, Ed relented, and quietly… ashamedly… walked out the door… and out of my life… forever.

It was at that time I began drinking any alcoholic beverage I could get my hands on… Boones Farm wine, Miller Lite ponies, cheap vodka… I started wearing my hair long, wore black rock and roll tee shirts to school every day, dropped my grades from above average to below… way below.

At fourteen, out of boredom and frustration, I and a friend of mine named Whitney Cass, whose father was our bus driver, and whose mom was a ganja smoking flower child, stole my former step-father's brand new GMC conversion van. Back then, it was The Thing to have, much like SUVs are today. Whitney also had three very hot sisters, all blondes and older than either one of us. The girls were rumored to be skiing in the intra-coastal waterway that day, while the rest of us suckers went to school. So, I told Whitney to walk to my house that day at lunch, skipping the afternoon classes. Whitney's dad was older than the mom by about twenty years. He was grey headed and having already raised a young hippie wife and two crazy daughters,

Whitney's skipping class was not a concern for him. So Whitney came over and I had the keys to the van. He managed to bum a doobie from his mom, and the girls would be happy to see us.

†

We were sitting at a stop light in the middle of Belle Chasse, the eight-track blaring distorted Lynyrd Skynyrd from its five inch speakers, the windows slightly cracked, passing the spliff back and forth and repeating that we would stop half way and save the rest for the girls. There was a bus stop on the corner where the railroad tracks intersected on our right, and an IGA grocery store next to the Ben Franklin on our left… and a Shell gas station. It's a four lane, and I am sitting next to an eighteen wheeler in the lane next to me, which prevents me from seeing the bus stop on the other side of it. Between us and the traffic light is a white Ford Galaxy full of men… workers coming back from a sulphur plant or oil refinery job, but white collar guys… probably engineers. I can see the red light and when it turns green, the brake lights on the Ford in front of us disappear, and it begins to move forward. I punched the gas pedal and we were off to good times… real women… wet bikini clad blondes with tits and nipples and manicured pubic hair.

Well, almost. The white Galaxy in front of me immediately slammed his brakes, I ran into his bumper, pushing him forward about twelve inches. The crash took a total of about two seconds.

I knew right away I was toast. The visions I was having of making out with high school chicks vanished. My gut went hollow. I told Whitney to hide the smoking torpedo, and I slowly opened my door, as I was met there by a tall white man from the car in front of me. He dressed a lot like my step-dad dressed. I noticed that a crowd was gathering in front of the Ford, and now saw at least fifteen black people converge there. As I followed the tall man to the front of the Galaxy, I saw an old black lady in a purple paisley patterned dress, with a purse on her arm, wearing a small flowery hat, sitting on the concrete, complaining of her back and hip hurting. One of the men from the car asked her if she would like to stand up, that he didn't think he'd really actually touched her with his bumper. Then the mob of coloreds began yelling advice to her not to get up, and then I heard someone ring out, "Hey, da's a ambu'lance ova de' getn gayce, go get 'em." The tall white man looked down at me and said, "Well, I'm afraid that's all she wrote boy. They take her off in that ambulance, your life will never be the same."

As the EMTs were putting the old lady on a stretcher, my poor mom was coming home from work, sitting at the intersection but across the railroad tracks, wondering what all the cops and commotion were about. She noticed the green and white conversion van that looked strangely like the one she inherited from her divorce from Ed. Then she recognized me as

I stood there giving my report to the officer. I suppose it was my mother's protection that saved me. She kept them from searching the van, and from bringing me to jail. The cops all had the same advice. "Lady, get a good lawyer cause yer gonna need one."

As it turned out, the Ford I hit at three miles an hour, happened to be a company vehicle full of guys who worked with my former step-dad.

The old black lady was actually sixty years old, hard-working and very sweet. The funny thing is, she was the maid to the attorney that represented my mom in her divorce from my father about eight years earlier. She was riding the bus route back home after work, was walking across the highway under a red light, when the light turned green before she could get all the way across. Neither I nor the driver in front of me was paying close enough attention. So said the attorney who now represented his housekeeper, and I would now agree that his estimation was correct. The van was covered under comprehensive insurance and uninsured motorist, but of course, without a license and not old enough to have one anyway, the insurer may have been able to get out of this lawsuit. But they didn't. They provided my legal counsel, and for four long dreadful years, we appeared in court each year to repeat questions and answers and procedures, until, finally a settlement was reached for three hundred and sixty thousand dollars, of which Freeport Sulpher Incorporated would be liable for ninety percent, and my mother for the remaining ten.

Mom then very shrewdly threatened to file for bankruptcy, as this amount was simply unattainable. In the end, Allstate paid our share. But my mother aged quickly during those years. She worried about things more than most folks anyway.

I remember the old black lady, Mrs. Vidalia Williams, as she gently grabbed my arm as I was exiting the witness stand, crying.

"Son," she said with sad grandma eyes, "Ise don't wanna hut you. Ise just needn my docta beels paid, dats all. You stop worryin now ya heea." I nodded to her gratefully. I never had another nightmare about that incident again. I was eighteen by the time a settlement was reached.

Shortly after the van incident, my mother had her second nervous breakdown. She took medical leave from her job, bleached her hair blonde, went shopping at boutiques she'd never even been in before, and one day came home with a new alpine white Mercedes 450SL convertible. I watched as she quickly and suddenly morphed into everything in a woman she'd always detested. And I witnessed, though I had no idea at the time how to express it, a woman who'd always been a victim, take charge of her life and "beat the men at their own game", she once told me.

"Mom are you okay?"

"Yes, I'm fine, why?"

"You've changed."

"I know, honey. Don't worry. I'm fine. I'm just doing what I have to do."

"What do you mean?"

"Sweetheart", she held my hands and looked at me gently, "I lost my job. And the jobs here that I qualify for just aren't available to me now. We don't have any money for rent… or your school clothes. So I had to do SOMETHING." Seems like I remember Dynasty or Dallas was playing on the console TV at the time. I didn't blame her.

I remember looking at her with a blank stare, wondering… fearing what she was telling me.

"I know you've been leaving me here alone at night."

"Oh, honey. I'm not leaving you alone. Mrs. Ostrander is looking after you while I'm at work. She checks on you while you're asleep."

"Are you sure… cuz I'm not seeing her, and I'm awake a lot."

"Yes, I'm positive. I would never leave you here without someone looking after you."

"So, what exactly do you do… in your new job?"

"Well, it's… it's really quite… uh… well, I… Do you remember Miss Betty? Well, she… uh… her brother runs a business that works at night, and he gave me a job."

"What kind of job?"

"Uh… well… I… when business men come to New Orleans for conventions…"

"What are conventions?"

"Business meetings. Big important business meetings. And when these, men, come to stay here they miss their homes, they miss their wives and kids. And they… they're lonely. They need companionship. So, I get paid to go to dinner with them, or attend after-meeting get togethers."

"You must be making lots of money."

"More than I ever made before. And soon, when I get caught up on all our bills, we're gonna take a long vacation together. How's that sound?"

"Why did you change your hair? And start wearing all these fancy dresses? You used to hate Mrs. Bush, and now you like a lot like her."

She tried her best to put a positive spin on it. But now she was growing impatient.

"Son, life is hard… so hard." She began crying, then sobbing, uncontrollably. I just sat there, resolute… and sad. To her, it must have looked like I was judging her. "Aren't you tired of being poor? I want to give you nice things."

"Why do they pay you so much money? A Mercedes Benz, Mom? Fur coats? New clothes? All in the last two weeks?"

She cried herself to sleep that night, calling into work sick. I laid on my bed, planning my next adventure.

†

When I was fifteen, I struck out on the road, literally, to find the father who never was, and in the process, found myself. Now, I look back and cannot fathom how all the experiences of my life could fit in the time I've spent here… and here is where I ended up. But that road, so to speak, was full of twisted turns, switchbacks and tall hills.

When I was sixteen, living with my old man, I got caught by a state trooper doing one hundred seventy miles an hour in my dad's Pantera, on interstate ten between New Orleans and Bayou Manchac.

When I was eighteen, just after the black lady's law suit was closed, I wrecked into another vehicle while turning right in my Mustang from the left hand lane, at seventy five miles an hour, in the pouring rain, at one a.m., with two high school friends in the car. Their parents both sued me for injuries my friends really didn't receive, and bought their sons new Mustangs.

I went to jail for DUI and possession, and called my dad to bail me out at three a.m. He said no. I called my mom. She called a girlfriend and they drove down to get me out. My dad sold the car after I worked offshore to pay to have it fixed. No matter, I didn't have a license anyway.

Life is full of irony and Karma. The court-ordered psychologist said I longed for my father's attention, and that I blamed my mother for all that was missing in my childish little mind. But when I went to live with him, without him actually asking me to, and against my step-monster's wishes all together, I didn't even like him. I found myself trying to be like someone I didn't really want to be. And through all my emotional crap, reaching out for attention by being a stupid ass, I end up incarcerated at the same prison where my father had his first real job.

Chapter Three

The Beast in Me

I was nineteen and Granddaddy, out of desperation, sent me to Louisiana State University hoping I would make something of myself. I was a rebel without a cause… finding trouble now and again, largely due to boredom and a restless spirit.

Aching for adventure, I continued to find trouble wherever I could. It was nighttime on a stretch of River Road along the Mississippi River, between Baton Rouge and Prairieville. After dropping acid, I had just blown the engine in my gold Nissan 280ZX, racing a couple of rich kids in a BMW. They kept going, leaving me stranded ten miles from the lights of town. I looked under the hood, but knew what happened as soon as the water gauge maxed out and the oil light came on. White smoke billowed from the tail pipes, a sure sign that water invaded the oil in the engine. The motor blew from the extreme pressures of driving at a hundred twenty miles an hour for the final five minutes of the run. There had been no way I was going to outrun the new beamer, and though I knew that, I didn't care. It was typical of my self-destructive mode. I, still a Toller son at the time, angry and lost, gulped down my last swallow of Busch beer and threw the can across the ditch onto the levee bank.

"FUCK!" I yelled out to the darkness. "FUCK! FUCK! FUCK!"

Tripping on LSD, stoned on skunk weed, and drunk on cheap beer, my head was half here and half way to hell. A filter-less Marlboro dangling from my lips, squinted eyes, I was dressed in khaki chinos and a white oxford, my hair cut in a "high and tight" style, like James Dean in Rebel Without a Cause. Up to this point in my life, I had accomplished nothing other than graduating high school without ever cracking a text book. Disowned by my father, (or was it I who disowned him?), I couldn't live up to my maternal grandfather's war hero expectations. I, John Toller, was a lost soul.

Going to God with my problems seemed too tame for a rebel. So, I yelled out to the devil instead. I'd read about such another disenfranchised character once in Rolling Stone magazine, a blues musician named Robert Johnson, who'd sold his soul to the devil in exchange for fortune and fame.

I walked away from the smoking sports car, one I'd paid for with student loans, pondering what I'd do next, when I came upon a crossroads... actually it was a tee in the road. There were three ways to go. One would take me to Baton Rouge. Another to Prairieville, a small town of around three hundred citizens… mostly black ones whose ancestors never left after the slaves were freed a hundred and fifty years earlier, and which reminded me of the small town near which I grew up. And the other, was unmarked on the reflective Kelly green sign, merely pointing another direction into the darkness. But, it was a place I hadn't been, yet.

On the corner, between the road that led to Baton Rouge and the other one which led to nowhere, lay the ruins of an old grey wood building. Only the rusty steel pipe that once held the proprietor's sign remained upright. In the gravel, at the base of the pipe, lay an old wooden sign, it, too, weather-beaten and faded. In crimson on a white background, it read, "The Wishing Well". I would later go on to record a song written by Ryan Bingham, called "Wishing Well". It's my favorite.

My buzz was wearing off fast from all the walking, except for the acid, and I sat in the middle of the road, my legs folded like an Indian, my arms stretched out behind me, hands on the asphalt, holding myself up, wishing a fast moving car or truck would drive through the junction and kill me dead, once and for all.

In the meantime, I made a conscious effort to conjure up Satan, much as a man would who was praying to God Almighty. I had absolutely no education in the ways of black magic, except for what I saw my step-monster perform with her candles and Latin sounding mumbo-jumbo. I didn't have candles and didn't know any Latin, so a direct request in English would have to do.

I sat silently as fog rolled in from the river, muting the sounds of the crickets and frogs and other crawlers of the night. A tug boat rolled quietly by on the opposite side of the levee, made apparent only by the sound of rippling water pushed aside by a long steel barge.

"Hey, Satan, you mother fucker! Answer me damn it!" I waited silently, looking in each direction for headlights. None. No sound. Not even a bug or a frog.

"Yes, John, I hear you." I almost pissed my pants, and jumped up quicker than shit.

"What the fuck!"

"You called me, John. And I am here."

My heart pounded in my throat. "I'm still high. Bad drugs."

"No John. You hear me. I am Lord Satan. And I am here for you. I have always been here for you, John." The voice was everywhere. It filled the air around me. There were no other sounds… only a surrounding deafness.

"I am everywhere on this earth, John. You see me everywhere. I was in the bar tonight. I was in your car. The way you felt at a hundred and twenty… that was me. Call me Lord Satan, your humble servant, John."

The conversation was typical I guess… "I hate my life. I hate my stepmother. I hate my father for loving her, and not loving me. I hate him for leaving me. I hate this world. I hate school. I hate the bullies that beat me up when I was a kid. I want bad things to happen to them. I want to be rich. I want to be famous. I want women to want me all the time. I want men to fear and respect me."

That old devil listened as I explained. Then he promised me all that I desired and all I had to do was give my soul to him. Deal!

I stood there at the crossroads, in front of The Wishing Well, on River Road Hwy 61, between Baton Rouge and Prairieville, as the lightning and thunder gave way to the crickets and frogs once again. A tugboat's horn was heard bluntly in the foggy distance. I wondered briefly if it were merely a strange dream. But I was convinced it was real, and would choose to believe so for many years.

Only seconds later, headlights were shining towards me from the distance. A dull red dually pick-up pulled up to the crossroads, pulling a long, faded red, beat-up old cattle trailer.

"Need a lift?" The toothless cowboy's windows were already down, and a stream of brown gooey syrup ran down the side of the driver's side from the door handle to the taillight. He spit onto the road in front of where I stood.

"I say do ya need a lift? Or you just standin' out here waitin' for the end of the world to come?"

I came to. Up to that point everything seemed surreal, and slow moving. "I… Yessir I could use a lift. My car broke down up the road."

"Hop in kid." The man's eyes were hollow, his gray whiskers and hair unkept and greasy. Hank Williams Sr. played out of a single dashboard speaker… Lost Highway.

I walked around the front end of the pick-up and got in, moving the pile of trash of coke bottles and Big Mac containers to make room for my feet on the floorboard.

"Where you headed?" I asked.

"I'm headed to the uni-vers'ty of higher ed-u-cation, boy." The old man smiled and cackled with a haunting rift, decaying parts of teeth exposing themselves. "They got a rodeo comin' up tomorra' and I'm providin' the stock. Thems bulls I got back there in the trailer."

I nodded my head.

"But… but LSU was that way."

“You a student boy?”

“Yessir. LSU.”

“Yeah, I figured. Well, if you don’t ‘member nothin’ else, boy, you ‘member this…”

The old man spit out another gob of brown tobacco syrup which ran down the driver’s side door and back towards the cattle in a gooey trail.

“…the road that ain’t marked… that’s the one less traveled, see. That’s the road fellas lak you and me are destined fer.”

The old cowboy wiped his chin whiskers and coughed. My reflection stared back at me from the inside of the windshield. I noticed the old man’s did not.

The radio played Lost Highway over and over again, seven times before we finally arrived at the South gate of campus.

“I’ll see ya at the rodeo.”

“Yessir. Maybe.”

“I’ll see you there.” The old man’s eyes glowed with firey flames and accented a most serious expression.

Two days later, I was drinking nickel drafts on a Monday afternoon, skipping class as usual. A couple of guys I knew from back home came in and started talking about how they’d just got back from the agriculture-center, about how they didn’t have enough bull riders for the student rodeo… then they started in on me and how an ex-motocross rider ought to be able to ride a bull… how much alike the two sports were. The next thing I knew I was at the Ag center signing up. By the time Thursday night came, it was too late to back out. They put me on a giant red bull with long horns that pointed out and upwards eighteen inches on both sides. Just before I was to climb into the chute, the old cowboy who delivered the bulls walked up to me and told me he'd picked this bull especially for me to ride tonight.

The giant angry animal came barreling out of the chute, and I didn't know what else to do so I just hung on with one hand and threw the other one in the air, as instructed by the old man. My long skinny legs were a benefit as I clung with my feet to the underside of his belly. The whistle blew and that was it… I was the only one to cover my bull… and won the whole thing. The guys all clapped, the girls all screamed. I got the respect I needed, and the attention I desired. Figuring it was easy, and not having any other real plans, I decided I'd turn pro and be the next world champ.

That was more than twenty years ago.

That same year, I was involved in three bar-room fighting incidents, one in which I broke a glass beer bottle over the side of a pool table and proceeded, Steve McQueen style, to slice the faces and hands of the muscle-heads I was fighting. With the aid of a drinking buddy, I escaped out of the back door of the bar. I had to get stitches in my right hand where the glass edges ripped my flesh open. I was learning that life was not a movie.

†

My grandfather's valiant attempt at reforming me through higher education failed to bring about positive results. Beginning with the second semester, I'd moved in with a guy I met through the fraternity I'd pledged. I kept this a secret from anyone in my family. Such foolishness as joining, furthermore, paying for, a fraternity would have been my ticket home. But, actually, I never paid a dime to that fraternity.

Fraternities exist for two purposes… so guys can fuck sorority girls and drink a lot of beer. This particular frat was known as the wildest one on campus. They were the Animal House of LSU. What I'd learned was that frats have pledge programs, whereby enough rich guys are recruited to make up for the few cool guys who didn't have any. The cool guys brought the women.

My claim to fame was the time, during a fraternity-sorority party, I rode my Harley Sportster through the front door, into the den, and up the staircase, all to the applause of sixty frat brothers and coeds drunk on jungle juice from a plastic garbage can. I made it half-way up the stairs when the weight of the bike came crashing through the floor and into the storage closet below. I was an instant smash hit, and so was the fraternity I represented.

The guy I'd met and moved in with was Mel Levitt. Mel was the quiet son of an Arizona psychiatrist, who purchased a swanky condo for Mel to live in while away at college. It was a gift to be living in a gated condo community, partying with rich frat boys and sorority chicks, free of charge, and spending student loan money on Harley parts.

It wasn't long however, that I began to find keeping up with the rich wasn't easy. Spring Break trips to Vail, summer parties in Daytona, gambling at the horse races… took a seemingly unending flow of cash. That's when Mel approached me with a "quick and easy way to make some serious bucks".

Mel worked part time as a bar tender at one of the many college bars around LSU's campus. He'd made contacts there that got him started in the coke trade, selling to the preppie Greek crowd, which was good money and limited risk. But now, his contacts were looking for a couple guys to sneak across the Texas-Mexico border, and swim a hundred pounds of pot across the Rio Grande River, where someone would be waiting to transport the bricks to wherever. Mel was a smart young man. I knew he wouldn't get involved in anything to risky. Texas has a long and vast border, he told me, and the likelihood of getting caught by the border patrol was highly improbable. The job would pay us two grand each.

What we didn't know was that the DEA had been tracking this particular cartel for months as a target in an even larger sting operation. At approximately three a.m. on the night of our swim, bright lights, sirens, and helicopters would convince me again that life is not a movie.

Mel and I were both caught with ten pound bricks taped to our legs. And it wasn't pot. I never saw the transporter. Mel and I were separated immediately, and brought to the same jail in Del Rio for interrogation. Before the arrest, Mel and I stayed up regularly, getting stoned on a four foot water bong, eating pizza, drinking beer, and watching Miami Vice reruns. We knew all about the good cop bad cop routine. They told me that Mel had told them who the contact people were, and was somehow throwing me under the bus. But I knew better.

Three months later, Mel and I both agreed to confess to the crime at the advice of my Grandfather's attorney, and threw ourselves on the mercy of the court. For that, I was sentenced to federal prison for no less than eighteen months, and no more than five years.

About that same time, Mel Levitt committed suicide by hanging himself with the pants legs of his tangerine orange prison uniform, a thousand miles from nowhere.

†

It was a medium security federal prison camp, in Pensacola, Florida. I was thinking about who I could call for conjugal visits, learning to play tennis and leaving with a nice tan. When I arrived there by bus, I was looking at what resembled a college dormitory, with a fence around it. It was actually part of an old navy base that once stood there. Upon settling in, I was to be assigned a job and even allowed family visitations once a month. But as luck would have it, the prison camp was suffering from extreme overcrowding due to the federal government's three strikes law.

When my attorney received a call from me the next day he immediately called my grandfather, who went to work trying to get me transferred to the Louisiana State Penitentiary. LSP was a maximum security prison, and by all comparisons, a hell hole for the worst kind of criminals. But Granddad's thinking was that if he could get me to Angola, where Great-Uncle Wingate was the warden, I could work as a Trusty. It would be a much shorter drive for visitations, and with Wingate's recommendation, I could be out in a few months.

The plan worked. I was bussed to the Tunica Hills where I lived as a child, and actually saw the old red brick house we lived in as the prison bus entered the grounds. After processing, I met Great Uncle Wingate, who acted toward me as though I were a huge pain in his ass, and immediately assigned to work the chicken farm.

"Chicken farm?" I asked, humbly. I never thought of chickens having their own farm. The farm was actually two three hundred foot long by forty foot wide curtain sided barns, made of wood and tin. The two barns housed around ten thousand chickens at a time, and were fed through three hundred feed baskets and as many drinking nipples. I was amazed at the size of the barns, the equipment that ran on timers, and the large number of birds.

Once at the farm, a guard introduced me to a fellow trusty in eighty year old Tobias McKlintock.

"Wus yo name boy?"

"John. Johnny Toller."

"Hmm. I see. Well, Johnny To-la, grab a bucket and let's get to workin' dese buhds."

Tobias was grey-haired and his hands shook slightly. He walked with a limp and his back was curved. The first thing he did was hand me a white plastic bucket and told me to start picking up any dead birds I saw. Two hours later it was break time, and I began asking questions.

"So why do ya'll spell trusty wrong?"

"Wutchew mean young fella?"

"Trusty. It should be spelled t-r-u-s-t-e-e."

The old man smiled, showing his gums and what few teeth he had left. "I dunno boy. I didn't know deah was anutha way." I later asked one of the guards, who explained that there were two versions of the word. Trustee, and trusty. Who says you can't learn new things in prison?

"Sooo, whadu do to end up in this place?"

"I shot my ol' lady for sleepin around."

"How long you been in?"

"Fifty yeahs."

"Fifty… they give you that for shooting your wife?"

"Well, deah was the boyfriend too."

"Oh, I see. Yeah, I suppose he should have died, too."

"You muss know sum-body in high places to be a trusty when you jus getn heah."

"Yeah, well, it's a long story. I was supposed to be in federal camp… medium security. But they were too crowded, so… here I am."

"MmmHmm. I see. So deys jus wantn to keeps you alive. Dats why dey put you heah wit me… somebody laks you." His smile was contagious, and made me feel like everything was going to be okay. He used to call me "Outlaw", but in a sarcastic way and playful way. He knew I was an angel compared to the cons who were there.

"Yeah. I suppose so." I replied. It was my granddaddy and his ties to Uncle Wingate that saved my life in that hell hole.

I learned that Tobias was the great-grandson of a slave. The owner of his grandfather was named McKlintock, which is the name he inherited when he was freed after the Civil war. Tobias McKlintock was sweet old man, and I could never picture him shooting anyone. But then again, I wasn't there when he walked in on his lover fucking some other dude.

Tobias was in the regular cell block, working the cotton and sugar cane fields every day, when the opportunity to work on the chicken farm came about. He considered it the best job for a convict. No one ever bothered us. And when Uncle Wingate sold the chickens every sixty days, if they finished heavy and healthy, he would give Tobias a little bonus in his spending account, which he would use to buy gifts for great-grandchildren he'd never met.

Six months after being introduced to raising chickens, I was beginning to learn animal husbandry, and was able to give Tobias a much-needed hand. In the chicken houses, it was just me and the birds. No one to fuck with me. No one to fuck with. And lots of time to think. I learned how to work on and replace electric fan motors, fix water lines and prepare the houses for baby chicks. I soon learned it was also a great place to grow marijuana. Tobias grew it, harvested it, and smoked it.

"Da only reason da Wauden let me have dis is cause I promise not to sell it to da population. Deys plenty pot and naucotics comin in heuh already, he don't need to worry 'bout me addin' to it." Tobias was shy and had a humble look about him… for a double homicidal murderer.

LSP had the big prison rodeo every year in August. It was a huge money bag. The cons made crafts and wood working stuff and were allowed to sell their wares at the arts and craft booths before and during the event. The inmates grew their own food, crops and cattle. And the ones who were talented in woodworking and such as that, provided they were well behaved, were allowed to sell their stuff to the visiting public during rodeo weekend. I asked Uncle Wingate if I could be entered into the bull riding contest, revealing to him that I had actually gotten some experience riding bulls at LSU. He relented.

"Boy, do you know that it was yo' fatha who made up this heuh ro-day-o bidness?"

"My father?" I thought back to my childhood here in the Tunica Hills.

"Yep. He was my Athletic Director back when you was just a chald, bout yay tall." He chomped on his sloppy wet cigar.

"Hea,hea. I gotta admit, I thought that man was craaaazy when he proposed the idea. But, it worked. And I'll be goddamned if it ain't the biggest and best prison rodeo anywauh. So, it don't surprise me none that you wanna ride those damn bulls, as crazy as you mat be!"

For the rodeo contestant cons, the best thing that could happen would be to break an arm or leg and have to go to the infirmary. Even better still, internal bleeding and an operation that would keep him out of cell block for a couple of weeks. But for me, it was about respect. It was about showing off in front of the cons and the civilians. And show off I did.

I rode three bulls in my first ever prison rodeo, and murderers, rapists and thieves hailed me as a hero.

†

Tobias, before he became a murderer, was an acoustic blues guitar picker. He had been teaching me the three basic chords of G, C, and D, which, he said, would cover almost any country or blues song I wanted.

Tobias' guitar picking was legendary at Angola, but he told me that he was too old to play anymore, as his hands grew more and more arthritic with each passing month. His old Gibson was as seasoned as he was. Guitars are not normally allowed of course, but the warden let Tobias keep his at the chicken farm, and he would teach me to play while on water breaks or at the end of the work day, before heading back to our cells.

Eventually, I would parlay my bull riding fame for a spot in the semi-annual convict concert for cons. The music festival of sorts was used by Uncle Wingate as an incentive for the convicts to behave themselves. Naughty cons were not allowed to attend.

My first ever performance was "Mama Tried", written by Merle Haggard. It was just me and Tobias' old Gibson, and a vintage microphone from the nineteen-forties, which hung from a single wire from eighteen feet above my head.

"Fresh meat!"

"Come 'ere boy I got sumpm for ya to play!"

The sneers and jeers continued as I walked slowly onto the small stage in the cafeteria. There were around fifty cons there, that Thanksgiving Eve night, in my nineteenth year. I was nervous as hell. I felt totally exposed. But, I knew I had a captive audience, so to speak, and once the guitar playing began, you could have heard a pin drop. I doubt I was very good, but they appreciated any entertainment they could get. They clapped when I was done, around three minutes after I'd begun. But absent were the hoorahs and the yippees I'd hoped for. I was a long way from Johnny Cash, but there was hope. At least I was living the song.

Thirteen months into my time, I was to be released on parole. The time had been cut to include time served in Texas, and for the good behavior I'd exemplified while a guest there. It was a happy time. But, in another way, not so much.

"A guy gets used to thangs", Tobias said. "I don't know wut I'd do if they let me out o' heuh. In heuh, I got a job. I gets good money compared to de otha cons. In here, I am somebody." And there was that gentle smile again.

And those were exactly the thoughts that plagued my mind the few days before I was to be released.

On my last day in the pen, Tobias hadn't been feeling well, and I'd gladly doubled up on my chores to see that his got done, too. I thought he might just be depressed that his new helper, whom he'd taken the time to train, was leaving the next morning. But that afternoon, by the time I'd washed my hands and began preparing for our final guitar lesson, I found Tobias McKlintock sitting in his old wooden ladder-back chair, leaning backwards against an old Spanish oak. After spending fifty years of his life there, he was dead.

I waited there, holding him in my arms, singing "Blues Man" to him, until the guard arrived to take us to our cell block. Oddly enough, to that date, working in those chicken houses, learning to play guitar during water breaks… talking about Tobias' life… these were the best years of my life.

When Uncle Wingate was notified at his home, he drove immediately to the chicken farm. I saw the sadness in his eyes as he instructed the guard to contact the infirmary. The old blues man had become a profound part of the warden's life.

"He was a good convict." Those were the last words I heard my Great Uncle say.

Chapter Four

Pay-Back

My grandfather was there to pick me up at six a.m. He'd driven a hundred and fifty miles, leaving his home earlier that morning.

Granddaddy was, by then, about as old as Tobias was when he died under the old Spanish oak. It caused me to think about him differently. I was profoundly sorry that I screwed things up so bad. At one time, I had been the favorite grandchild… "The Golden Boy" my uncles, aunts and cousins would call me. But the gold was tarnished. And only Granddad had any time left for me.

Granddad was a career soldier. He served twenty years in artillery, working his way up to Major, a world war two veteran, a Korean War veteran, and served in Vietnam as a "civilian contractor" after he retired from the military. He kept his hair as a flat-top all of his adult life. He stood at around five feet eight, a hundred and sixty pounds, but had a commanding voice that could cause any soldier to shit himself. And he could back it up.

The trip to Baton Rouge was mostly silent. He still drove the same old GMC pick-up, with a little Shriner bobble-head stuck to his dash, and a pack of green Wrigley's Spearmint gum in his console. The radio was tuned to country music on an am station, and the volume was barely audible.

Granddaddy liked beer. He drank Busch in a can from ten each morning until six in the evening, when it was time to eat supper. But whiskey was the potion that allowed his demons to come out. And about every three or four months or so, he'd go on a three day drinking binge. And during these times, everyone who could, got out of his way. But I'd stay close to him, even though he got meaner with every drink. It was during these times that he'd talk about the war years… the stench of death, the evil in the world, and the curse of living, knowing you'd killed so many.

I didn't know why we were going to Baton Rouge, and I really didn't care. I had been freed from prison and that's all I cared about. That, and getting laid.

As we approached the city, Granddad turned down the radio and began to speak.

"Son, you've done a good job of screwing up your life so far, but it isn't even half over yet. You've learned a lot that others your age will never know. But you've also cost your family, and the government, a lot of time and money. It's time you gave something back. With the help of Judge Causey, an old Army friend, I've had your criminal record expunged. None of this ever happened. Now is your time to begin again. This time, get it right. You he-uh? Now… there's been another war started while you were in prison, son. You may have heard about it. It's over in the Persian Gulf, place called Iraq. So, you'll probably be sent over there. Now, bein' a grunt in a place like the desert ain't fun. So I advise you to join up with the Air Force, or the Navy if you have a hankerin' for water."

I had a sneaky suspicion my joining the military was part of the deal Granddad made with the judge. Granddad had done way too much for me to not obey his wishes at that point.

By noon on a Thursday, I was standing in line at the U.S. Military Entrance Processing Station. On the advisement of my maternal grandfather, I joined the Air Force. The year was 1990, and I was twenty-one years old.

After basic training in San Antonio, I was sent to train at a mobile aerial port and forward air controller school. Right after graduation, I was sent to Fort Benning, Georgia to learn how to jump out of perfectly good airplanes. Then, ironically, I was assigned as an Air Force liason to the First Special Forces Group at Ft. Lewis, Washington… an Army special ops group. I would be a grunt in the shit after all.

†

The Air Force, and the Army, for me, was a whole lot of life, real fast. You get close to guys you fight with. You depend on each other. You hear some cry at night, dreaming of seeing their wives and kids again. Afraid they won't… Others, especially in the spec ops community, don't say much, or hide their feelings really well. They're trained to.

In ninety-one, I was deployed to an American base outside of Al Kharj, Saudi Arabia, which was a city about fifty miles south of Riyadh. There, I would be introduced to daytime temperatures in excess of one hundred ten degrees Fahrenheit, and night temps around freezing. Chemical warfare gear is a bitch in hundred degree temperature. The sand storms were frequent, and sand permeated everything in your body and your equipment. Fortunately, my expertise was not as valuable in the desert as it was the mountains or jungles, and I was flown back to base after just a couple of months there.

On the next deployment, attached to a Special Ops unit, I found myself overlooking the once thriving old city of Sarajevo.

I could see the Latin Bridge, where Archduke Ferninad was assassinated, triggering World War One.

There were rapid rivers like the Neretva to raft on, with steep canyon walls and emerald green water to behold. I was seeing the world.

But, as we all know, war changes things. Now, at this point in time, I was looking at all this through the matt lenses of binoculars, from high atop an unnamed mountain ridge.

Nearly 700 members of the Army Special Operations Command and their "special attachments" deployed to Bosnia in mid-December 1992, and began numerous operations throughout the Balkan region. I was included among them, along with civil affairs and psychological warfare specialists. On this mission, I was to act as special liaison to the Army, training, coordinating and spearheading the airlift into and out of the theater of war. Most airmen, especially the married ones, wanted only short temporary duty assignments that kept them in four star hotels and paid high per diem rates. I wanted to sleep on the ground with the grunts.

On the afternoon of April 6, 1992, a "peace and unity" demonstration in the Bosnian capital of Sarajevo was disrupted when Bosnian Serbs fired shots into the crowd and killed several demonstrators. The civil war erupted, and for the next three and a half years two hundred and fifty thousand people would be killed. At least four out of every five deaths would be noncombatants. Twelve thousand women were raped. Five hundred and twenty thousand Bosnians found themselves homeless. Ethnic cleansing created one point three million refugees.

Only a few years earlier Bosnia's capital, Sarajevo, was the site of the 1984 Winter Olympics.

But I also recalled my maternal grandfather's stories of how the region had a turbulent history that dated back as far as the first century. "It's where World Wars One and Two started", he said. In Bosnia, people tended to align by their ethnic and religious allegiances. Slovenes and Croats associated with the Catholic West, usually Italy and Austria. Serbs identified with the Russians and the Orthodox East. Bosnian Muslims favored the Islamic Turks. I could understand the schism between the Muslims and the Christians. But the one between the Orthodox Christians and the Catholic Christians puzzled me.

The CIA was already aware that the turmoil in the Balkan region was a perfect condition for the Muslim fundamentalists from the Middle-East-Mujahideen to spread their terror efforts. Then Secretary of State Warren Christopher stated, it was "the problem from Hell."

†

One late rainy afternoon in Bosnia, sitting in a fox hole, talking to this short skinny freckle faced red headed kid from North Carolina… Steven Barbee… reminded me of the MADD magazine kid… we're sitting there in our hole, our Kevlar helmets and our Gortex parkas and pants, trying to stay as dry as possible, trying to stay warm and literally shaking in our boots…. rockets firing over our heads from across the valley by the Serbs. It's zero two hundred hours, we're talking… telling stories of back home, trying to keep each other sane and awake… swapping MRE desserts and sides… I had a brownie and he had potatoes au gratin, so we swapped… he was one funny son of a bitch. He had me laughing my ass off in an insane world.

We sat there in the insanity, trying to recall lyrics of Hank Williams Jr. songs, singing at the top our lungs, and you still couldn't hear for the explosions all around us.

There we were, sitting in a fox hole, a six foot by six foot bomb crater, about four foot deep, deep enough that you could sit against the north wall, and I'd have to really stretch my neck upwards to see over the south wall, which was the direction we were looking out over. The crater was from a Serbian shell that exploded there two days prior, before A-10 Warthogs drove their line south of the city. There we were, talking in the dark about what our favorite MRE entrees and sides were… and all of a sudden, he wasn't talking back. He was supposed to talk next, like he had been… only… nothing. So, you know it's dark and it's raining, and water is pouring over my eyes. I look at him and shine my chem-light on his face; His face is all pale and white. My eyes were open and staring. I thought he was fucking with me. I grabbed the back of his neck… to, you know… get him to stop fucking with me… and I feel this jelly shit, all slimy and warm. It was really warm. And I looked at my hand with the chem-light… it was fluorescent green… the light I mean. And I saw it. I saw it was dark, dark red and white. I could feel chunks of brain and shards of bone between my fingers. Steven Barbee from North Carolina was dead… by a sniper's bullet through the Kevlar helmet, through his frontal lobe and out of the back of his head. Matter had exploded silently on the earthen wall behind him, and I couldn't see it. Life was definitely not a movie.

Sergeant Erslick… everybody called him ET, because he looked like ET, as in "ET phone home". But he was well liked and well respected among his men and his commanders. Sarnt E. found me at sundown when neither I nor Steven answered the radio call. He said I was conscious when he found me, but I was just sitting there looking at my hands.

I was flown back to base, evaluated, and sent back stateside for thirty days rest and relaxation. I kept thinking, everyone has a story to tell… and some stories are too damn short.

†

Between deployments to Europe, I made trips to Haiti, under Operation Uphold Democracy, and Rwanda, the mission-name of which I can't remember, nor has it been declassified.

In Rwanda, I was helping with the insertion of a five man squad of Special Forces commandos, a mission which is still classified. While on this mission, we were disguised as trainers supporting the Joint/Combined Exchange Training (JCET) unit, teaching tactical skills, land navigation, first aid, and basic marksmanship to seventy-two Rwandan Patriotic Army officers.

While in country, walking through a Tutsi controlled village near Sheli, southwest of Kigali, I would witness a horror of war from which I would never recover. There was not anything in sight that had not been altered or destroyed by fighting. Tutsi women and children were gathering their belongings as the men had long since been killed in battle and genocide.

Captain Bill Tassler, Wild Bill, was on point, of our five man squad, conversing with our interpreter about the fighting the villagers here had seen. Cap'n Tassler had a hard-bitten aura about him, as though he'd spent his whole life in places no one back home could imagine. He had a reputation as someone who'd back his men no matter what, even if it meant demotion down to captain. His salt and pepper flat top made me guess he was around forty five or fifty, but he reminded me of my granddad. He had a leathery face, tanned bronze by the majority of his years in the sun. We all wore red ball caps, and Specialist Cory Butcher had his hat on backwards. Cory, from Vermont, and I, had become friends riding bulls together on the armed forces rodeo team. He had black hair and steel blue eyes, six feet of solid muscle. He carried an M14 and the laptop that could link up to a satellite and provide live feed from command post, sat maps, even call in air strikes. I carried my M4 Carbine, shorter and lighter than the traditional M16, and the Army's weapon of choice for close combat. Tassler brandished an M9 Beretta and an M4. Turbo, a mustached little grunt from Portland, Maine, liked his experimental MK16 with its fourteen inch barrel and effective range of five hundred meters. The interpreter, a local village leader hired by Cap'n Bill and paid off in MREs and meds for his clan, carried an old Vietnam era M16.

The little black boy could not have been more than twenty-four inches tall. Naked, he walked blindly into walls of huts, tripping over rocks and debris, his head flailing side to side, at first we just looked at him from about forty meters away. As he came toward us, I wondered if he was mined. Had the Jihadists trained the Hutu to make him swallow a bomb that they would detonate when he reached us? He walked toward our squad, toward Cap'n Tassler and the terp. We could all hear the boy's high pitched whine, like a hair-raising moan of terror more than a cry. I wanted to shoot the kid… it was like being forced to listen while your own kids are tortured and raped. I still hear him in my dreams.

I walked slowly up to Wild Bill, as the boy continued in slow ovals toward us. It looked like someone had given PCP or LSD to this kid, the way he was acting. Now just twenty clicks away from us, we saw his disfigured and tortured face. His eyes had been burned out with a torch or heated instrument of some kind.

"Oh my God." Tassler gulped. The terp looked away.

When the child cried aloud again, it was revealed to us that his teeth had all been busted out, most likely with the butt of club, his gums like mushy ground meat, bleeding through cracked lips. It was like being on a far-away planet, communicating and dealing with a species that is totally foreign to you. The barbarism could be, at times, soul sucking.

The interpreter, a member of the Patriotic Front militia, explained to Cap'n Bill that the Hutus had blinded the boy first, then busted out his teeth for more pleasure with him. They had probably raped him for weeks. While I was trained in first aid, none of us had the knowledge or supplies to help the poor child. I still considered shooting him.

Tassler told the terp to tell the village elders where they could bring the boy for medical help… forty five kilometers away in Kigali.

We boarded our two Humvees, and drove away.

†

For my service, I had been awarded the Air Force Commendation medal, the Joint Services Commendation Medal, and the 1995 Air Force Airman of the Year award.

Chapter Five

Money for Nothin' and Chicks for Free

After my hitch in the service, with all that I'd been through and brought down upon myself, I was ramping up for something big. That's what I decided. Now I was ready. I'd paid my debt to society, and would someday do the same for my family. Immediately upon exiting the service, I began calling myself Johnny Outlaw, in honor of Tobias McKlintock.

I was fearless. There was nothing anyone could do or say, nothing I could behold, that would be any worse than what I'd seen or done. In my mind I was a very prepared actor, ready to walk on to wide screens around the world. And, other than killing people and breaking things, the only things I knew how to do were raising chickens and riding bulls. So, I struck out on my own with fifteen hundred dollars and a black 1978 Cadillac Coupe DeVille that I purchased for eight hundred bucks at a used car lot just outside of the Air Force base.

I signed up for local rodeos at first, and more than a couple of bull riding clinics, learning the bulls and the riders, and placing in a few small events. It didn't take long for me to learn that if someone's going to make it in the rodeo business, they're going to have to think big. And that's what I did.

At Rollie's Tavern one night in 1995, I ran into Captain Wild Bill Tassler, who was now retired and working as Vice President of Team Air Express, an air cargo company in Seattle. He asked what I was doing for a living, and offered me a job. I appreciated it, I told him, but my plans were to become the world champion of bull riding, and make a million dollars. The problem, I told him, was that I needed a sponsor to pay my fees and gas to get me to the rodeos across the country. Twelve beers later, I was officially sponsored by the company, for which I would advertise by sticking the corporate brand on my competition shirts. I was on my way.

One day in the fall of 1995, at nearly twenty-six, I was riding in Jackson, Mississippi at the Tri-State Rodeo Dixie Nationals, and won my event. I won twenty-five hundred dollars and a gold belt buckle. After the show and autograph session, to the bar I went. It was at the Tumble-In Bar that I met my soon to be betrothed, Beth. Beth was what we, in the rodeo industry, called a buckle bunny. Like groupies are to rock bands, so too are buckle bunnies to the rodeo elite. We were married under my original last name of Toller by Christmas, and nine months later, in ninety-six, my son Marshall was born. He looked just like me, and I was absolutely thrilled at the prospect of being a dad.

But making a living on the road while my wife was at home, was going to take a lot more commitment than I was able to give. I wanted fame and fortune. Beth wanted a double-wide somewhere close to where she grew up.

At first she traveled everywhere with me. But as her pregnancy went on, she stayed home more and more. By the end of the rodeo season, our marriage was on the rocks, and she wanted another child. So, having grown up an only child myself, and realizing that our marriage probably would not last, it sounded good to me.

Matthew was born in March of ninety-seven. Beth and I divorced in the fall of the same year, and I joined the Professional Rodeo Cowboys Association, which took me more places and more often. In ninety-eight, I was the biggest money winner ever for a single PRCA season. I was invited to join up with a new organization called the Bull Riders Only.

The BRO was actually the first organization to make bull riding a separate event from all the other rodeo events. It was also the first sanctioning body to pay contestants just to show up. In December of that same year, I won the first ever prime-time bull riding event, sanctioned by the BRO and aired on Fox. To this day, it is the largest rating ever for a rodeo event at a viewing share of four point one. Johnny Outlaw was making a name for himself.

Eventually, the Bull Riders Only Tour would be bought out by an organization calling itself the Pro Bull Riders, or PBR.

In nineteen ninety-nine, at the age of thirty, I still looked ten years younger. I began shopping for an agent to acquire more, and more lucrative, sponsors. Based on my performances in the PRCA and the BRO, I was allowed in to the new premier PBR through its pro touring division, and earned my way into the elite Built Ford Tough Series, the PBR's elite group.

In two thousand, I was the PBR's Rookie of the Year by placing tenth in the money and making it through the last eight rounds at the championship in Vegas.

In two thousand one, I would win my first PBR World Bull Riding crown, along with the four hundred fifty thousand dollars in winnings, and a million dollar bonus award for winning the championship. Now, I had agents looking for me.

†

Ari Pei worked in the mail room at William Morris in the early eighties, paying his dues and getting to know the real players in Hollywood. He learned to love the art of the deal. Back then, he was the stereotypical manager/agent; visible chest hair, rolodex, shaded eyeglasses and a mini afro hairstyle, walking the stretch of Wilshire and Santa Monica Boulevards that links Beverly Hills with the skyscrapers of nearby Century City, saying things like "we'll max it out at three hundred thou".

Ari left William Morris in 1985, using his wife's fortune to found Victory Arts Agency, or VAA, and stealing Morris' top three clients in the process. They were little known then; Angelina Jolie, Billy Bob Thornton, and Ted Dansen. He helped turn talent management into a fine art and a disciplined science, willing to crawl on broken glass for his clients.

Today, he wears sharp tailored black or grey business suits, sports a year-round tan, keeps his silver curls close to his head with a trimmed white beard, against piercing grey eyes, and constantly works his iPhone or iPad for up-to-the-second news and gossip that might play in favor or against one of his boys.

I was one of Ari's hottest commodities then… not the richest, yet, but the hottest… and I knew it wouldn't last forever, so better take advantage of that service for which I was paying. Ari would keep track of the schedule of appearances, sponsor banquets, and commercial shoots I was to attend in any given week. He also reminded me of important dates and birthdays, thanks in large part to his assistant's attention to details.

Rebecca was a self-described nerd in high school. From a Los Angeles suburb, she, for whatever reason, never dreamed bigger than being a secretary for a law firm or talent agency. She never married, as her work was everything in her life, except her two dogs. Over the five year period between graduating from some technical school in office management and now, sleeping with the dangerous outlaw was the most exciting thing she'd ever done. One night she had too much to drink, and proclaimed her love for me… From that moment on I took her for granted. I believed Rebecca would always keep my best interests at heart, being sure to text me that it was my Mom's birthday, or that my son had an important game coming up, even going to lengths of buying Christmas gifts for those on my list. By balling her until she was raw and begging me to stop, and causing her vagina to be sore the next morning as she walked around her office building, I would earn her loyalty and respect. That's how I was programmed to think about women.

†

"Hollywood", "Primetime", "The Outlaw", "The Man", "The GOAT" (Greatest of All Time)… I'd been called all of these by this time in my career. I was at the pinnacle. And I knew it.

"When he's not drinking and carousing and carryin' on, he's all business... most of the time.", said fellow competitor and friend, Tuff Hedeman, now retired a millionaire and commentating for CMT at bull riding events. "I'd say he's a cowboy's cowboy!"

Tuff continued, "Our sport just has never seen anyone like him. He's got that raw kind of talent, which by the way he's too darn humble to admit, but... I rode down many a mile with The Outlaw, and I can tell you, right now, right here, tonight, he is the best." And such was the common theme whenever I was behind the chutes and the prime time cameras were searching for ratings. I was who people tuned in to watch. And that made me valuable.

As it turned out, two thousand two was a year I would just as soon forget. Riddled with injuries, I failed to compete the second half of the season, and bought some farm property in Mississippi, where the boys were living with their mother at the time. I began teaching bull riding clinics to locals, and wrote a book called Fundamentals of Bull Riding. I sold a few hundred copies, mostly to my friend Dudley Rogers' western store chain. I didn't promote the book at all. Then came the idea of me putting on bull riding clinics, where I sold a few more.

O'three was a good year. I was healthy again, rested and eager to show the world I was not a flash in the pan. I totally dominated the sport that year, winning the championship and one point five million dollars. I was thirty-four.

†

That year, the week-long finale of the ten month tour, our last night at the MGM Grand, I was in second place with only one ride left for myself and the number one cowboy in the points chase, Trip Lloyd. Trip won four major events that year, which propelled him into the points lead going into the finals, but his weakness was inconsistency. Once Lloyd was falling off, he would probably do so for the next few rounds, until something happened to change momentum… like maybe when the previous five riders all cover their respective bulls, and the crowd is hollering and standing up, cheering for more! There's a vibe in the air, a kind of Karma that insists any rider must hang on for eight.

But that night wasn't like that at all. Lloyd had fallen off his previous bull, upsetting his chances to cover all seven for the week. I was catching up, and the crowd loves the underdog. Former World Champ, Dan Bumpers, was on our heels in third. I knew I was in just the right position to slingshot into first in the last round. I was very confident. I'd seen it all in my dreams the morning before. I suffered from insomnia, which no doubt was made worse by my lifestyle of whiskey and pain pills. The Devil had plans and reasons for my success. Why else would I have made it so far for so long?

American Cowboy Magazine, online, December issue:

It was like a scene out of Rocky. Johnny Outlaw, comes out of the breezeway that leads back to the dressing room that the bull riders shared, their gear bags on the ground beneath the oak stained, bench seats; the lockers, most half opened, with riders' second pair of jeans dangling from the locker door; a set of spurs or a rope dangling on the inside. He walks out like a rock star as he approaches the stage, only in this case the stage is a dirt filled arena, more fit for modern day gladiators. The cameraman for CMT, the sponsoring cable-television network is in his face, walking backwards to get the facial close-up. But on this day, The Outlaw is focused, and his squinting eyes are the proof. He is armed only with a seven plait, braided nylon rope with a leather pad tied to the handle and a big brass bell dangling from the loop, clanging with every Clint Eastwood step.

Truth is… I get very insecure when a camera is in my face. I made the cover of Roundup magazine once, and I had a nose hair poking out from under my nostril. *They should have never used that photograph*! *You can't trust anyone.* Besides, close crowding like that, kind of freaks me out. I think I got that from my time in Africa. Tribesmen had a bad habit of crowding Americans to inspect our weapons and canteens and such. Problem was, you never knew who might stab you with a spear.

The announcer has just alerted the crowd that the man they have all paid to see is about to enter the arena behind the chutes. The crowd is in a cyclonic frenzy. The pressure to perform greatly is overwhelming.

A wide brimmed hat came in handy in my effort to avoid eye contact with anyone, especially those with cameras flashing at me. I neared the outside edge of the stands, and I pass this kid, I figured twelve years old or so, who obviously suffered from Down's… maybe more. I walk another ten steps, thinking *if I stop they'll say it was just a photo op. Then I stopped*, causing the CMT camera man to walk into the promoter walking beside me, then turned around in slow motion, walked back to the kid, and bent down on one knee, eye level. *Hell with everybody else.*

"Hi little buddy. I'm Johnny. What's your name?"

"Marcuth." We both knew this was a moment… a moment for one as much as the other. It defined who we were. Why we were here, now, right now, in all this chaos. Immediately around us seemed a sea of calm, and everywhere else was a blur of noise and color.

"Hi Marcus. I sure do like that hat." I noticed the Bolo High and Tight shirt with faux pearl snap buttons, the Rebel jeans. Marcus had his black Outlaw hat pulled down on his head, as if to cover his eyes, "Johnny the Outlaw" style. I could hear myself breathing.

I looked up at who I presumed to be the mom. "What size hat does he wear?"

"Seven and three eights." She was smiling thankfully.

And with that I took my own hat off, signed the inside of the crown with a black Sharpee that Marcus held in his hand, and with my other hand gently took Marcus' hat, and replaced it with my own. Mine had been custom made in California in a sponsorship deal by a hat company. It was worth about three hundred dollars in almost pure beaver felt. Marcus got his wool-blend hat at his local western store for around forty-five bucks. I loved giving something to him.

The roar of the crowd began to overshadow our moment. The fans were growing restless, for only the closer folks who could see what was going on were respectively quiet. The announcer was struggling to be heard over the vibrating bass drum of AC/DC's Back in Black… my calling card. The arena was shaking with energy.

I shook Marcus' hand, winked at him, looked up at his mom, and dressed in my black leather chaps with leather images of pearl handled silver pistols and camel brown holsters sewn on the hips, and a shirt that had more sponsor logos than a Sprint Cup car… I walked into the light.

I was aware of the moment, almost every time there was one. Good or bad. I could see the bar room fights before they happened. Pushing the photographer in the face outside a nightclub in Los Angeles and having my picture taken at just that moment... and the law suit that followed… I saw it happening before it actually did.

The girl-friend break ups, the arguing… If breaking up is a done deal, there's really no sense at all in talking about it. I hated to argue with a woman, knowing it was fruitless, and would rather walk out or hang up than say a word in retaliation or explanation. This drove women crazy.

I did nothing to interfere with my destiny. If a bar room brawl was eminent, I might as well get it started. If that guy takes my picture after I politely ask him not to, then the guy ought to get a punch in the nose. That's what John Wayne would have done.

I give plenty of time to the paparazzi guys. I know they are, in a harsh way, mostly responsible for my fortune. But I won't put up with bad behavior.

As I walked by Marcus, I knew I had to go forth and fulfill my destiny. Not once did I ever consider that the prophecies were self-fulfilling. I was merely doing what I saw was supposed to happen. But, it wasn't always easy.

"Jet lag is jet lag," I would explain to the boys in the locker room, just before this night's show started, "private jet or not!" All laughed and kidded one another, as if they also understood how it was meant to be. Yep, victory was mine, preordained. I would be two-time PBR World Champ. I was totally confident, but not relaxed. Inside, my guts were wrenching with an intense pressure to perform.

If anything goes wrong… anything. If the bull gets crazy in the chute, get off 'im quick as hell. Make sure they use a rope to keep his goddamned head down. Keep yer feet up. Last time this sunofabitch broke your ankles.

Funny how one can show one side of themselves by telling jokes in the locker room before a match, and be so freaked out inside. Don't get me wrong, its normal I think. You want to be up for it… excited, nervous energy is a propellant. Adrenaline. All good. It was the times I didn't feel that energy that I got hurt.

†

Watching the video later, it looked for the first two seconds like it was going to be just another day at the office. And just as I began spurring with my right foot, to score more points, the bull made a move that had not been seen since the great

Bodacious… D&H Cattle Company's "The Storm", weighing in at a mere eighteen hundred and fifty pounds, stopped spinning left, and in one gigantic leap went straight upwards, coming dangerously close to my already beaten head, pulling downward with the thrust of a missile, slamming my upper body into the bull's hard skull and that one funky horn dangling, his hauntingly zombie-like eyes looking upward at his victim like a soul-less shark. I held on with my legs, squeezing my weakened knees together, and without thinking, pulling myself back up to the rope from where I was sliding, all the while keeping my back arched so as not to let my back pockets get too close to the tail end. I recall the audience was a blur of various colors of the rainbow. The announcer's voice had become a record playing backwards. My eyes were open but I couldn't focus. All I could do was feel the bull and anticipate his next violent move. It was all will power from that moment on.

The bull was now spinning the other direction to the right and away from my riding hand. All the cowboy contestants, even the leader cheered me on from the tops of the chutes, as the crowd of forty thousand lived in slow motion for the remaining four seconds.

My body was rigid, and then limp and out of control. Later, I would confide to Bobby that I "felt the hand of this strange long haired dude holding me up and telling me to hang on, and eventually, guiding me back to the gate". It wasn't a pretty ride by any means. Not stylish as usual. But very technically perfect. The ride was half over and I was giving all I had to just hang on. The bull, genetically superior, yet young and inexperienced, gave all he had in his arsenal too early in the battle, and I rode out the remaining seconds with what seemed to everyone else, relative ease. I slid off the side of the bull on a twist toward the bullfighters, and looked for the chute gates to exit the arena. The bull fighter, looking like the cross between a circus clown and a rugby player, with black ink oxide under his intense adrenaline filled eyes, yelled my name, "Hey Outlaw, here's your rope cowboy!" The television camera caught the action and the audio from its camera on a suspended wire above us. Michael Gaffney, former PBR Champ himself, now married to a doctor in Colorado, was technical commentator for the night's event, accompanying host Brock Stricklin. He noticed that I was limping on my left side, and my riding arm was dangling, my eyes were glazed, no one was home. "And Johnny Outlaw is hurt, folks. He's dazed and confused, no one is home." Michael, The G-Man, as I called him, sounded concerned, but only in a rough cowboy humor sort of way. "I don't know how the heck that man is walking around out there right now, much less that he just rode that bull for eight seconds. (Laughing) Damn, I don't know why I'm surprised… it is The Outlaw and he is the best in this business!"

As I approached the gate to exit, the event coordinator pointed me back out to the arena floor, where I would stand under the spotlight and throw my hat into the air, for the people in the stands I could barely see for the darkness out there and the light in my eyes. Fans foamed at their mouths and cheered. Fellow gladiators patted me on the back, as I retreated momentarily out of the spotlight to gather myself.

The television commentators, with the aid of slow motion replay, critiqued the ride as follows;

"Let's take a look from our overhead camera here… Look at his timing. Look at how every time that bull jumps and goes left, so does he. He's not behind the bull and he's not ahead of the bull. He just finds that groove at the end, you know, and he rides it out. He knows what he has to do to win this event, and he does it. He gets the job done, and really, really puts on a fantastic show here for these great fans."

"Yes he does certainly do that Michael, and just look at that, "The Storm"… aptly named by the owners of D&H Cattle Company, twisting and belly rolling, and turning, all at the same time, and then changes direction… I just can't believe the quality of bulls we have in our stables tonight. And Johnny 'The Outlaw', some say he's possessed, some say he's obsessed… either way he has taken over the points lead, and listen to the fans as the announcer tells them the score… oh my!"

"Wow! And look at The Outlaw just as cool and calm as he could be… the fans are up on their feet, stomping and chanting John-ny, John-ny… this truly is a scene out of Rocky."

"I think I saw a tear in the G-Man's eyes folks, it is truly a celebration taking place here now. Folks are all up out of their seats, yelling the name of Johnny Outlaw, and here he comes... here he comes..."

"Oh Man. I'm speechless. Let's just watch and listen..." The G-Man's voice was cracking.

It was the moment, on worldwide television, displaying energy of forty thousand screaming, loyal, hard-working American fans; last round... three great riders... and the last ride of the night. Just like the dream.

And with that, the announcers silenced themselves, as I limped from back of the chutes made of premium square aluminum tubing and adorned with sponsors' ads and logos, into the white hot light beaming from above.

"The Storm" scored forty-six out of a possible fifty points for his performance. And I, the new record holder of the most career earnings in rodeo and bull riding history, scored forty-seven out of a possible fifty, which gave me a combined score of ninety-three points in the final round, and a total score for the three rounds of two hundred sixty-six point five... enough to beat Trip Lloyd by one point. It was like when Dale, Jr. takes the lead at Talladega Motor Speedway. The decibels from the devoted followers are deafening.

I was still dizzy, and holding on to one of the bull fighters, when the two sexy buckle bunnies in black leather pants and lace bras came out with the giant cardboard check that bore my name and a cash award for the top money winner of one million dollars, along with yet another gold buckle with the event's prestigious insignia emblazoned with gold block letters and red rubies. The Brazilians who always hung together, walked down from the chute's wooden deck, smiling ear to ear, marveling at my ability to ride out "The Storm", clapping and slapping me on the back between the blades. Lloyd walked over to congratulate me, the crowd cheered, both my fans and his. Trip was a classy cowboy, and the rodeo lovers paid him off with an ovation.

For most of the competitors, it was time to retreat back to hotels and motels with hot tubs and hot meals… comfortable beds. As for me, it was anything but. The rock stars, the actors, the junkies, the groupies, the models, the agents, the law suits, the any press is good press… it was insanity. And Hollywood made it all seem so common place. And that was because, I figured out, they all had issues. And the more you get people with issues together, the more chaos and insanity perpetuates.

†

I had by now seen so many ordinary people with special talents, and some with no talents at all, shoot like stars and explode into fiery flames… and so few who actually had the power to remain lit. It seemed to me that the smart ones knew their place… they had situational awareness that guided some celebrities slowly away from Hollywood and New York, and more towards the serenity of rural places. And while I tried to fit in to the scene, and actually enjoyed the fame my bad boy behavior brought me, I was tired of the phony bullshit that seemed to now plague my life. And though I had carefully tried to balance my work life with my role as father, I was failing… I couldn't help but feel the urgency to settle down while the boys were young. I was, after all, making the choice to stay amongst the screwed up Hollywood elite. I'd abandoned the gypsy train of rodeo contestants who traveled up and down and all around the highways and back roads of America, riding and roping their dreams together. That wasn't really my thing either. Instead, I made a conscious decision to leave the nest of those fellow performers who supported me, for a life far more glamorous and groundbreaking. I thought best to make enough money now and to never have to work again, and spend the rest of my years loving my sons… and generally just screwing off and having fun. The real fear I faced was the idea that this was all a one-time shot. My fifteen minutes of fame turned into a lot longer, and I wasn't ready to let it all go. Also, the fact that females can be so… easy… is downright discouraging to any man who really wants to get married, and it was sobering to realize that not one of them were ever around long enough to get to know me… by my own choice. And I've got to admit, if ever I was addicted to anything, it would be women. I love women! And I loved their attention.

I recall the only advice my dad ever gave me… "Son, women are like sheep on the mountain side. You can run down the slope and catch one, or you can walk down and fuck 'em all." *Where did he get THAT analogy?*

The Johnny Outlaw business was never better. It seemed that I could do no wrong. It had been reported on some blogs and lesser-known web sites that I was an illicit drug user. People talked about it. Some cared. Some didn't. Olympic phenom Michael Phelps had been caught on someone's phone cam smoking pot from a bong while at a party, and it aired on every news cast. He lost his Cheerios sponsorship, but after a year went by, the public forgot or didn't care. He went on to capture more victories and more sponsors with big pockets. I saw the same kind of things happen to Charlie Sheen and Kid Rock. The more they rebelled, the more famous and wealthy they became.

No competitor or stock contractor or promoter ever accused me of it. I had never appeared under the influence behind or in front of the chutes. And most of the competitors had seen me drunk before. Hell, most of us went up the ranks together, and there wasn't any hiding that I was a partier. They'd seen me hung over plenty of times, too. Cody Lambert, of the movie, Eight Seconds, and one of the founding fathers of the PBR, liked to tease, "He got his money for nothin' and his chicks for free." Cody knew better, though. No one wins a PBR championship without dedication and determination, much less two championships. I just made it look easy.

Chapter Six

High and Tight

"60 minutes wants to interview you Johnny." Ari's voicemail was fast and direct. "How the hell are we supposed to talk about this, when you tell me to call you back I call you back. Then you don't answer. Call me Johnny! ... Please."

I always screened my calls. I was really quite anti-social, which was difficult for most people to believe, what with all the showing off for the fans, the TV appearances, the interviews, the provocative poses on magazine covers… even sexy posters of me half clothed in low-rise Rebel Yell jeans with the top two buttons undone, and my manhood showing through the denim. But the truth was that I felt more and more anti-social every day. I was pulling away slowly from all the hoopla and attention that I once craved for myself. I was tired of being The Outlaw. I was… just tired of being somebody, and longed for the day when my destiny played out… I longed for a day when the boys and I were living a nice normal life in a remote natural environment, and, still, I fantasized about the girl who would share our lives and perhaps even have more children together. But I knew the farming business would not sustain a family without first investing a sizable amount of cash for property and equipment.

Bull Riding was my ticket. I thought sure that by now, after ten years on the circuit, I would have collected enough money to retire and go home. But the money seemed to flow in and out again… as if I was just holding the money for a day or so, before it was routed somewhere else. The fact was, my bad boy image was costly. The very vehicle that carried me to fame and fortune was also very high maintenance. Lawsuits and attorneys cost money… lots of money. And so do managers and agents. And publicists. And doctor bills.

"Ari. It's me." I spoke quietly, in a low tone.

"Johnny, good to hear from you… listen, Rebecca's got a jet chartered for you waiting at the airport. You need to be in Connecticut by tomorrow 9 am, that's a different time zone. Oh and…"

"Wait a minute, what? Connecticut? What the hell's in fucking Connecticut?"

"The ESPN studios Johnny. Follow me here. We talked about this."

"Damn it Ari I was calling about the 60 Minutes thing." I was now speaking as if I had been irritated by the spontaneity of the trip.

"I know it's a lot Johnny. But remember our conversation the other day about…"

"I know. I know. Ari, damn it." Johnny said shortly. "Put me on with Rebecca. You don't know shit."

"Johnny… you need to really be appealing this time. APPEALING! Johnny! That means you need to smile Outlaw, and shave for Christ's sake. Wear some clean clothes Johnny. You know what I mean? Johnny? Johnny are you there? The Outlaw image is wearing thin, Johnny. The fans want to see you do something… heroic! Like Robin Hood, or that Irish guy, what's his name? Wallace?"

"Ari, have I ever let you down before?"

"Yes Johnny, you have!"

"Aw come on." Speaking again in my low tone phone voice. Patronizing Ari, and Ari knew it.

"Johnny, I've gotta tell you, you're not going to be riding much longer. You have this one window of opportunity to…"

"Make as much money as I can for you and me… I know I know."

"It is what it is Baby." Ari said in his best star manager lingo.

†

The next morning found me headed promptly to the small municipal airport south of Carmel. It was an airport built for the small private planes and jets that transported so many of the world's rich and famous to and fro. Upon my arrival, I looked out the tinted windows at the limos that lined the curb. The parking lot looked like a European auto show. Jags, Mercedes, Ferraris, tricked out Hummers, a couple of Lamborghinis… I thought … and not a single pick-up truck… not a single muscle car.

Just as the jet began rolling off its parking spot, Clint Eastwood came out of the operations building and was walking towards a white Gulf Stream, stairs down, door open, engines running. His plane would be taking off right behind mine.

Clint Eastwood! I grew up watching you tame the ugly west, even if it was Italy. And here we are… taking off in private jets from the same runway, not five minutes apart. I couldn't help but smile.

My clothes were clean. But I had ordered the house cleaning service to not iron my clothes. I wanted them washed and dried at home, and wrinkled was fine with me. "No creases!" was my chief demand. I even rolled my clothes up and twisted them to make them look "lived in". So I always looked like I just woke from an all-night party, whether I really was or not. My hair, usually just air dried and pushed back, was all one length to just above my shoulders… not as long as Bobby's but certainly long for any cowboy.

Some of the other bull riders and stock contractors had, one night at a honky-tonk outside of Pendleton, dubbed me the "Hippie Cowboy." I was comfortable being a little different, as long as it was accepted and respected by my peers. Winning took care of that. Respect was a big deal to me. And I knew from experience that I could earn the respect by working hard and being the best. Because being good demanded respect, no matter what you wore. And whatever the winner is wearing, folks tend to like. I wore my jeans legs extra long. The sleeves of my retro snap button western shirt were rolled up almost to the shoulder. I termed it the "High and Tight", and Bolo used it as their slogan for the Outlaw Wear segment.

On my left forearm is inked the word **OUTLAW**, designed in block lettering like on an old fashioned wanted poster, and taking up the entire part between my wrist and the crease of my elbow. My upper right arm is tattooed with skull and crossbones… and you could barely see the bottom of it coming from out of the rolled up sleeve. My left shoulder down to my elbow is a tattoo of a vintage microphone, like Cash or Elvis would have used… and wrapped around it is a ribbon that hold the names of my two sons, and, originally had two blank spaces where I might one day have permanently inked my future wife and new baby's names. My right forearm reads, **Spiritus Invictus**, which means unconquerable spirit. Later, while in the service, I had **INFIDEL** tattooed across the width of my chest in big bold letters. I figured, the enemy calls us that on their radios all the time. Why not be proud of it and spit it back in their rotten faces? On the top part of my left arm is a rattlesnake that reads **Don't Tread on Me**! The snake represents liberty, and goes back to the founding fathers of our great nation.

My earrings, one small silver loop in each earlobe, were considered extremely radical for the rodeo cowboy culture. My jeans, torn, stained, and faded, were also extreme compared to the starched and creased blue jeans most contestants wore.

The PRCA and the PBR had rules for contestants' attire. Shirts must be long sleeve with collar. Long pants required. Contestants must enter the arena with a cowboy hat, even if it flies off as soon as the animal starts to run. I played within the rules, but only barely. My torn and thread bare jeans were enough to cause an emergency session of the council just before the PBR and the PRCA enacted new rules mandating that contestants are required to wear long pants that are appropriate as deemed by the council, which were as follows; may not be faded or worn to the point of becoming unprofessional. I pushed the envelope further than any cowboy ever had. My boots were leather square toed bull rider types, with red shafts and fancy stitching. I walked with a slight limp and I, when attending social events, carried a rosewood walking cane for effect. It always reminds me of Evel Knievel. I was in my element. The planets had lined up just so...

Once again, I was being interviewed by a female. It was if I had a guardian angel looking over me. I didn't feel comfortable spilling my guts to the male variety. Apparently the producers and agents of the world knew this about me, for rarely did The Outlaw give interviews, and television shows and glossy magazines weren't about to screw things up. I preferred candid shots in places where the public would never think I would be, like Los Angeles coming out of the Troubadour after hanging out with Slash and... strippers... one on each arm.

By now, I was no rookie, and had been on TV and radio enough to know what I looked and sounded like on the airwaves. I knew what the people wanted. They wanted their outlaw. They wanted a tall, good looking, ass-kicker to put the rest of the world in their place. They wanted someone out there to do for them what they themselves could not or would not. Like Clint did in High Plains drifter, when he made the townsfolk paint their own town red, and then left all their asses to deal with the bad guys on their own.

But at the same time, my fans wouldn't allow their outlaw to be disrespectful to women or children, nor would they allow their outlaw to disrespect the fans who put him here. They wanted a real bad boy, but one who knew where the line was… you can be bad, but don't hurt any innocents in the process.

†

The show was taped just thirty minutes prior to airing. Erin Answer and I arrived in the parking lot at the same time. I got out of the limo quickly (Ari always insisted on Limos for my appearances… it was all about image… and keeping me from getting any DUIs, something the public would be slow to forgive), limped over to her car and escorted her through the front doors, talking about the weather and how she liked her Lexus as we walked. I reminded her that we had met once before at a get together somewhere… maybe last New Year's Eve party? Erin said, "No it was at my sister's wedding. Karin? She married your friend, Wade."

I stopped walking, staring at her without thinking of it, and instead focused my memory on recalling "the wedding". It wasn't so much the wedding, I recalled, but the party afterwards. We had been talking for about fifteen minutes or so when I began to feel as though she was crossing the line between party small talk and an interview. "Jesus, lady, why don't you just give it a rest, huh!" And, abruptly, running my fingers through my hair and replacing my Stetson, I walked away, disappearing purposefully into the crowd and out the other side of the room. I was whiskey drunk.

"NOW you remember! Damn, Outlaw, don't you have any brain cells left? Or have the bulls finally beat 'em out of you? How are those precious boys of yours?" And I wondered briefly how she would know anything about the boys, and settled that I must have talked about them that night at the after-wedding blow out.

"They're really, really well. Thank you for asking." I opened the glass door to the ESPN studios, and motioned her to enter before me.

Smiling, Erin's face turned red.

What's that all about?" I asked as we approached the chrome framed elevator.

"The only time the men here open my door is when they still think they have a chance of getting in my pants."

"And this makes you blush?"

She didn't say anything.

"So you think I wanna get in your pants, Ms. Answer?"

The elevator door slid smoothly open, we stepped in, her before me, and I pushed the button. We made eye contact for the first time since the wedding, and our eyes locked on each other. I put my hand on the small of her back, moving only my thumb, up and down, softly feeling her skin through the silk blouse.

Thoughtfully, carefully, respectfully… Erin, turning and looking up at me in an admiring sort of way… whispers, "I think you're sick and tired of women throwing themselves at you. It's disgusting after a while, even to a womanizer like you."

Then she smiled… and I smiled… and the door opened again to the business at hand… creating a TV show.

After being led to our respective little dressing rooms (My dressing room door had a star made of construction paper, about the size of my hand, with glue and glitter on the outside edge, yellowish gold, with my name written in black marker. JOHNNY OUTLAW. *Someone took great care to create it,* I thought… *in kindergarten.* Erin had her own dressing room. Her star WAS gold, at least it looked gold. Her name was engraved. I thought it might have been a gift from her parents or something. I was in and out of the makeup room as quick as possible. I hated mirrors… especially when the room was all lit up in fluorescent lighting.

The makeup girls, two of them, a blonde and a brunette, seemed to be battling for position, anticipating I would sit in their chair. I chose the brunette. She wasn't as chatty as the blonde. Erin entered as I was getting out of my chair, my base coat of flesh colored face paint giving me a youthful fresh appearance, even covering the dark circles under my eyes. I was asked specifically NOT to wear the sunglasses today. Almost begging, Marty the director proclaims, "The camera loves your beautiful green eyes Johnny…. The people want to see into your heart, Johnny. Johnny, believe me… huh, Johnny trust me on this ok, my girls back there… will make you look ten years younger, ok. Just drop the shades and I'll let you keep the hat! Come on Baby, we roll in twenty."

I hung around in the green room, occasionally glancing at one of the three monitors hanging in the corners, to see how things were going on the set. But most of the time it was just a bright green screen, with a black and pink stripe at the bottom. Six minutes to show time, Erin walked in, and trying to be funny, says something about the chunks of green melon on the glass plate on the glass table by the Ralph Lauren sofa in the green room.

She nods toward the set, where Marty the director walked around talking to cameramen. We both said hi to the director, and followed instructions to sit at the twin chairs under the lights. At the last minute, the make-up girls pranced up to each of us, powdering our noses and cheek bones, patting our hair. The blonde had me this time. Then as quick as they came they were gone again. Leaving Erin and I alone for what some crew member yelled "five minutes til queue".

"Ok, cowboy... you've done this before, I know. But just think to yourself, 'Relax'. I'll ask the questions and you just answer in your own words. Just let it flow."

"Damn Erin Answer, you sound like that director over there... let it flow... Ha! I am relaxed. I popped a Xanax about a half hour ago... and one before that at the airport just before we took off." I smiled at her, exposing her own very sensitive insecurities as a woman in a man's world of sports broadcasting, and she turned red again, probably wondering if I had been one of those guys who googled her name to watch the "Peephole" video. Had I seen her naked? But then again, I doubt I gave off that kind of vibe to her. She felt like I would be one of those superheroes who comes from out of nowhere to save the damsel in spite of the odds... then disappears into the moonlit sky, stopping atop the hill and turning on his horse's hind hooves, looking at her from afar, smiling as if he was thinking 'wow, what a vision', waves his hat at her out of admiration and respect, turns back... and rides off, leaving the place better than when he found it.

"One minute!" came the voice from the shadows.

"Erin, Darlin, you're like the sister I never had", and gave a warm wink and a trademark smile. I only said that to make Erin comfortable, when inside I had the same desires as any other single, healthy, heterosexual man should have. I wanted to jump her bones back there in the elevator. But I sensed something damaged about Erin. Her feelings were hurt… by men. She trusted them to a point, to be professional and respectful. And they failed her. And for this reason, I supposed, I made a rule for myself. *Hands off Erin.* I wouldn't be the man to break her heart again. This would be a fast business trip, and its back home to see Marshall and Matthew.

"Hello everyone, I'm Erin Answer and this is ESPN's ***In The Arena***. Tonight, we're talking to a different kind of athlete, from a different kind of sport. A sport where the men AND the bulls are athletes, and the consequences for fouling out can be death. Unless you've been sleeping under a rock somewhere, you've heard of him. You've seen him on newsstands everywhere, doing cameos on hit TV shows such as Two and a Half Men, late night programs such as Jimmy Kimmel, Conan, and the Tonight Show. You know he's good… you know he's popular… in fact, he's a shoe-in for the Rodeo Hall Of Fame, the PRCA Cowboy Hall of Fame, the PBR… and this reporter would have to imagine even the American Sports Hall of Fame. We've got 'em here with us in the studio and we're going to be talking about his reign as his sport's King, his thoughts on the drug testing fiasco, and more… right after this."

Drug testing fiasco? What drug testing fiasco? There was no drug testing in rodeo. Is someone trying to do that?

The interview continued after a three minute commercial break, during which time the television monitors hanging on every wall were a constant bright green color. Then it was "one, two, three, you're on!"

"One PRCA championship… Four Bull Riders Only-event wins in one of the only two years of its existence… And now, as of last week, two-time PBR World Bull Riding Champion, pro bull riding's premier class. Nascar has Junior Nation… and rodeo has Outlaw Nation." (She turns away from the camera and toward me.)

"You came into the sport just ten years ago, albeit somewhat uh… well… not quite as an imposing figure in the rodeo world, but, even then, a little rogue… a little rebellious. But always… respectful of rodeo's traditions and the fan base. Somehow… somehow, Johnny, you managed to bring people into the arenas to spend their money who may not have ever even THOUGHT about going to a rodeo."

Nodding slightly and neither smiling nor not, I listened to the accolades, processing them in my mind, thinking… *Damn, I can't believe this is my life. I'm on ESPN, Nationwide Baby! Sitting here with fuckin Erin Answer. Damn! Damn!* I bit my lip to keep from smiling outwardly.

"The PBR announced four or five months ago that they had concerns that some of the bull athletes have been given steroids to gain muscle mass. Have you ever seen bulls being given steroids, or seen any symptoms of steroids in bulls in the PBR?"

"No. Absolutely not. I mean… I've seen results of roids in bulls, usually at auctions. You can always tell… their eyes are bulging out and looking like crazed idiots. As soon as you get them back to the ranch, they start losing weight and going through withdrawals. Anytime there's money to be made, some folks, a small minority, are gonna try things. But, to shoot roids in a bull athlete of the caliber that PBR bulls are… naw. The side effects are too bad. No stock contractor wants to do that to their money maker. They take excellent care of those bulls, I promise you."

"Well, regardless, the PBR has announced that it will begin testing bulls at the finals next year."

"Yeah, well, it's in the best interest of the sport to reassure the fans and the cowboys that it's not happening. Cody Lambert, the VP in charge of stock contracting, has been workin' with veterinarians for the last couple years, working on a special test that'll work. The PBR doesn't need any outsiders comin' in and requiring anything. They're a first class organization, and the PBR can regulate itself." *The shareholders of the PBR should appreciate that swingin' endorsement.*

"You were the first cowboy I can remember to have the announcing booth play hard driving rock and roll when you climbed into the chute."

"Yep. That was me… AC/DC, Back in Black…" There was an awkward silent moment to fill, and I, ever the professional interviewee nowadays, obliged and decided to elaborate. "It was the BRO. We were in St. Louis. They had used lighter fluid… they squirted lighter fluid on the dirt floor in a foot wide strip around the top ten cowboys and lit it on fire, before the contestants were announced by name, one by one. The night was feeling electric. The energy was apparent. The crowd was pretty pumped. I don't know… I just had the idea so I went and got the CD out of Wade's truck and brought it to the announcer… asked him to play track one after he announced my name. It worked perfectly. It was raw and loud, and the lights were going crazy."

"You won that event."

"Yes, I sure did", nodding thoughtfully. *Boy, she did her homework.*

"I noticed the other day that you've changed your calling card to 'Cowboy' by Kid Rock, who most of us know by now is a good friend of yours."

"Yeah, I've always liked that song…it gets me pumped."

"What is it, Johnny, that makes the professional rodeo cowboy… specifically the bull riders… different, or the same, as professional football players or hockey players?"

Clearing my throat. "Well, I think we have to have, ya know, a competitive spirit. We all have that to start with. And whatever life hands us, whatever it is we get exposed to, whether its football or hockey or whatever… checkers… ya know (smiling sarcastically), certain sums of us will excel at it. (I pushed my hat back again, and scratched my forehead, James Dean style.) And for the lucky ones who survive, ya know, uhmmm, injuries and other unfortunate circumstances, those of us willing to work hard and, and practice and… Mostly it's that we like the physical-ness of it all. We are men, and we don't have the luxury of combat as an everyday way of life. We are regulated to what we can do in a sports arena. And the mud and the blood is an important part of who we are."

"Bull riding is sooo brutal. How long do you see yourself doing this?"

"Ohhh, I dunno know. I guess one day I'll wake up and know it's time to hang up my spurs." Smiling one more time… for Erin's ratings and her value as a female broadcaster in a man's wide world of sports. I thought my time on the hot seat was nearing its end, but Erin Answer the reporter had one more question…

"You used to teach bull riding classes, or clinics I guess. And… a horrible tragedy… happened… uhmm (Sincere look here)… back in… where you were residing at the time… Aaaaand (Erin is hesitating, dreading the question, and the answer)… there was an accident… one of your young teenage students… was crushed… when the bull he was riding bucked him off and stepped on the boys chest. He had on a safety vest, but… died… How did it affect you as a bull rider, as a father yourself, with two young sons?"

Erin was trying to be sincere. She had given ample thought to the accident and how horrible it must be for anyone to live with something like that. But somehow, under the bright hot lights, with all these crew members standing around, looking, and me, the OUTLAW, the bad boy, not just of rodeo, but bad boy of everything… her sincerity gave way to a more scornful look, and hint of blame in her voice.

(Silence). My smile and warm caring look gave way to instant anger and an intense glare. My face turned beet red. She shouldn't have asked me that. She sold me out to get me to react… for ratings, or possibly it was at the insistence of the dickhead director. Her hands were balled into fists, her knuckles turned yellow as if she was nervous that I was about to throw the table at her or something.

I came out of my chair, took the one step needed to lean over into Erin's face, stared her straight in the eyes, and harshly whispered, "He didn't die in my school you idiot. Get your facts straight. And you can just shove it up your ass."

And with that said, grabbed my cane, stormed off the set to my dressing room to get my bag, and my sunglasses, out the door into the stairwell, and out the side door to the parking lot, to the awaiting black limo. I caught the driver napping. I knocked hard on the driver's window, scaring the bejesus out of him. The show aired fifty minutes later… the walk-out scene was deleted for a couple of two hundred thousand dollar commercial spots.

Chapter Seven

The James Bond Accident

As much as I hated to think of it, Erin Answer caused my mind to tromp back through my dark memories of when a young boy who I had given lessons to, died as a result of injuries sustained in a bull riding crash. It had been nearly three years since then, during the spring of yet another rodeo season, and I was still recuperating from a mind numbing head injury that spring in two thousand two.

I would never be able to shave my head, I considered. The scar was literally from ear to ear across my skull. Surgery to relieve critical swelling of the tissue was in time enough to save most of my normal brain functions, except that I did tend to stutter, a chronic condition that I blamed on my drinking and pain pills… and my short term memory loss was beginning to be problematic.

I had set up my modest homestead, a seventeen acre farm in Mississippi, so as to be closer to the boys' mom, Beth, making it possible for us to share custody during school weeks, when I could be there.

Immediately upon arriving home to begin my long rehab program, I began to be inundated with requests to appear at club luncheons, church meetings, et cetera. It was while at the rotary club discussing, for fifteen minutes, "The Business of Bull Riding", that I first had the vision of a bull riding clinic.

"Like your business… whether it's a car wash or a restaurant… we have to give the customers what they pay for. In my case, people pay to see the worst wrecks or the best rides." And with that I asked one of the Rotarians to play the DVD of my worst wrecks and best rides.

I had a personal invitation to sit at the same table as the mayor, the police chief, the city attorney, and the clerk of court. The table, oddly enough, was in the back corner of the Days Inn motel ball room. The room was filled with tables, around twenty-five of them. The banquet room was full of everyday managers and small business owners, small town politicians. And the most influential… the most powerful and the most corrupt, the dirty joke bunch, sat in the back.

It was the old city attorney who gave me the idea of having cowboy suppers for boys who didn't have fathers around. Even in Magnolia there were the projects. And most of those boys didn't have dads.

I played with the idea in my head for a couple of weeks. Then sat down one afternoon while my ex had the boys, and wrote a how-to manual called **The Fundamentals of Bull Riding**. It was rather short at a hundred pages. Only a few black and white photos of a bull riding glove or a rope and a bell, other such equipment and a sketch of the proper positioning of the rider, that sort of thing. In my mind this was just practice.

How hard can it be to get a book published? I thought. Selling it will be the problem. This was before everyone had access to the internet and carried an iphone in their pocket. *THAT's where the cowboy suppers can come in*, I announced in my mind. *Hell, I'll have bull riding school. I'll show 'em how to ride bulls, and then I'll sell 'em the book. Let's see… twenty students… a two day clinic… make that a day and a half… we'll watch and ride all day Saturday, and have cowboy brisket and beans, with a real covered wagon and a cook, and a big ol fire… we'll sleep under the stars in our sleeping bags… and the next morning we'll eat fireside biscuits and go to cowboy church under that pin oak… then we'll ride and watch videos of them riding, and ride again one last time, and then we'll sell the book. Let's see… twenty riders at… a hundred and fifty bucks… that's three thousand dollars for a day and half. And I'll use that money to put on the cowboy camps for kids. The school money, and the book money… it'll all go back to the camp, for the kids. Yeah!*

Two fingers pecking away at my laptop, I finished my little how-to book in three days. Ari's assistant, Rebecca, sent the disc to a self-help publisher named Majors, and then I sold the book on my own web site, but under my publishing brand of Six-Gun Publishing. And with that I was in operation by the end of that May.

School year ending, summer in the hot muggy air, local rodeos were going on everywhere, every weekend. Once I announced my plans to the city attorney, volunteers came out of the woodwork. I had horsemen and horses, a chuck-wagon and bucking stock. A portable arena made of Priefert blue steel section panels was erected by the local western store, by a man named Dudley Rogers. Dudley was a champion roper, and as was typical among ropers in those parts, came from money. He looked like a short George Strait. He was too cocky for most men to take, but he always had a good looking lady on his arm, waiting on him, dressing up for him. Dudley became heavily involved in the recruiting of the volunteer cowboys, which greatly increased my standing at the First Baptist Church of Magnolia.

The cowboy suppers under the stars went well, but proved too much trouble for the volunteers to do more than twice a year. I proposed paying them a small incentive for their troubles, but that didn't seem to help. Twice a year would have to be enough for now, and I set out to make it a big affair that would eventually host hundreds of kids. And the idea for a clinic… well that seemed like a good one. There was plenty of interest. Even the high school rodeo coach was interested in sending some of their athletes to the school. Cowboys and wanna-be bull riders all over the Tri-State circuit were buzzing about the news that Johnny Outlaw was opening up a bull riding clinic. "Right here in Miss'ippi."

It was late June, and my third clinic, when I met James Bond (Yes, Really) James was a thirteen year old kid who grew up on a cattle farm outside of Jackson. He'd heard about the bull riding school among some of his friends who were into rodeo, and begged his mom to let him go. He'd worked "mightily hard at mowing yards to pay for this" James told me when handing me the money order for the hundred and fifty bucks.

James Bond was all country, nothing like the name would suggest. He was an eager and energetic boy with a ten gallon hat and boots that were too big "cuz momma said I was growin too fast." He always had a smile on his face. He was never intimidating to anyone, though his size, a bit taller and heavier than others his age, would allow him to be. Instead, James was just a good 'ol boy from rural Miss'ippi, with a dream of being a world champion someday. I was taken with the boy almost as soon as I met him. The way he smiled and his eyes glistened in the Saturday sun. I saw the desire. I saw the hurt.

"Your daddy ride bulls?"

"No Sir."

"I mean I don't rightly know… he's not around anymore." Right away this boy had my heart.

"So… how'd you get to likin bulls?"

"Oh I had a friend of mine take me to a rodeo some years back. I always liked the bull ridin' best."

"Yeah. I understand that… and they get more girls too." (Trademark smile, eyes glistening with a boyish eagerness to walk down and…)

"Awww, I ain't all that intersted in girls yet… right now I'm just wantin' to cover my bulls. "

"Well, then… James… do what I tell you today, and you'll ride 'em alright."

The school went well for James. He met Marshall and Matthew, and they had a grand old time riding horses and running around annoying the older teenagers in the group. When the clinic was over the next day, I gave all my students compliments, leaving them with positive messages about a strong work ethic and a big heart. "If you combine those two things, you will be successful. Don't get intimidated by all the commotion going on behind the chutes, or IN the chutes. You are cowboys. Practice. Stay focused. Stay away from the bad stuff… you know what I mean… girls! And booze. And drugs. Stay away from that stuff. You wanna stay alive; you wanna be the best…. Keep your head clear." I felt like such a hypocrite saying it. But I knew it was the truth and best for the kids to hear. James exchanged phone numbers with Marshall and Matthew, and I told him to keep in touch.

"Here's my address. Write me a post card sometime... let me know how your doin. Ok? Send me some pictures of you ridin' those bulls." Folded into the page with my address on it was the entrance fee refund of a hundred and fifty dollars... cash.

"Yessir." James replied gratefully, oblivious to the refund, and ran out to the driveway where his mom was waiting and honking the horn, waiving at me and the other cowboys who were still hanging around.

One month later, I was nearing the completion of my therapy, looking through my mail, and was surprised to see an envelope from James Bond. In it a five by seven color photograph on glossy paper, of James covering his first steer at a Little Britches Rodeo. On it, James wrote, "Mr. Outlaw, Thanks for the inspiration. Good luck to Marshall and Matthew." And signed his name. I imagined James, wearing a bright white Stetson, one day signing autographs in some arena somewhere. And smiled.

After a physical by, first my own physician, one I'd found in the yellow pages of Magnolia, and then PBR Sports medicine chief, Dr. Tandy Freeman, I was back on tour by late August. I rode in two events in one month, then, with doctor's orders to ease into it, went back home to rest for another couple of weeks, putting me into the middle of September before I was again full time on the circuit. My mathematical chances of winning the championship were nil. For the rest of the season it was just practice and building momentum for the following season.

And Ari reminded me, "You still got bills to pay, Johnny… winning a few events wouldn't be a bad idea yunno!"

On the second day of my first week home, I again went to the mailbox. "Bills, bills, bills. I don't know why I bother." And these were just my local municipalities… water, power, garbage pick-up… the really big bills were sent to Rebecca. I laid the pile on the kitchen table, and played outside with the kids until dark, then it was cooking supper, getting baths, and watching Toy Story, before putting the curtain climbers to bed.

It wasn't until then that I sat down to drink a cold beer, pull up a trash can, and started ciphering through the mail, mostly junk ads on cheap paper. Half way through I saw an envelope addressed to me, in a woman's writing, but no return address. Curious, I opened it, but slowly, for somehow I just felt odd about it. It wasn't a greeting card envelope. It wasn't sprayed with perfume or kissed with red lipstick. It didn't have hearts drawn on it with x's and o's. It wasn't a business envelope. So I opened it.

Dear Mr. Outlaw (or whatever your real name is)

You don't know me. But my son, James, attended one of your bull riding schools this past summer. He always talked about meeting Johnny Outlaw the Mighty Bull Rider. He has your poster on his bedroom wall. And he always puts his hat upside down when he's not wearing it, just like you told him to. He sent you a photo a while back, you may have gotten it. He really loved riding those damn bulls.

James' funeral was today… this morning… in the rain.

My eyes dropped slowly down the handwriting on the page, noticing the big black letters that said, *I HATE YOU!*

I dropped my beer can on the floor, spewing foam all around my feet. I placed the letter down softly, then, thought of the kids, folded it up into a small rectangle, and put it in my denim shirt pocket.

I never finished reading it. I just walked away from the table, and its big pile of bills and junk mail, and the foaming beer on the floor, went outside, opened the gate to the pasture, walked about two hundred yards, using the moon for light, through the fescue to the acre sized pond. I sat on the bank, in the dark, looking up at the stars, thinking about rain, numb to her words, and ignoring the ache in my heart. I longed for a cave to hide in. My throat was tight. I couldn't swallow. Tears rolled down my cheeks and neck, and I was ringing my hands tightly. It wasn't long ago I was at the top of my game… I could do no wrong… I appeared on ESPN and Letterman… the Tonight Show, and Saturday Night Live. Then I have a horrible crash… a life changing event. But I live to ride another day. I curse out loud, drink too damn much… smoke… hang out with bad people doing bad things… and yet, it's some kid like James Bond who gets killed.

"Why!!!!!!!" I shouted into the night sky at God. And then to the Devil.

"Why him?"

Chapter Eight

Ever Been to Jamaica?

Normally, I'd just let voicemail pick up, but it was Ari.

"Hello."

"Johnny, where are you right now?" It was Rebecca, Ari's assistant.

I looked at the young red head next to me, lying naked in my hotel bed… she whispers to me, "You're in Santa Fe sweetie."

"Mmmm, Santa Fe, Sweetie." My voice was especially hoarse after hooting and hollering at the nightclub last night.

"Yeah I heard her. Who is she this time? Never mind, you couldn't possibly know her name, and I wouldn't want to put you in the embarrassing situation of having to ask her! Ari needs to speak with you. Do you have a minute?" Rebecca was not happy or in the mood to be happy. She was very concise and void of any personal greetings following her first question.

"Johnny have you seen the television lately, no never mind, of course you haven't seen anything further than the bottom of your beer glass." Rebecca took on the tone of my Mom.

"I drink out of the bottle."

Meanwhile, at Ari's insistence, Rebecca turned the line over to him.

"Whatever the fuck Johnny. I swear, kid, you are impossible to reach, you know that? I mean, we need to change this. I need you when I need you. Timing is everything!"

I was now sitting up in bed, my head slightly spinning, mostly the result of so many concussions over the years than the after effects of the booze. I fumbled to open the child proof lid, and popped in a five hundred mil Vicodin.

"You walked out on the Answer interview I understand."

"She deserved it." I was still preoccupied with swallowing my pain killer, slurping warm beer out of a bottle and cringing.

"Yeah, well. Whatever went on between you two, they cut it off the end of the program, and I get this call from the director and producer of the show, eating my ass out about how they're short on program material... Anyway, Johnny, someone else picked up on the story and all hell's breakin' loose Johnny."

"About what?" My stomach feeling more and more queezy. Tight. Nauseating feeling.

"What the fuck Ari Pei! Tell me what happened!"

"Somebody found out about your past, Johnny. They know you're an ex-con. They know you're name isn't really Johnny Outlaw."

"Hmmm"... I got up from the bed and walked toward the closed curtains... half believing the seriousness of the call, I continued, "They can't find anything. It's all been expunged. There's no record of any of that stuff. And Ari, EVERYBODY knows my name isn't really Johnny Outlaw."

"I realize that. But we never gave a reason for anyone to really investigate your life. Now they have this damn YouTube video of you getting high with some strippers, and questions being raised about your athletic performance..."

"Ari, there's no way anyone can say pot helps my athletic performance."

"True. But don't you think the PBR, the PRCA, and everyone else wants to protect their business image? You think your sponsors want their Outlaw smoking pot on freakin' television news media every sixty minutes? And, let me ask you... don't you think there's a record in the courthouse down there in Africa fuckin' Louisiana that shows the records were expunged? And don't you think that if some reporter out there knows who you're not, that maybe he's on the trail to who you are? If he knows who you are, he'll get where you're from. And then he'll find your mother."

"Angola… Angola Louisiana. Not Africa." I proclaimed, as if to minimize what it was that Ari was so freaked about. The red head was looking strangely at me. I'd forgotten she was there.

"Every tabloid in the world will have shit shovelers out there digging stuff up on you. You're front page news, for all the wrong reasons. You're supposed to be the Robin Hood of Outlaws, John. They'll find someone, and they'll pay big bucks to get the information. That's what these fuckers do."

Silence. The red head wrapped a sheet around her innocence and tip toed to the bathroom. I can't remember her name.

"Ari, I built my career on being a bad ass. This is going to make punching the reporter in the nose look tame. Why are you so worried?"

"John, I know. But the public is a very fickle thing. They build you up into this god, and…" Ari snaps his fingers and I can hear it through the phone. "The public likes to tear down what they build up every now and then. It's a power thing. Being The Outlaw is cool, as long as you're just a good guy with a few bad habits. Cross the line and they'll leave you hangin' on the goddamned street corner."

"Aaand, you think my jail time is a deal breaker?"

"Not the jail time… but possession of cocaine, intent to distribute, Mexico… I mean… I don't know. But we need to be smart here… we need to take advantage of the press. Let me put my spin into action. Meanwhile, I want you to leave town for a while… let me work things out."

"Fine with me. I'll fly home and get the kids."

"I'm afraid that's not smart… you need to freakin' disappear. Now, I've got a vacation home in the islands. It'll be some time before anyone finds you there. And by then you'll be gone anyway. Rebecca's gonna… Rebecca honey, come here… send my jet to Santa Fe. She'll call you with the details in a few minutes. Get there Johnny. Get to the fuckin' airport and don't tell anyone where you're going."

"Hell I don't even know where I'm goin."

A few minutes passed, I kissed the girl goodbye, and quickly hurried her out the door explaining that I had an emergency come up and needed to go. She was disappointed about the separation, but was "just happy I got to meet you, Johnny." Her index finger in the corner of her mouth, "Will I see you again?"

"I've got your number Hun. I'll give you a call sometime… next time I'm in Santa Fe."

"Aren't you ridin tonight?"

"Uh, well… no darlin', I'm not. Now you have a good day now hear. And take care. You're a beautiful woman." I eased down to her and kissed her like a gentleman on her pouting pink lips.

And with that she was gone, as I took a quick hot shower. Then the phone rang before I could wash the soap off good.

"Johnny, this is Rebecca. I've got the airport directions for you. Got a pen?"

"Hang on, Rebecca." I could tell she was excited, and remembered she didn't get out much.

I trampled across the carpeted floor with wet feet and droplets trailed to the desktop as I reached to get a pen and paper.

"We're gonna have you go to a rural airport, about forty miles outside of town. South of Santa Fe. Take a cab there. I'm sure the driver will know how to get there. It's the Dry Gulch municipal air strip."

"Dry Gulch. *Of course it is.* Fifteen miles. Got it."

"Where am I going Rebecca?"

"To Ari's place in Jamaica. He used to vacation there quite a lot. Now he just pays for someone to take care of the place."

"Jamaica? Okay. Shit. I still don't see the urgency. I'm supposed to ride tonight. I need to talk to my boys. Ok. Rebecca thanks."

†

The shiny white Lear landed in Ocho Rios three hours late. Bobby sat in the small airport lobby, drinking his third Mountain Dew, watching Fox News play the same stories every thirty minute cycle. *Just like radio.*

I had no idea who was meeting me at the airport, only that someone would be there to pick me up. I expected it would be the caretaker of the property, whoever that was. I figured the property meant some kind of estate.

After all, Ari must be very wealthy. But why Jamaica?

Jamaica I knew absolutely nothing about. Only that it was mostly black, and that Bob Marley was from here. I expected pink and aqua-blue shanties, set against rusty old bicycles and garbage lined roads.

The jet landed, I poured myself one last Maker's Mark and Seven on the rocks, stirred it gently with a red plastic straw, and waited a moment as the co-pilot pulled my camel-tan saddle leather gear bag from the four foot by four foot baggage compartment. The lack of weight in the bag surprised the guy, as he pulled way too hard and nearly fell on his ass. I drank and laughed. Already I was beginning to relax. I missed the boys.

One thing I didn't particularly like about the plane was, though fast and extremely convenient, I could not stand up in it. Either my knees were bent or my body bent at the waist. Even when pissing. And my knees were beginning to throb. My back always hurt, but mostly in silence except for the occasional groan when getting up out of a chair… any chair. I certainly enjoyed the privacy, and the alcohol, and not having to go through public airports. One of the biggest advantages flying by private jet was there is seldom any security to hassle with.

As I limped down the four small steps that hung from the side of the aircraft, grabbing my bag from Dufus the co-pilot, I squinted across the tarmac to the lobby windows. They were tinted and I couldn't see a damn thing other than my reflection. Before I could take three steps I heard Bobby yelling my name. At first I thought I must be mistaken, then less than a moment later I saw Kid Rock strutting over the concrete surface, through an oil slick where a plane had been, smoking a fat cigar, wearing Bermuda shorts, house slippers, a wife beater tee shirt, his stringy blonde hair in a pony-tail, and a straw fedora with a rainbow colored hat band. *Man, what a pleasant surprise.* I smiled from ear to ear and my pace quickened.

"What the fuck took so long dickhead?"

"Mountain Dew?" I asked Bobby while I drank from my cocktail glass and looked mockingly at the rock star.

Bobby drank his last warm gulp, slammed the aluminum can into his forehead, crushing its thin sides into a palm sized Frisbee, and tossed it into my chest.

"I didn't know you were gonna be here or I woulda called you. Didn't Rebecca or anybody call you?"

"There ain't no fuckin cell phones out here Man… which I ain't complainin' know what I mean, but there ain't no way to communicate out here except with a land line or a satellite phone, if you're one of the rich people who can afford it."

"But, you are rich. And I'm sure Ari Pei can afford a land line."

Bobby smiles and dumps his cigar ashes on the sweltering concrete below. We are both beginning to sweat just standing and talking. The airport is void of human activity. Only planes, mostly small business class jets tied down with steel cables to steel hooks that protrude out of the concrete tarmac. There is a distinct smell of jet fuel in the air. The air is heavy, and I realized quickly I was way over-dressed.

"I can't believe you wear that." I remarked quickly.

"What? You don't like it? Man, you wouldn't know fashion if your name was fuckin' Christian Audiger."

"Who?" I was truly perplexed at the statement. "Who's Christian Audiger?"

"Nevermind." Said The Kid.

"Is that all you've had to drink today is Mountain Dew?" I asked.

"What time do you think it is Outlaw?"

"I don't know queer-bait, let me see." And I looked up at the sky, blinded by the scorching sun, put my free hand over my eyes, thinking the sun is almost straight up above us…

"I'd say it's around noon."

"Lucky bastard… So I'm up rather fuckin' early you know what I mean. I had to get my ass out of bed and rush my ass over here to pick your lazy ass up. Why can't you fuckin' WALK like I did?"

"You didn't walk." I was pulling my baggage with one hand, and drinking with the other, somehow managing to hold the glass temporarily with my teeth and pull the door open to the lobby area. Bobby walks through.

"Thanks Sweetheart." Bobby quipped.

The TV was barely audible from across the room, and there was an unmanned counter with a table behind that, on top which sat the radio and telephone equipment. There was a computer monitor visible, and the glare from the radar screen reflected against the glass covered trophy case that hung on the back wall, which was being utilized as a storage compartment for such necessities as extra radio batteries and what looked like a couple of folded up maps.

"Seen anybody here?"

"I saw one dude", Bobby assured me, and yelled out, "Hey Airport Dude, we're leavin'!" And we both shrugged their shoulders as we exited the small Jamaican terminal without fanfare of any kind. Not a soul. Not a single camera. Not a single groupie.

†

"Who's Jeep?"

"Ari's"

"Bet this comes in handy."

"Yep."

"So, I have all these questions running around in my head…"

"Ari sent me here to take care of your stupid ass for a while." I said to him.

"Yeah, right! I watch the news mother fucker. How long is a while?"

"I dunno. He'll need time to pull all his forces together." I replied mockingly.

"Ari's at his best in times like these… hey that sounds like a song. In times like theeese."

"So… all I know is that Ari told me over the phone that somebody finally found out that I was a con, and that Outlaw isn't my real name."

"WHAT! Outlaw isn't yur real name, Dude? Oh My God!"

"I know, right. So I really fail to see what the big deal is. I mean this Jamaican vacation is nice, but, I don't think I'll be here very long. I haven't seen my kids in weeks…"

"Well, I'm just tellin ya dude, it could be longer than you think."

"You speak from experience I guess."

"Yep. Remember my Waffle House incident? He turned that into a real life bad ass story… turned out to be good publicity. Of course it cost me ten grand to buy the mother fucker I hit."

Is that all? Ten grand? Wish I could out that cheap.

Besides, Ari likes to feel important… take credit for pullin' your ass outa the shit."

Bob's comment immediately made me think of Captain Bill Tassler. *How many times had he pulled us outa the shit?*

There was a long silence as the Jeep traversed the chip seal road from the air strip to the coast line.

"It's an o'eight model. Fucker's only got two thousand miles on it, man. Just sits in the fuckin' garage. CD player works, but I don't have any CDs."

No iPod port I noticed. "So tell me about Jamaica and this place we're headed to."

Smiling, Bobby puffs his eighteen dollar Cohiba Esplendidos, hands one over to me, and I, in turn, accept and pull out my own lighter.

"Here Man, use a REAL lighter." Bobby hands me a mini-torch.

"Jamaica… Capital city, Kingston… Population, just under three million… an island roughly the size of Connecticut… annual average temperature eighty two degrees… the official language is English."

Bobby stops his lecture for another puff. The Jeep hits a pot hole while he's trying to light it.

"FUCK. Where'd that come from Man."

"I don't know. Want me to drive?"

"You don't know where we're goin… Besides, they drive on the wrong side of the fuckin road here, Man."

"So I'd still do better than you."

"Shut up you crazy fuckin' bull rider. Jesus H Christ, Man, whatever possesses you to get on those crazy fuckin' animals anyway? You do that 'cuz you ain't got no fuckin' ball sack, and you're trying to compensate."

"Somebody very important to me once told me I couldn't do it."

There was another silent moment, until Bobby broke silence.

"There are all kinds of cultures here, Man. You said you were familiar with New Orleens?"

"Ha. It's not New Orleens. It's New Orlins. Or as the residents there say, New Awlins! And yes, I am, or used to be familiar with it."

"Well, I've been to the Big Easy a few times, and I can tell you this is a lot like it. Only instead of everything being fuckin' Cajun, its Curry and Jerk."

"Sounds good. They got cold beer here?"

"It ain't THAT good, brotha. Oh yeah. Ari's house is stocked, Man. It's got everything you'll need or want, even pussy. Just get on the land line and call the guy."

I knew there was a land line. "The guy?"

"You're not ready yet."

"There's a lotta fuckin' Africans here. From the slave trade days. You gotta watch em too Man.

"You're from Detroit. How bad could it be?" I looked at him with crooked eyes.

"The Rostamon fuckers will rip your ass off big time. They prey on tourists. And NEVER buy pot from those fuckers on the beach… cuz it ain't real pot. There's a lot of ethnic groups here though from all over Europe. Spain. Portugal. Great Britain. Even German and Irish. Result of the sugar and citrus and coffee that they could purchase here and trade back in Europe."

"Didn't Columbus discover this island?"

"Yep. Columbus… The Jamaican motto is 'Out of many, One people'."

"Sounds familiar… Huh, well it does sound like quite the melting pot. Food must be damn good then. Got any women?"

"Yeah, some. I mean, you know, you gotta look around if you want the local talent. They're in the back street bars and shops and schools."

Schools? I wondered to myself what kind of teachers live in Jamaica where most people are black, and full of Rostamen. Bobby lit a fat boy and passed it.

"I got it off a web site, Man, about Jamaica. Gave me all I needed to know in one fuckin' page." Smiling.

I smiled and laughed. Passed the torpedo back to the driver. There's an intersection coming up… a busier street with lines on the pavement and one green sign directing traffic. Bobby slows down, sees no one coming, and rolls through the stop without ever applying his brakes.

"Holy Shit!" I shouted as I grabbed the dash handle in front of me.

"Fuck!" Bobby spit out his doobie onto his lap, hopped up and down in his seat a couple time, swearing all the while, and the spliff fell to the floorboard.

A small horn sound erupted from the oncoming vehicle, a tiny Datsun B-210 from the dark ages, painted in various colors of the rainbow, but mostly light blue.

"Son of a bitch Outlaw! Why didn't you tell me he was comin?"

I looked at Bobby with surprised eyeballs.

"Fuck you Kid." And I looked over to the beach, just a hundred yards or so from us.

There is silence now as we gather our nerves and find our smokes.

"This is highway A3." Puff, choke, breathe in… breathe out. Pass it over.

"There ain't much chance of getting lost around here, just stay on A-three or A-one… it's the only state highway system."

"Shouldn't you be drivin' on the other side?"

"There's another set of roads called B-one, B-two, and so on, over on the other side of the island. A-three runs along the coast line pretty much. A-one and A-three run basically north and south, across the island… pretty much. Everything else is back roads. Dirt, sand, gravel. Some pretty big fuckin' estates out here, Man. Especially back there in the hills. Lots of old plantations. Some of 'em are on like, five hundred acres of prime real estate, and you can be drivin' down their fuckin' driveway and not realize it 'til some son of a bitch chases you down in his little fuckin' police scooter. Five hundred acres on an island that's only four thousand square miles."

"You okay Man. You sound like you're havin' a flashback."

"Take the wheel." I reached over, took over seamlessly as Bobby reached back and grabbed two longneck Coors Originals from under the back rumble seat. I steered the vehicle back to the left side of the road, which no longer had yellow marking on the pavement, but instead looked like miles of pavement in the middle of nowhere.

"You're on the wrong side of the road Dufus!" Bobby yelled.

"What?"

"That's why we almost crashed back there. We were on the wrong side of the fuckin' road, Man."

"YOU were on the wrong side of the fuckin' road. You were drivin'. I was way over here." Bobby could be maddening at times.

I abruptly put the drab green Sahara Wrangler in to the left lane, and dropped the wheel. Bobby steered with his knees until he got his twist cap off his cold beer, lit his cigar with his torch, and put the remainder of the doobie in the ash tray.

"Coors."

"Yep."

"Cold."

"Yep."

"Long neck."

"What's your point?" Bobby glares over.

"You like me." I smiled my trademark smirk and winked.

"Fuck you."

"So, what's it like for kids growing up here?"

"Why? You ain't plannin' on movin' here are ya?" Bobby grinned.

"You never know."

"I was datin' this chick one time, a short time… when I was here before… she was a local. Creole I'd call it I guess. Beautiful… I mean fuckin' BEAUTIFUL! Brown skin with white features… green eyes. But a baaaad temper Man. Bad temper. Bitch chased me with a knife. She was gonna cut my fuckin' dick off."

With his beer now between his thighs, his Cuban cigar safely tucked into the crook in his mouth, his teeth clinching it, Bobby came to a rolling stop at the intersection of highway A3 and the Coast highway that ran almost westerly toward areas like Saint Ann's Bay, Steer Town, and Discovery Bay… on to Rio Bueno, and highway A1, and then to Montego Bay.

I was smiling and looking occasionally to the road in front, and the ocean that was now to my right, on the other side of the road, and there was a sugar sand beach between us.

"Anyway, she had a son… he was eight. They called him Bambi."

I gave up trying to light my cigar in the rushing wind, and had too much pride to ask Bobby again for his torch. I instead concentrated on my cold Coors in a bottle. I had the feeling this was a special treat on the island. Why else would Bobby have gone to the trouble?

"Kids here play a game… called Dandy Shandy. No shit that's the name of it. And another one is uh 'lou do'. 'Lou do.'"

"Lou do?"

"Yeah."

"What the heck does that mean?"

"Hell if I know Man. Hell if I know."

I noticed a smaller green sign that read Saint Ann Parish.

"Parishes instead of counties", Bobby informed.

"Yeah, I saw that. It is a lot like Louisiana. They call 'em parishes too."

The road wound around and away from and back to the white beach, and immature palms looked as though they might have been planted recently. Hurricanes wreaked havoc on the island, and if one looked carefully, he could see the water marks, the wind damage, and the occasional demolished structure of wood and tin crumpled up into a pile of leafy vegetation and sand. The coast land appeared to actually be below sea level as the crystal blue waters rolled up the shoreline, in direct contrast to the awesome looking foothills and mountains to my left. Below sea level reminded me of New Orleans… and the gulf coast. This was the month of February, and it felt like August in southern "Miss'ippi". In a way, I was glad to be away from the world. In another, I was sick to my stomach missing the boys. I wondered what they were doing right at that moment. I felt too far away. The beer was good, but didn't fill the emptiness in me. It had only been around thirty minutes since I landed in Ari's private Leer jet, and an hour or so before that I was in Orlando. And four hours before that I had been in Santa Fe. In bed with a nameless red head who liked to call me Sweetie, and expected me to ride tonight. Or was that last night?

"What day is this?"

Bobby looked at me and smiled empathetically.

"Saturday. One pm. Jamaica time!" Bobby looked at his cell phone, barely charged, and which was now acting only as a time piece.

I looked again out at the endless sea, as the sunlight shattered the waves, and wondered what it would be like to be a pirate in the days of the explorers. I recalled Jimmy Buffet's Lighthouse novel. The way Jimmy colored the pictures for the reader, like he did in his music. The water, the salty air, the people… mostly the people… how colorful his characters were… how seemingly outlandish to most, but how very real for those who had been there. I was here, in Ocho Rios, Jamaica. With a rock legend named Kid Rock. Riding in a Jeep, heading to a place I knew nothing about, sitting out the storm, waiting for my time to re-emerge. I looked at my cell for antennae bars. One bar. Then it was gone again. No service.

Chapter Nine

Mount Plenty

Bobby explained it was about half way between Ocho Rios and Montego Bay, on a magnificent point that protruded out into the ocean. There was a cutaway that formed a kind of swimming pool of calm azure water of the Caribbean, and a man-made beach for lying out or playing volleyball or whatever. There was also a heated swimming pool and a hot tub beside the house, off the terrace, nestled in amongst the trees and a beautiful flower garden. The house was a mansion Bobby proclaimed, and that meant something, as I knew Bobby's Carmel house to be one of the largest I'd ever been in.

We soon passed a four foot by three foot wooden sign, painted white with yellow trim, engraved with the name *Mount Plenty Great House.* We drove down the long meandering pea-gravel drive, through a field of sweet juicy sugar cane, past some silk-cotton and cinnamon trees, to the Plantation. I had Bobby stop long enough that I might cut a piece of cane and chew on what reminded me more and more of Louisiana.

It was indeed grand. As large and exquisite as anything I'd seen in Hollywood, or Carmel, or anywhere. It reminded me of the old plantations back home, where you could tour the grounds and see costumed volunteers in their olden day wears, blacksmithing or cooking over open fires in cast iron pots. Only this was in Jamaica of all places… on its own strip of private beach. It felt as though we were on our own island.

The grand manor, nestled nicely between the azure sea and a lush tropical rainforest, all cheery yellow with white accents of wooden shutters and Greek columns, green lawns circuiting the home with allamanda-draped terraces and beds of blue plumbago, stood as a magnificent monument to someone's good old days. It had fifteen bedrooms on three floors. The kitchen and bathroom floors were made of granite, along with the counter tops in every bathroom and in the gourmet kitchen, more fitting for a small restaurant.

The wrap-around porch hosted huge white columns and front steps reminded me of something from **Gone with the Wind**. Enormous brick chimneys arose, one on each end of the house. As I looked to the south I noticed there were the Mountains of Saint James, according to the tourist guide and map I'd grabbed at the airport.

It was covered in thick vegetation, most of it in rows like crops. These were rows and rows of coffee groves and pineapple plants, Bobby explained. They were nestled in the foothills between the coast line and the Catadupa mountain range. The place was covered in lush vegetation, and I was seeing what I thought were probably rain forests further up into the hill country. The canopy looked like a solid carpet of various shades of green. We were both sweating. The humidity reminded me of Louisiana, too… only worse.

We pulled up to the west side of the house, to the portico, unloaded our bodies and I grabbed my bag. I followed Bobby to the massive side door, of mahogany and glass. A massive crystal chandelier suspended overhead, light cruised in through a menagerie of windows. We walked inside and I dropped my gear. I walked through a large visiting room which opened up to an old library of classic literature and leather bound chairs with deep red colored tables.

I was losing my sense of direction until I happened upon the entranceway, which through its massive walls of sash windows, and the wrap around veranda, I viewed the beautiful Caribbean sea… due north. Ninety miles north of where I was standing was Cuba. I noticed a laminated brochure dangling from a rich cherry table by the umbrella stand. I picked it up and began to read. I could hear Bobby in the background, slamming doors and walking up the stairs.

Overlooking the beautiful Caribbean Sea, on the hills of the former Rose Hall plantation, sits this Great House, made of wood with a cut granite stone foundation. It has a wrap-around veranda and sash windows which help keep the house cool.

At the front of the Great House is an elegant porte cochere with massive thirty foot square wooden columns that greet visitors. The bay area is octagonal in shape with fixed glass panels, louvre windows and lattice work above. The roof is cedar shingles with cap and comb and finials. This would suggest the house was built after the Georgian age when homes were adapted to the climate.

Mount Plenty was for a long time the home of Custos of St. Ann, Honourable I Hiatt, who was born in 1722. He was 98 years of age when he died. He was buried here at Mt. Plenty. Much later the estate was owned by St. Thomas Roxborough, and finally Pat and Bernard Cooke. It was the Cookes who renovated the building and added the four car garage, along with the custom bay pool.

The property was famous for its production of pineapple, and later coffee. There were slaves on the property until emancipation. Now, the land around the estate is leased to the Walker Company, and they care for the land under strict guidelines from the owners.

Mt. Plenty is a three story building. Beneath it is a basement made from cut stone which elevates the granite portion off the ground. This granite is the foundation to the wood framed main level.

The second level is clad with wood shingles on the low portion of the walls, with a series of louvre panels, sash windows, and small portions of walls taking up the rest of the wall space. The third level is the finished attic and has within it a sweeping cedar shingle hip roof. Additional habitable space is created on the third level using large dormer windows.

"Mrs. Cooke was Ari's mom." Bobby whispered but still caught me by surprise.

"There's a lot about this house that's… interesting. But enough of that for now ol' boy, let's get you settled in. I'm putting you on the second floor with me, but I'll warn you… I keep my door locked."

"In your dreams rock star." I said.

"Yeah, okay… whatever!" Bob replied.

Bobby showed me my new digs… nothing less than fantastic.

I wish the boys were here to see this. I could picture it and hear them running around from room to room, hey daddy look at this… no daddy look at this one…

I unloaded my gear and threw my stuff in the chest of drawers, laid out my bathroom bag on the marble counter top, and tossed my empty leather bag into the closet. I ran my fingers under the water from the tap and then through my hair, looking into the mirror only for a split second.

I had a whim to change into something a little more… tropical, as opposed to the shit kickers and jeans I was donning since yesterday in Santa Fe. I hung my Stetson on a lamp, quickly disrobed, tossing my Rebel jeans and Bolo High and Tight into a pile under the nightstand, and donned a pair of thread-bare khaki Duckhead cutoffs, flip flops, a Hemingway's Restaurant t-shirt, and a sky blue Hobie ball cap, backwards. Instantly, I was an ex-patriot, ready to settle into what I'd hoped would be a very short vacation. I thought about Marshall and Matthew constantly.

Bobby knocked on my door, which was only half closed, and walked in.

"You knock like you drive through stop signs." I noticed.

"Hey at least I fuckin' knocked." Bobby handed me the ice cold Coors Light in a can.

I looked at the Light, looked at Bobby.

"Hey Man, we're in fuckin' JAMAICA! You're lucky it's not Red Stripe or some bullshit like that."

And with that I understood how fortunate I was, and drank my second beer on Jamaican soil.

"So where'd you get the Coors Original in a bottle?"

"I had a few left over when I got here yesterday. I saved you the last one."

"Thanks Man."

"Hey Man, I'm always thinkin' about ya… You poor bastard… I see you opted for the room with a view."

I replied, "Yep. It sure is nice. Can't wait to see the sun come up over that water."

"Yeah, well, if I have my way, you'll still be up when that happens Outlaw."

"Got plans do we?"

"Come on, I want you to meet somebody."

"Who?"

"Just come on. That is… if you're finished primpin' in here."

Bobby left the room, leading the way down the hall way to the huge mahogany stairs to the main floor. I was still captivated by the grandeur of the place.

"Some kind of prince live here before?"

"Well, actually, Ari's mother married a wealthy man who had business here… brokering citrus and coffee… shit like that. Anyway, she died, and left the place to Ari."

"Some guys are just born with it."

We walked from room to room, and eventually to the awesome game room. There was a pool table, a hockey table, dart board, a completely furnished bar, and a movie theater with reclining leather seats. On the north side, we walked out under the veranda and, after a few short steps up, to the heated swimming pool and hot tub area.

"I should have just unpacked down here."

"I hear ya Man. Nice. Nuther beer?"

I handed Bobby my empty can, and saw framed pictures on the shelf next to the elongated mirror behind the rich mahogany bar.

"Who's that?"

Well, that's Ari right there."

"Damn, really?"

"I know, huh… and that's Ari's wife and son with him in this one over here."

His wife? His son? "I didn't know Ari was divorced?"

"He's not." Bob replied. "Hey, I told you this place was interesting."

I looked at Bobby, me on the receiving side of the bar, Bobby on the bartender side. But Bobby's attention was soon robbed as his eyes glanced across the room where she was entering.

“Oh, hey…” Bobby walked out from behind the bar, past me and toward her.

“Uhhhh…. Jasmin… sweetheart, I want you to meet a good friend of mine. Jasmin, this is Johnny.”

“Hi, Jasmin.” And with that I held out my hand to greet her.

“Jasmin here is Breezy’s daughter. Breezy is our house keeper. Ari lets Breezy bring her kids to work with her. Jasmin likes to lay out by the pool… don’t you honey.” The two held hands while Bobby looked her over.

Jasmin looked to be about sixteen or seventeen. Perhaps she was eighteen. It was hard to tell these days. I always got real cautious around teenage girls. American ones could be very aggressive.

†

I remembered all too well an episode in Pendleton, Oregon a few years ago… Short on motel space, and long on economic need, some residents and rodeo enthusiasts volunteered to put cowboy contestants up during their stay for the week long festivities. I stayed with the Blakely family… Father Ralph, Mother Marge, Son Roger, and Daughter Mori.

Mori was an exuberant and ambitious sixteen year old, intent on making the most of her fortunate happenstance. The fact that it was The Outlaw himself staying at their residence was all she could talk about with her friends. One night, after I got drunk at the Rodeo dance and stumbled back to the Blakely's home, Mori had three of her friends staying over for a slumber party. Once I was settled in to my pallet on the floor in the garage that had been made in to an entertainment room, the girls decided to drop in to say hello.

"Johnny."

"Hmm."

"J-o-h-n-n-eeeeeeeeeeeee."

"Hmm, what? What is it?"

"Johnny" the female voice whispered, "I want you to meet some of my friends." Giggling ensued, and becoming more aware of my situation, pulled the comforter tighter to my chin.

"Are you wearing anything under there?"

"Yes." More giggling.

"This is Kerri."

"Hi, Kerri."

"Hello."

"This is her sister Kimmie."

"Hi, Kimmie."

"Hello."

"And this is Becky."

"Hello Miss Becky."

"Hi, Johnny." All three said in unison with more giggling.

"So, what have you been up to tonight?" Mori, with one finger in her mouth, and the opposite hand holding a golf iron and trying to pull back the only cover I had between my nakedness and teenage curiosity.

"Oh, nothing much. Just went to the dance for a while. How 'bout you ladies?" If I hadn't been in HER house, I'd have been insistent that they leave. I'd met too many cons who warned how just one little sex act with one teenage girl, even if SHE is the instigator, can lead to decades behind prison walls.

Shy little Becky until now, all of a sudden turned on a small lamp behind them that sat on a pile of American Geographic magazines. I saw they were wearing only oversized tee shirts and skimpy little panties that were more lace than anything else… each of them. My heart started pounding, more and more, out of fear of what Ralph would do if he woke up and caught them there with me. I could already see the headline in the local paper. "Pro Bull Rider takes advantage of local citizens' kindness and fucks their underage daughter, who is a choir girl at the First Baptist Church of Pendleton."

"Oh, nothing much. We're too young to get into the dance, so we just stayed here and waited for you."

"Yeah, well, uh, now girls…" I propped myself up on my elbows, looking up at the girls with an eye full of teenage skin and exuberance.

"Now, now, as much as I'd like to visit, ya'll are gonna… have to… get out of here before someone comes in here and thinks we're up to somethin'."

The girls all laughed devilishly, making fun of my sheepishness.

"Why, Johnny, don't you like what we're wearing for you?" Mori smiled her sexiest smile and glared at me lying there on my pallet, in the added-on guest room which was once a single car garage, in Pendleton Oregon, in Ralph's house.

"No. Hell no. I'm not going to jail for any one. Now ya'll run along and play now. And I'll see you in the morning at breakfast. Now ya'll GET OUT!" I said it loud enough that Ralph would hear it if he was up looking around, threw my pillow at Mori and the girls all laughed, as they walked one by one out of the garage and back into the main house.

I lay there, trying to shake off the hard-on and reminding myself that they may think they want it now, but chances are they would hate me for my selfishness later. And I recalled guys I'd known in my life that would not have forsaken such a bounty of virgins… and I was proud of myself that I had the decency. The Devil was frowning.

†

So that was the way I saw the female persuasion. If they were eighteen, and breathing… I was probably game. But under eighteen… it was hands off and avoid the situation. Period. Jasmin was no exception.

She seemed quite educated, and spoke well. Her skin was like hot cocoa. Her ears were pierced, along with her bellybutton and her tongue. Her hair was black, so black it was almost midnight blue, shined like silk, and looked soft like a white woman's hair. She was wearing a string bikini and barefooted. *Nice feet.*

"What are you guys doing?" Jasmin asked. Her Jamaican dialect was immediately apparent.

"I'm just showin' Johnny Cakes here around the palace. How 'bout you?"

Looking me up and down, as if sizing me up for a feast or something, Jasmin replied, "I'm just layin' out by da pool, takin' it easy, listnin' to the waves crash on da shore." She removed her leopard print bikini top, which really only covered her nipples, as she spoke. Jasmin's fingers from her right hand ran softly and slowly up and down the length of her torso, between her tender breasts, as she waited for a reply from either one of us. Her left hand twisted playfully with a lock of hair that hung gently over her face. I saw trouble, and all I could think about was getting away from the situation.

"So, Bobby, you haven't finished showing me around the place yet. How 'bout we finish our tour now?" It was rude, abrupt and out of place to say it, but I knew there wasn't any time for beating around the proverbial bush. Bobby looked at me with bent eyebrows. I check-mated Bobby by putting my left hand on his shoulder, smiling intently and demanding with my eyes we go now.

"Oooooh-Kaaaaay? Well, Jasmin, will you be spending time with us this weekend?" He burns the end of his cigar again, trying to get it to light quickly but it doesn't.

"May be… if you are lucky." Her hand now on her hip and her fingers still twirling that one lock of hair.

"Goood… well we'll see you around then okay." Then Bob leaned in to her ear and spoke so quietly I couldn't hear.

Jasmin walked away slowly, back to her lounge chair and beach towel, her tight ass cheeks beckoning to her prey, and looked back over her shoulder at us boys to see if we were looking… We were.

"Jesus H. Christ! What the hell are you thinking, Man? 'Cause even in Jamaica I'm pretty sure she's fucking jailbait!"

"Hey Man, I know. Believe me I know. I've been putting up with her shit for the last two days. Man, I'd like to fuck her brains out. Aw, I'm just teasin' that's all."

"Yeah, well… I met guys who thought the same way, Bob, and they're locked up tighter than a Mason jar. I'm not getting anywhere around that package of dynamite, Bro. That shit's trouble, trouble. T-R-O-U-B-L-E. Trouble!"

"Okay Outlaw. I know. How about another beer."

Reloaded with beverages of the Gods, we ventured away from the poolside nymph and back upstairs. The main floor was enough to witness, chocked with historical artifacts from a bygone era of plantations and sugar cane, and slaves.

Slave labor obviously built the mansions and tended the fields and crops, and Outlaw was more reminiscent of the pre-civil war South than I would have ever expected. Out the east wing of the main floor, about two football fields out, was an ancient looking slave quarters. Attention had been paid to it recently, as the grass and trees around it were mowed and trimmed, and walls that had once been falling down were tastefully mended with weathered wood and like-materials.

The tour was only half over, Bobby explained, but we were growing tired of walking, and Bobby's throat was becoming rather scratchy. Time for another beer, and we walked together to the kitchen, which really was a commercial set-up that would rival the finest restaurants anywhere. The refrigerator freezer unit was six feet wide and six feet tall. The large gas Viking cook stove, with six big burners, and a massive stainless hood vent suspended over it, was the center piece of the room. Under it were two ovens, one large gas oven and one electric bread and pastry oven.

I'd day-dreamed about cooking in a kitchen like this, and peaked into the massive arrangement of dark cherry wood cabinets for possible ingredients for a midnight meal. There wasn't much. A few spice bottles. Some angel hair pasta in a zip lock bag, a fresh loaf of bread. The fridge was stocked mainly with Red Stripe, Coors Light and Bud Light… a few Dr. Peppers… a couple of Mountain Dews, some drink brands I didn't recognize… and a bottle of ketchup. A bag of Blue Mountain coffee in the freezer, along with a couple of ice packs and a half gone box of popsicles. It was obvious that the Great House was not lived in often. I wondered if maybe Breezy and her daughter were inconvenienced by our visit. The mere size of the home might require full time dusting, whether anyone was staying here or not.

The time was now five pm, and the sun showed signs of waning as it appeared more to the west. Shadows began appearing around the lawn, mainly from the massive building we were in. I memorized the lay-out as much as possible… where the entertainment room was… where the kitchen was… and how to navigate from the west entrance to the main one… the bar… and how to get to my room from the huge mahogany stair case. And that was enough for one day. We decided we would each do our own thing for a while, and agreed to rendezvous back at the entertainment room in an hour to discuss evening plans.

Montego Bay was about an hour and a half drive, and Bobby suggested we venture out on this Saturday night to get a feel for the city. I wasn't sure, as it had really been a long day. I felt a thousand miles away from my world and my boys, and I was not in the mood for a vacation.

Chapter Ten

The Locked Door

It was Monday, two and a half days after my arrival, around seven pm Jamaica time. The sun was going down and I walked out onto my own little bedroom porch to witness the setting over the Caribbean Sea. I ached in all the normal places… my lower back… between my shoulder blades… my right shoulder… my head… my riding hand… my knees… my ankles… my toes… I wondered what Bobby was up to.

I splashed hot water on my face, ran my wet fingers through my hair… which was beginning to take on a salty surfer-dude appearance… rinsed with a travel bottle of Scope, and limped down the stairs to the entertainment room to find Bobby sitting there watching a tabloid show on the big screen.

"Hey Man, check this out!" Bobby was looking back at me, as I was entering the room, smoking another Cuban… or possibly the same one.

He was half-way, it appeared, into an exclusive investigative report by Extra! on bull rider Johnny Outlaw. Mario Lopez was hosting, amid a collage of photographs and video of "the rodeo star" that blanketed the screen, one scene of me after another.

Me, leaving the Troubadour nightclub in west L.A. with two barely dressed women, presumed strippers I'd escorted to the Guns concert…

Me, at the Cannes Film Festival with the ultimate porn star, Virgin Madsen…

Me, with a cigarette dangling from my lips walking towards the camera, in my three day beard and unbuttoned shirt, leaving the upscale condo of Paris Hilton's from a party there the night before…

Me, hanging out with Charlie Sheen, before a reported "binge of drugs, alcohol and prostitutes"…

Me, on stage with Slash, again at the Troubadour, yelling into the microphone trying to sing "Sweet Child of Mine"… Me, doing a cameo in a Kid Rock music video, "Mirrors", in which I played the role of a drug dealer in a leopard skin box hat…

Me, at the porn video awards show in Vegas with Jennie James… *I almost fell in love with her, but I knew better.*

Me, naked in Playgirl, the photos of which they were showing were digitally censored…

My pictorial from GQ… *pretty tame compared to the Playgirl pictorial.*

Me, getting in Erin's face… *Damn I look mad.*

Me, walking off the set at ESPN… *I didn't think anyone would release those.*

Then came the mug shots.

In just a matter of seconds my years of playing the bad ass were all flashing on the tube, and I hoped desperately the boys weren't seeing any of it. It was like watching someone else. I reached for and found the edge of the sofa and fell into it. I was numb all over.

"Damn, Johnny, lookin' at this shit, I'd have to think you were some kind of… Outlaw." Bobby looked over at me with a reassuring grin. He saw it all as entertainment, and was obviously glad it wasn't him for a change.

Then, he said, "Don't sweat it, Dude. It's the rep you've been grooming since you got into this biz. Hell, it's what the fans love about you. All this press is just making you a rich man."

I recalled what Ari warned me about. "Bobby… I'm in the rodeo business. Rodeo fans are all about the American flag and apple pie. The cowboys I ride against have always hated me for changing the game. The image. They're eatin' this shit up, Man. They're watchin' me fall, and they like it." My eyes were tearing up, and my face was flush. "Did you know that my contract with the PBR has a morality clause? They can kick me out any time they want."

"Watching you fall? Johnny. Take it easy. In all that footage, did you see one shot of you riding a bull? You're way beyond the rodeo business, Man. You're in the entertainment biz, Cowboy! It will all work out for the best. I promise. Ari ain't stupid. He's been expecting something like this for a while. Believe me, he'll have this whole thing working for you in a matter of days, if he hasn't already. If I had to guess, he sent ET those photos and videos, or at least got them to do the story."

Bobby switched channels during the commercial break to Showbiz Tonight on HLN. There, Brooke Lynn, a pretty blonde with bright white veneers and green eyes, was reading her teleprompter for the Making News Today segment.

> "Big News Breaking! Bull Riding Champ Johnny Outlaw: Good Guy or Bad? (*Up pops a photo of me on the television screen.*) Recent investigations have uncovered the truth behind the mysterious man in the black cowboy hat.

Johnny Outlaw, frequently referred to as The Outlaw, the Pro Bull Riders World Champ, REALLY IS an outlaw.

Turns out his given birth name is Toller. (Another mug shot appears, my short hair is a rat's nest, my eyes bloodshot, dark circles under my eyes. I am so young.) Toller, who has a rap sheet of various misdemeanors and drug and alcohol related charges, pled guilty to 'Intent to deliver and distribute twenty pounds of cocaine back in nineteen eighty-eight. *(I swear I thought it was pot.)*

He, and his college roommate at the time, a Mr. Mel Levitt, was apprehended during a DEA sting operation, which involved U.S. and Mexican authorities. Mr. Levitt, his partner in crime, actually committed suicide by hanging himself while in custody at a detention center in Del Rio, Texas.

Now, while he was attending college at LSU, he received a then-mandatory prison sentence of ten years in a minimum security federal prison camp in Florida. BUT, due to prison overcrowding at the Pensacola facility, Toller was reassigned to a maximum security prison in Louisiana's State Penitentiary, also known as Angola. The man we've all come to know as Johnny Outlaw served just over eighteen months and, was released on parole for good behavior.

Now, according to court documents, part of his early release deal was that he would have to serve at least four years in the military branch of his choice. (*Additional court records pop up on the screen, which are supposed to be about my early release, though the multiple pages are lined up together and too small to make out.*)

Toller served with distinction and received several medals, including the Joint Services Commendation Medal for his service in the Bosnian War. The Bosnian War, you may recall, was between the Serbs and the Croats, and a U.S. led NATO force intervened.

Now, Toller, who reportedly began riding bulls while in college, made quite a reputation for himself as a bull rider in the annual Louisiana State Prison Rodeo, AND actually rode bulls while serving in the military! (*A mug shot appears again. It's my LSP identification picture. I didn't know they could get that.)*

Did you know that the armed forces had a rodeo team? How's that for responsible government spending huh? So, apparently he was even better at cowboying than he was at soldiering. He completed one term in the military and hit the rodeo tour. After exiting the service Toller legally changed his name to Johnny Outlaw. And the rest, as they say, is history." I thought to myself, *Hell it's all history dumbass.*

(A video clip showcasing my two thousand three, championship winning ride appears.)

On the spilt screen to the right of Ms. Lynn's talking head is K. Foxx, a pretty black woman in her early thirties, with a retro afro and hip blue eye shadow, New York Radio Host on HOT 97, and guest entertainment expert on Showbiz this night, was asked by Ms. Lynn of her opinion.

> "Hey, look, he's not the clean cut Gene Autry Cowboy people came to expect from the rodeo world. He's not Roy Rogers. He's more of a Clint Eastwood type guy ya know. (The host and guest laugh in unison.) You're more likely to see him on a Fox sitcom or some late night show than CMT, okay. He's a... a rock star. He brings raw energy and sexy good looks and let's face it... we all love the bad boys don't we? He's a rock star and that's exactly what we need, to keep us even remotely interested in bull riding and that whole business. Rodeo NEEDS a Johnny Outlaw more than he needs them... The Outlaw is a whole lot more interesting than Dan Bumpers or any of the other so called rodeo stars. But make no mistake, Johnny Outlaw has become, over the years, a character who transcends the rodeo world. He's so much bigger than that. I love him. I love his style. I love the way he gives back to charities. And honestly, I don't see him as Bad, but rather a good guy with a few bad habits."

Good guy, Bad habits. That's what Ari said. Hmmm.

Next, Ms. Lynn invites "Brotha Fred", syndicated Talk Show Host on 103.5 KISS FM in Chicago, another expert, to give his opinion of the man he's never met. By the way he speaks, and his hand breaks the plain when he gestures, I'd say he was gay.

> "Hey, well ya know, he changed his name to Outlaw… I mean, what else do we need to know. He's the most popular rodeo guy in the world. He's really much, much bigger than that… he's by all accounts a Hollywood star. Much like Lance Armstrong used to be, the difference between the two being that Johnny Outlaw doesn't lie about his transgressions. Armstrong used to act like he was such a good guy, but Outlaw doesn't hide his dark side. And, I mean, he is one of the rat pack. HELLOOOOO! He's never tried to act like an angel. And, to that extent, he is what we perceive him to be. He is definitely the Real Thing!
>
> Look at Kid Rock, look at Slash, and Charlie Sheen… these guys are all into the same things basically… sex, drugs, and rock and roll, Baby! They live their lives to excess as, we, the viewing public, live vicariously through them. And now that same viewing public is ready to pounce on the news that he's an ex-convict? Give me a

break! Look, after this news wears off, Johnny Outlaw will be bigger than ever."

"If he doesn't die in the process." Says host Brooke Lynn.

"Especially if he dies in the process!" Brotha Fred replies excitedly.

Click.

I had reached over the square coffee table and turned off the one of the three flat screens that hung in the upper left corner of the room.

Not a word was spoken as Bobby looked at me holding the remote, choosing not to say anything. He was pretty good at that… knowing when to talk and when to shut up. Besides, he didn't have to say anything he hadn't already said.

I placed the remote on the table, on top of a stack of picture books, quietly eased back in to the sofa, and asked, "Do you ever feel like you sold your soul to the devil?"

I knew Ari Pei had worked his magic. The press was already falling into his trap. He was right. People in our society are obsessed with celebrities. And the celebs are so narcissistic, they learn to feed on the paparazzi just as the paparazzi feeds on them. Successful managers, publicists and agents, know how to move the machine. And I was part of that machine.

I was pale, and the room was spinning uncomfortably.

"Men have been trading their souls since the beginning of time." Bobby replied, thoughtfully. "We all think that we can sin like crazy and repent just before we die, and go to heaven, having had the best of both worlds… having our proverbial cake and eating it, too."

"It's a helluva chance we're taking." I said lost in thought. Still processing it all. I couldn't really believe that I was THAT FAMOUS that folks would take the time and expense to do an entire show about me.

"It's who we are." Said Kid.

"Is it?"

"Hey." Bobby moved forward to the edge of his recliner, putting his elbows on his knees, looking intently into my confused eyes. "We are more than who they perceive us to be. We are bad asses. We are outlaws. But we're also compassionate, intelligent, creative men. We are Johnny Outlaw AND Kid Rock… but we are also John and Bobby. Most men only dream of being everything they are inside. We've had the awesome responsibility of living up to our potential. Good and Bad. Don't lose sight of yourself… who you really are. And most importantly, don't look away from the Outlaw in you. It is a part of you. But be careful where you let him come out to play." It never failed. Bobby's smile loosened the load.

My headache was back, pounding in my forehead and at the top my skull.

"Hey, Man, I'm not feelin' too good. Think I'll pass on the road trip tonight."

Bobby was clearly disappointed and it showed on his face.

"Bullshit." Bobby stood up rather abruptly, walked between the coffee table and the sofa I was sitting on, and slapped my knee with medium force. "What you need is to forget about things for a while. Clear your head. You need the Jeep. Come on. Let's go Cowboy." Bobby walked past my position, and out of the room toward the kitchen.

My head was spinning. What were the boys up to? Hope they hadn't seen anything on the TV. She was good about that… keeping them away from news about their father. Even as hard as Bobby was trying, I felt lonely anyway. I felt very, very alone. I did not want to go for a Jeep ride through the jungles of Jamaica to go to a city full of Rasta thieves, and nasty islanders. I just wanted to go back up to my room and take two Xanax, and doze off until tomorrow.

But Bobby was back refusing to take no for an answer. I soon relented and took the cold beverage Bobby was forcing on me.

"Here. Let's have a toast."

I looked at Bobby like, please is this all you've got in your medical bag? I opened my beer can, trying my best to remain miserable looking.

"To adventure."

I raised my Coors Light to Bobby's Coors Light, only to cause that rather weak sound of aluminum filled with liquid crashing into another aluminum vessel filled with liquid.

"Very dramatic."

"Fuck you, let's go."

And with that we were rounding up flip flops and hats, a couple of Montecristo "A" models, Bobby's torch, and a small cooler full of beer and ice, and a liter of Maker's Mark from the bar. Then it was off to the Jeep which was still parked outside under the carport under the portico. Dew had settled in on the interior of the vehicle, and there was a slight mist in the stagnant air on the estate. Fog lights on, and loaded with provisions, we began our journey.

†

Nine pm, first night in Jamaica - The sandy gravel road Bobby called the driveway was narrow already, but seemed especially so at night. We turned right out of the drive onto another only slightly wider chip seal road, when all of a sudden the right rear tire exploded leaving shreds of rubber behind us.

"Shit!"

Bobby pressed on the brakes and slammed the tranny into park. We just looked at each other, Bobby with more disgust than me, who was actually relieved we weren't about to spend the second or third consecutive night partying.

Still not a word spoken between us, Bobby takes a torpedo out of his cigar box, lights it, smokes it and hands it over to me, who gladly receives it. It was just one of those moments. Nothing needed to be, or ought to be, said. Just two normal guys, sitting in a borrowed jeep with blown out treads, on a narrow road, in the middle of the night, living out of a plantation that was built in the eighteen hundreds, smoking a joint and looking at the stars.

"Whadya do, rig it so the fuckin' tire would blow up?"

"Yep. I'm that smart." I replied with a smile.

"No you ain't!"

"We'll go tomorrow."

"Yeah. Well. You wanna walk back or change the tire?"

"Let's just change it tomorrow. It's not that far back to the house."

"I don't want some fuckin' Rostaman to steal this fucker, Man. It's the only ride we got."

"I'm sure Ari would understand."

And with that we both smiled and sat there, amateur astronomers and philosophers for the moment, discussing the odds that God does and doesn't exist, agreeing eventually that He does indeed, but not in the form that most humans can imagine. He was bigger than that. Bigger than the Bible, written and edited by policy-makers and arm-benders who insisted everyone think and act accordingly.

We stumbled down the dark and unfamiliar road, taking turns carrying the ice chest, which was growing lighter by each beer we drank, and passing the Maker's Mark occasionally, for straight shots, to keep sharp and focused. It was a little over a mile, we both considered, and by the time we fell down, got up again, strayed from the road from time to time to piss, got lost, and zigged-zagged our way, it was more likely three miles. Bobby told a string of jokes, which were in bad taste, but kept my mind off of my dilemma anyway.

"Why does Helen Keller wear tight pants?"

"Don't tell me." I said.

"So you can read her lips."

"I told you not to tell me."

"Ha, Ha. That's still funny!"

"It's juvenile, Bro. You know my sister is blind."

Bobby stopped in his tracks, looked at me for a moment, and said, "Naw, you're fuckin' with me."

"Hey I got another one. A woman sued the hospital back in my home state of Michigan. She claimed her husband had lost his sex drive after the operation he had. The hospital spokesperson explained to the wife that they'd performed surgery to correct his eye sight." I couldn't help but laugh, even if it was just at Bob's attempts to humor me.

I felt obligated to oblige. "Ok, here's something. One time, I bought a Tiger Woods video, titled 'my favorite eighteen holes'. Turns out it's about fucking golf! Total waste of money." That one had us both laughing again, until we had to stop and rest.

While we were sitting there on the ground in the dark, we gather ourselves, and I come up with another gut buster. "I think it's terrible how everybody is treating Lance Armstrong. Especially after all he achieved, winning seven Tours, and the whole time taking drugs… When I'm on drugs I can't even FIND my bike!"

And that was what I cherished about our relationship. We could find ways to get through the shit. Neither one of us took life too seriously. With our stomachs sore from laughing raucously, we were standing and moving forward again.

I asked Bob, "So, what's up with Ari? What's up with the wife and kid I don't know about? Why doesn't he talk about them?"

Bobby told me the story. "Ari married his high school sweetheart. Kathleen. Nice looker in her day. She was from Nevada. Typical couple, I guess, with the American dream of working hard and being successful and raising kids… Turns out Kathleen couldn't have kids. So they adopted one… Timothy.

Ari was making his way through the business, starting with the talent agency in Vegas. Eventually, they moved to L.A. where Ari really began to hone his skills and making contacts…

Anyway, there was something wrong with Tim… he was never quite right, ya know. Then Ari's mom passes away, and in her will she asked that Ari scatter her ashes, here, at Mount Plenty. She left him this place, and asked that he never sell it. Ari and Kathleen loved it here, for obvious reasons, and came here to spend time with Tim more and more, as Ari made more money.

One night, when Tim was thirteen, I think, he snuck out of the house. The next morning when Kathleen went to check on him, he wasn't there."

"No shit." I was taking it all in, and was impressed with Bobby's story telling skills. We stopped once more to pee in the middle of the road, and Bobby kept talking.

"So the locals all got together to search for 'im. They found 'im on the beach a couple miles down, drowned. In fact, I think it was Breezy's ex-old man who found him."

"Damn."

The story was paused as we could see the lights glowing from behind the bushes and the trees, Mount Plenty marking her territory.

"So, where's Kathleen?"

She tried to commit suicide a couple of times, unsuccessfully. She's in Santa Barbara… in a mental institution. Ari still visits her every weekend. He drives or flies down from L.A. She doesn't even know who he is anymore."

"Damn." That's all I could say. I filtered it through my mind. Everyone has a story to tell, I thought. This one was tragic. And Ari made it out okay. He was doing alright. I supposed he was, anyway. Come to think of it, I'd never asked him.

As we approached the rear of the house, I asked, "So what's behind the locked door?"

Bobby looked at me with knowing eyes, but relinquished nothing.

Bobby unlocked the door that led us through a mud room and the washers and dryers where I assumed Breezy did her work. A few more steps and we were back in civilization, with gourmet kitchen and flat screens and air conditioning. We automatically settled in the entertainment room, where I looked for dials to operate the sound system, and Bobby fetched another couple of beers out of the cooler.

"You gotta use the remote penis brain." Bobby found the device under a Maxim magazine, and tossed it to me.

I eventually got the jam going, using all the smarts my mother gave me, and was relieved to finally be done with the task, settling into one of the leather recliners for another cold beer and a Xanax. Bobby came back with his guitar in hand and began strumming familiar tunes he'd cut.

"Single Father. Part time Mother. When I'm not one, then I'm the other…"

Then, without stopping, Bobby played a melody of memories that I knew were directly from the rock star's life, reminding me, yet again, that EVERYONE has a story to tell. And I greatly admired the man. Kid Rock. Self-made. Took shit from nobody. Did things his own way. And made it to the top without sacrificing his dignity, finding himself along the way.

When Bobby did stop playing and singing, it was to take a large swig of "pearl pop with foam on top".

"My granddaddy used to say that. Pearl pop with foam on top. Where'd you get that from?" I asked.

"I had a granddaddy too."

"Yeah, but you're a fuckin' Yankee." I quipped.

We smiled, content with listening and drinking our beers slowly, the Xanax kicking in mellowing me out to the point that I felt like part of the chair.

"So, you been practicing your guitar?"

"Yeah. Some. I bought a new Martin... Auditorium 15... satin finish mahogany. Nice sound. But, you know, it's one step forward and two back. I learn, then, I forget and have to learn again. And it hurts my fingers."

"It hurts my fingers! It hurts! Ouch! Pussy!" Mocking me.

"Fuck you." I replied loudly.

"Think you could play the three cords in this progression?"

I used the remote to mute the sounds coming from the small but big sound Bose speakers that hung almost secretly from the corners of the recessed ceiling. And so it went until I was playing one of Bobby's Martins, and Bobby the other.

"Your heart's on the loose. You rolled them sevens with nothing to lose. And this ain't no place for the weary kind. You called all your shots, shootin' eight ball at the corner truck stop. Somehow this don't feel like home anymore."

Good one, Man. See you can fuckin' sing. Just let it hang out. There ain't nobody here to laugh at you."

"Thanks a lot asshole."

"You know what I mean. Hey about this one?"

"If I had a boat, I'd go out on the ocean. And if I had a pony, I'd ride him on my boat."

And then I joined in… together we sang and played, like two brothers at Christmas.

"If I was Roy Rogers, couldn't bring myself to marryin' ol' Dale. It'd just be me and Trigger, we'd go ridin' through them movies, we'd buy a boat, and on the sea we'd sail."

"If I had a boat, I'd go out on the ocean. And if I had a pony, I'd ride him on my boat. And we could all together go out on the ocean, me upon my pony on my boat."

Then I ventured enough to do a solo, as Bobby backed off the vocals and continued with his guitar playing.

"The mystery masked man was smart, he got himself a Tonto, 'cause Tonto did the dirty work for free. But Tonto he was smarter, and one day said Kemasabe, kiss my ass I bought a boat, I'm goin' out to sea. And if I had a boat, I'd go out on the ocean. And if I had a pony I'd ride him on my boat. And we would all together go out on the ocean, me upon my pony on my boat. Yeah, me upon my pony on my boat."

Laughter ensued and we drank to one another, finishing our beers and pulling two more from the ice chest that sat on the dark wooden floor beside us.

Bobby set his Martin down leaning against the side of the sofa, and got up abruptly.

"What's up?"

"Come on."

"What the fuck, Man?"

"Just come on. I wanna show you somethin'."

I followed closely behind, so as to not lose my friend in the halls of the mansion. Bobby walked through the library, across antique oriental rugs, under chandeliers, and past crystal lamps, into the main entrance of the home, and to the other side of the house, to the locked door. I couldn't help thinking about the **Chronicals Of Narnia** that I had watched one night with the kids.

I knew Bobby was about to let me in on the big secret, but intently subdued my anticipation by swigging a large gulp of Coors light. By the time my beer hit my gut, the key was in, the knob turned, and the door opened to darkness. Bobby searched with his free hand for the switch, and, boom, like the spotlight at the World Finals, all was bright.

The room was huge. *The size of Granddaddy's entire basement.* It was nothing less than a professional grade recording studio, with three sound proof rooms, a small stage complete with colored lights, strobes, Pearl drums, Marshall amps and speakers, old Gibsons and Martins and a Les Paul. There was even a polished brass sax and an entire mixing board with a Mac that ran the entire process. It was an analog system, but plugged in to a digital program, the perfect combination.

The walls were made of finely finished cherry. The ceiling was constructed of special black acoustical tiles that aided in the recording of music. The way things were laid out, and evidenced by the dust, this was a holy place, and I knew not to touch anything. My mouth was open in surprise and wonderment. My eyes loomed large.

"This was Timothy's room…sss Ari doesn't come here much anymore… if ever. I've never seen him come in here. He gave me a key one day and said I could use it if I wanted to. But I never did. I come in here when I'm bored. But I never touch anything. I keep my guitar in here."

"I've got chills on my arms, Man." I whispered.

"Yeah, I know. Me, too."

"This is a lot of shit for a thirteen year old." I said back.

"Well, I'm sure this was Ari's idea of something they could do together."

"Yeah… Damn… so sad."

"Yep."

"Everybody's got a story." I claimed.

"Yep, everybody's got a story. And if they don't, they ain't livin'." Replied the Kid.

"Right on Brotha."

Bobby sat down on the brown leather high back on wheels that was perched under the big oak desk, where the computer was, and lit another doobie. After passing it to me, he laid out four long lines of cocaine on the desk-top. It was time for this. Our time of reflection, to soak it all in, to wonder what it must have been like in here, with Ari and his son, Tim… playing music together, isolated from the world's problems and just… being.

After what seemed like an hour, but was actually only half, we finished christening the holy place, stopped by for another cold Coors, grabbing the ice chest and a Martin, too, and went outside to the swimming pool and sat at one of the outdoor tables.

"You goin' swimmin'?" He asked.

"I don't know I might. Later."

Bobby kicked off his flip flops, tossed his fedora on the glass table top, laid his wife beater shirt on his chair back, revealing a tattoo that covered the width of his back across the shoulder blades that read "American Bad Ass", and dove in… forgetting to take his cigar out of his mouth. Upon Bobby's surfacing, I noticed the dumb-ass move, and roared with laughter.

"Dufus!" I said to him laughing.

"Fuck."

"Throw it over here and I'll hang it up to dry!"

"Yeah, right. Man, that's a twenty dollar cigar!" Bobby threw the soggy tobacco plug over the shrubs into Neverland, and dove again. I, content with my buzz and looking out over a vast and dark ocean under glistening night sky, wondered how my boys were doing. I wondered if they'd heard of their father's previous life, my criminal record, my jail time, my wild party pals, the strippers and whores. And I longed to be with them, or to have them with me.

Chapter Eleven

Nice Hooters

The next day I awoke to the sounds of bare footsteps pitter pattering up and down the stairs and up and down the hallways. Judging by the light and shadows, it was mid-morning, and neither I nor Bobby would have had more than two or three hours of sleep yet. Tired but not hung over, I eased out of bed, stretching my aching body parts, grunting and groaning against what was otherwise, quiet.

I thought to myself that Breezy and the maid service had probably arrived around eight that morning, and were working their way upstairs. I was in their way of getting their work done, and proceeded to the bathroom where I brushed my teeth and hair, and washed my face. Only then did I dare to glance into the large picture framed mirror over the sink.

It was only a glance, my trained eye looking for any renegade hairs that seemed to grow longer and faster than the others on my face.

I looked quickly at my eyebrows and my ears… places and crevices I'd not had to concern myself with in previous years. Sliding my feet back toward the bedside, next to the window, which I opened to a mind clearing tropical breeze, dampened by oceanic winds and warmed by the mid-morning sun, I fumbled through the chest of drawers for fresh shorts and a tee shirt.

I flip-flopped my way down the hall to Bobby's room, knocked hard once, and opened the large and heavy mahogany door.

"Hey Kid Rock! Get your ass up! It's time to party!"

"Rrrrrrrrrr."

I picked a decorative pillow off the wood floor and chucked it at Bobby's head, who responded by simply covering his head with a pillow.

"Come on man, the ladies are trying to clean up after our lazy asses. Get your ass up and let's go get the Jeep. Come on! Get up! You gettin' up? It's ten o'clock."

"YES. Yes, yes, yes… I'm FUCKIN' getting' up!!! You asshole!"

"Whoa, now… no need to get nasty."

"Well, I'm not ready to get up yet. So get out and go find somethin' to do."

"Okay, Dick." And with that I walked downstairs, said a polite and thankful hello to Breezy and her nymph daughter Jasmin, who even now seemed to be suggesting with her eyes that the two of us go find a bedroom and have sex. I felt nervous instantly and my instincts drove me outside to meander around the grounds and wait for Bobby to make his entrance into the outdoors.

Fifteen minutes later the stringy haired kid from Detroit wrapped his arm around my neck, made a kissing sound in my ear, and offered his apology… a Jamaican torpedo compliments of Breezy.

"Let's start the day right."

"Let's go get the Jeep."

"Let's do both."

"Sounds good."

Down the old faded grey chip-seal road, we recalled last night's conversations, minus the jokes, and re-made plans to attempt our trip to Montego Bay. We chased bugs of various types… the forked tongue lizard, the island hair spider, the purple haze butterfly… each of us trying to show our best Bear Gryllis techniques… laughing at each other, like the Lost Boys of the Pan Kingdom.

The Jeep was still there. Just like we left it… right rear flat. CD player was still there. No signs that anyone else had ever been there. I pulled the manual out of the dash door.

I told Bob, "The jack's under there", first pointing and then deciding *to hell with it I'll do it myself, it's easier that way.*

I was the jack man, and made high speed air wrench sounds as Bobby wrenched the lug nuts off. The air wrench sound led to who was going to win the next NASCAR championship.

The job went off surprisingly well, and we hit the road. Then, Bobby laid the news on me.

"Tomorrow's Wednesday. I'm leavin' in the mornin'..."

Silence followed for the next three miles.

"My son needs my attention. Seems he doesn't need me as often as he used to, so… when he calls I'm there, ya know."

"Yep. You're right in doin' so." I replied.

With that I pulled out my cell phone, turned it on, skipping the messages and going straight to Beth's number to talk to the boys. No service.

"Shit. I should've called from the landline."

"You'll get service when we get to Mo Bay."

†

Montego Bay was a typical enough tourist trap. Vivid colors to attract money spenders from around the world, one could recognize the various languages, accents and dialects from sidewalk cafes and bars.

Mo Bay defies description… Posh resort town, package tour playground, market town, commercial center, seaport, slum. Its disparate elements coexist without blending. The result is an atmosphere of schizophrenic energy, especially at night.

Columbus sailed into the bay in 1494 and named it "el Golfo de Buen Tiempo" or Fair Weather Bay. Today, Montego Bay has the greatest concentration of tourist accommodations on the island of Jamaica. Luxury properties like Half Moon, Round Hill, and Tryall, large multi-stories like Rosehall Beach and Country Club, Holiday Inn, Seawind, and Fantasy, apartment hotels like Montego Bay Club and Seacastles, small inns like Wexford Inn, Blue Harbour, Royal Court, Toby Inn and Reading Reef. All-inclusive resorts are the latest thing, including the Sandals chain, Club Paradise, and Jack Tar at Montego Beach.

Of all the little restaurants and bars on the strip along Cornwall Beach… Rotis, Brigadoon, The Native, The Diplomat and Mickey's Montegonian… Hooters was the only one that had a full parking lot. A Johnny Cash cover band could be heard on the backside of the restaurant, and there were more people going in than were coming out.

"Jesus, Man, you come all the way to Montego Bay Jamaica to go to a fuckin Hooters?" I was not into crowds.

"Hey, what's good is good, no matter where." Bobby proclaimed.

"Yeah, ok, and I suppose you just like the food."

"It's like McDonald's Man, you always know what you're gonna get." He smiled.

"Uh,huh." I rolled my eyes.

"Besides, I get tired of eatin' jerk chicken all the fuckin' time. You want Coors Light. They got Coors Light here. Nowhere else on this island will you find it."

"Coors! I want Coors. Not Coors Light."

"Well you ain't gonna find that here. So can't you just be happy with Coors Light. It's all the same shit."

"Whatever." I said under my breath.

"Man, Johnny, you sure are pissy today. Got a signal yet?"

"It comes and goes." I checked my cell and had full bars. It was two hours later here, than in Louisiana. They were still in church.

Bobby opened the door to the restaurant, but I just stood there, looking dejected.

"Johnny."

"John."

"Hey Outlaw!"

I looked up at Bobby with a blank stare.

"Come on, Man. Let's get us some beers and some hot wings. Make you feel better. Come on, let's see if they got any hot chicks in here."

Bobby put his arm around me and we walked in, me in my blue Hobie ball cap pulled down over my eyes, and Bobby in a straw fedora today.

It was the usual scene as at most any Hooters. Babes in white tank tops, outdated orange up-your-ass shorts, and those stupid stockings covering their legs, with thick-ass Jazzercize socks over that.

"I hate those stockings."

"Well, maybe you'll talk em out of 'em."

"Yeah, maybe." I said sarcastically.

"Hi guys, welcome to Hooters. Just the two of you today?"

I simply nodded without saying a word, but Bobby just had to say something.

"Yep, just the two of us, honey. And how is your day going so far?"

"It's goin' fine, thank you for asking."

She was all of about five feet tall, with big D cup tits, bleached blonde hair, a tanning bed glow, and thick thighs.

"Bobby."

"Yes John."

"What color are her eyes?"

Bobby smiled and shrugged his shoulders as the hostess walked us to our table.

"I don't know but her voice sounds familiar."

"Yeah, Minnie Mouse."

Bobby let out a raucous laugh that got the attention of everyone in the place. Even over all the TVs and the Jay Geils Band on the sound system.

"Ok, fellas, your server is Caroline, and she'll be right over to get you guys started on drinks ok."

I was so freaking embarrassed. Attention just wasn't my game. I was more about laying low, hanging out in the shadows, mystery man and all that.

"Oh, Man, I hope that one's ours." I proclaimed as the only brunette in the joint cruised from one table to the bar and back to the table again, smiling and carrying on with her customers, two Frenchmen trying to woo her with fancy adjectives.

"Here she comes."

"Hi. I'm Caroline, and I'll be taking care of you today."

"Will you really?" Bobby smiled his best grin and got Caroline to look at him for the first time. I was hating him at that moment.

"I'll make sure the food is good and the beer is cold."

"And deliver it with a smile?" Bobby said, grinning.

"Well, sure, that's my job." She replied quickly.

Oh, Caroline I'm going to like you, I thought.

She didn't even look at me. Caroline was coldly professional, as if she had heard it all and was well beyond falling for any bullshit from horny, hard-leg customers.

"Stuck up bitch!" Bobby said to me as he scoped out the dining room for more talent.

"Why 'cuz she dissed you?"

"No cuz she don't know a fuckin star when she sees one."

The beers arrived in a couple of minutes, and shortly afterwards the hot wings and extra napkins. Not a word was said between us until the meat was chewed off the bones and the first two bottles of beer were spent. At which time Caroline was there to replenish, smiling and making only small talk.

"So where are you from?" She looked at Bobby first, then at me. And she spoke very articulately, with a clear and concise kind of east-coast accent.

"Well I'm from Carmel… that's in California… and this… this is…"

I looked at Bobby, unsure what he was going to say. You never knew what Bobby would say to shock someone, especially some chick in Hooters a thousand miles from stateside.

"… John. From Louisiana."

"Really? From Louisiana? Are you from New Orleens?" Caroline looked at me for the first time with any real interest at all. "I've always wanted to go to New Orleens."

"My mother lives close to New Awlins, but I grew up more around the Looziana-Texas lon." I felt the urge to mock southern stereotypes.

"Ok. So I'm pronouncing New Orleens incorrectly aren't I? I know I am but I just say it like its spelled."

"That's ok. Few things in Looziana are pronounced the way they're spelled." I smiled at her, and she smiled back with perfect teeth. I thought of the Farrah Fawcett poster I had on my wall as a boy.

"So, what brings you two here to Mo'Bay?"

"Vacation." Said Bobby quickly.

"Just taking some time away from the stress of daily life in the states." I talked softly as Caroline's eyes never left mine.

"Caroline!" Minnie Mouse hollered her name from across the dining room and over the volume of flat screens, clambering plates, and chatty customers.

"Gotta go guys. Would you like to order an entrée?"

Naw, that's alright, we'll just drink our beers and watch you work the room." Bobby wasn't giving up yet.

As Caroline walked away, Bobby looked at me. "I bet you're dying to tell her who you really are", he said.

"I doubt she would care. She doesn't even watch bull riding on TV." I replied to him.

"Well, I guess yur right. But I can't believe she didn't recognize me."

"You're just a lot uglier in person." I said back, still watching Caroline balancing plates and drinks and a highchair.

"Fuck you. I bet she's talking to her friends right now trying to figure out where she's seen me before."

"Yeah, you're probably right." I smiled, gulped down the last swallow of my beer, and began the next.

While Bobby was enamored with sports on the flat screen overhead, I couldn't take my eyes off Caroline. She reminded me of Audrey Hepburn in Breakfast at Tiffany's. You could dress this girl in a potato sack, and she'd still be beautiful. Her silky raven hair caressed her shoulders as she went from table to table, pleasing her customers with an endearing Farrah Fawcett smile.

She was five foot five. A hundred and ten pounds. Sea blue eyes. Nice perky c cup breasts. Small tight round ass. Runner's legs. She walked with confidence, her head and chin held high, like she was on a mission. Her uniform didn't do her justice. She would have looked perfect in a bikini, or nude.

She was obviously educated and well-traveled by the way she talked and engaged so easily in conversation. She had an heir of sophistication about her that led me to believe she was different from other servers here. She was well-bred. And as the hour drew on, I wondered more about her.

"Ready for another round?" This time she looked at me, and only me. To which I replied with a smile, "yes".

"I didn't ask where you're from, Caroline."

"Yeah, Caroline, where are you from darlin'?" Bobby was back in the game.

"Oh, I'm from Florida."

"Really, what part?" Bobby asked before I could get it out.

"Ocala." She looked at Bobby and then back at me again.

Ha, Ha motherfucker, she likes me, not you!

"Ocala. Lots of horse ranches in Ocala. It's nice there." I looked into her beautiful eyes as the words came pouring out.

"You've been there?" She asked intuitively, her perfect lips glistening in the light from above our table.

"Yeah, I've been through there a few times." I replied.

Caroline was engaging in conversation with me more easily. And she paid Bobby only the professional courtesy of placing a new cardboard coaster under his beer.

"So, I'll ask the inevitable… how's a beautiful, educated girl like you end up working at Hooters in Jamaica, of all places?"

"Can you think of a better place to end up?"

Caroline and I laughed at her statement, while Bobby was already looking behind toward the beach. She had a self-deprecating humor that was attractive, especially when she looked so perfect.

"Maybe." I smiled at her again, and she reciprocated.

"Actually, I worked at the Hooters in Jacksonville while I was going to college. I took a job teaching second grade here in Montego. So, it was easy for me to get a summer job here. It's fun. I'm a people person, so I like the interaction with the customers… most of the time. So how did you come to choose Jamaica for your vacation?"

"Oh, it's more like Jamaica chose me." I replied.

And just when I thought they were making a connection, she was off again picking up orders and moving effortlessly across the brick-red stained concrete floor.

A school teacher… teaching poor black kids. Wow, how cool is that?

"She's rich. I can tell by the way she talks. She's here teaching poor black kids cuz she feels guilty for the comfortable life she had back in Florida. Hey, Johnny Cash is back on stage." Bobby said facetiously.

"Oh, she had a good upbringin', that's for sure. And she is well-bred. Very well, indeed. Now, don't you go blowin' our cover, Man. I just want to eat and drink quietly and be anonymous. Maybe I can get Caroline's number."

"I know. I know. Come on let's move out to the sundeck and listen to the band."

"But then we won't have Caroline."

"Whatever. I'm goin' outside. You comin?"

"Naw, I'll hang here for a while. I'll come find you."

A few minutes later Caroline came back to my table to check on things.

"Do you have a minute to sit down and talk to me, Miss Caroline?"

"You have a southern accent. I like that… I can't stay long, but for a couple minutes." She gave one glance over her left shoulder toward the kitchen to be certain she didn't have any orders up.

I pushed Bobby's chair out from the table with my right flip-flop, and quickly got up to push her chair under her as she sat down.

"My goodness. I bet you open doors for women too."

"Always."

"So chivalry does still exist."

"For some I suppose."

"So your name is John. And you're from Louisiana. Close to Texas… are you a real outlaw?"

She was looking at my forearm tattoo.

"I have been." I said quietly.

Caroline smiled.

"Are you single, John?"

"Yes." I responded without hesitation and looked into her eyes appropriately.

I looked at her left hand. No engagement ring.

Noticing my glance, she replied, "Oh, no I'm not married. But believe me, if I was, I'd have at least a two carat diamond on white gold. I like the classic look… a round diamond on white gold… a six prong setting." She smiled, I smiled back with astonishment, with conflicting thoughts of *run, run away!* and *man, this chick knows exactly what she wants!*

And after an awkward two-second silent period… "I want to apologize for my friend. He gets a little full of himself. But he really is a good guy."

"Yeah, I see lot of guys like him in here. Kid Rock wanna-bes. They don't really bother me. I see 'em come and go."

"I'm not like that." I confided.

Caroline paused to look into my eyes and then softly said to me, "I believe you."

"But you're the mysterious type, Mr. John Outlaw. And I'll have to know more about you if we're to see one another outside of this place."

"I'll tell you whatever you want to know."

"Whatever?"

"In time… but you owe me an answer to a question."

"OK. What do you want to know?"

"What's your last name?"

"Goodbody", she said with a sigh and a half-smile, expecting some lewd comment afterwards.

But I kept eye contact, and without making any facial expressions, simply replied, "Perfect."

And with that she excused herself and was off helping her customers once again. I just watched her as often as I could without seeming like some strange stalker, taking my eyes off of her occasionally to sip beer or check out the flat screen in my view. On it was the Outdoor Channel, showing footage of whitetail deer hunting in Texas. I thought how strange it was to be in such a tropical place and still be inundated with scenes of the heartland. Just then, an advertising spot came on showing Johnny Outlaw's picture and five second glimpses of some of my better rides… Shark Bait, Phoenix, Arizona. The volume was muted, but I could tell it was promoting the next round of championship bull riding on the Outdoor Channel… an event I would not even be participating in. My heart pounding and my face turning flush red, I ducked my head and pulled my cap visor down over my forehead, my sandy brown hair falling nearly to my shoulders.

It was now closer to six in the evening, and the dinner crowd was arriving. Caroline stopped by to bring me another beer, and to let me know that she was about to get very busy. I asked her if I could see her again, to which she replied, "I'm working a double. I'll be here until closing, and again for the lunch shift tomorrow."

"I've got to see you again… soon." I wanted to say more, like… *You're the most naturally beautiful woman I've ever seen. Your teeth are whiter than the clouds. Your raven hair is so thick and beautiful, naturally curly, like the angel in my dreams. Your hair smells like flowers in springtime. I want to bury my face in your breasts. I want grab your ass with both hands and pull you to me and ram my engorged cock into you repeatedly. I want to suck your neck, and caress your shoulders. Your skin is so… tan and supple. I want to kiss you long and slow. I want to watch you on your knees as you suck me, your beautiful blue eyes looking subserviently upward at me. I want to make you my wife and treat you like a princess for the rest of your life.*

She quickly wrote her cell number on a cardboard beer coaster. "Here. Call me around ten tonight if you want to do something. I know this really cool hangout I think you'd enjoy. I go there sometimes after a long shift to unwind. We can talk there."

I looked at her hand writing. Smooth and neat. And pretty. Like her, I thought. "I will…"

"I don't give my number out, and I rarely tell my last name, so consider yourself… special." Caroline smiled like Farrah one more time, and began to turn away.

"Princess…"

"Yes?"

Stuttering, I said, "Tha', Thank you. I really… look forward to getting to know you."

She kept smiling, but her eyes, I could tell, had a momentary look of concern. Or maybe it was just my imagination.

Oh Jesus! I sounded like a freakin' retard! I considered worriedly as I walked out the side door of the restaurant.

Damn it! I can't BELIEVE I said that. Tha'… tha'… thank you? Dumb ass!

And as I walked absent mindedly across the concrete parking lot, I secretly wondered where the heck the Jeep was, and where I was going to spend the next five hours waiting to call her.

I feel like a schoolboy.

I found the Jeep, but only after casing the perimeter of the parking lot and realizing the vehicle was on the OTHER side of the building.

Dumbass Bobby, had to park over here in the fuckin' sand! And she's probably in there laughin' her ass off at me right now… probably been watchin' me with all the other waitresses.

And just then, "Oh Shit. Bobby! I forgot all about him." I froze in mid-motion as I was sliding the key into the ignition, and contemplated my next move.

Hell, he don't even know I'm gone, yet. I considered carefully. *He'll go home with some chick and call me later.*

With that, I cranked the Jeep, rolled onto the Hip Strip, checked my cell for missed calls… nine of them and one was from Ari. The rest were all girls I'd spent time with in various places across the United States… it was difficult to put names with faces, but I knew I'd been so fucked up out of my mind that I'd given them my correct cell phone number. I knew I'd call Ari back sooner than usual, with all that was going on. But first, I'd drink the half full Coors Light I'd walked out of the restaurant with, and turned up the volume on the tuner, which was set to a funky reggae and dance hall station.

As I pulled out on to A3 and headed west, my cell phone vibrated in my pocket. I threw down the paper map of the island I'd found in the glove compartment, and struggled to get the cell from my shorts. It was Bobby.

"What!"

"Where'd you go Dick!"

"Is that a question or a statement?"

"You know damn well what it is."

Both of us were laughing and the music in the background was muffled.

"Where are you, in the closet or somethin'?" I inquired.

"Actually, I'm in the men's restroom… getting a blow job."

"Oh, shit, you told on yourself."

"They figured it out." Bobby said convincingly.

"No they didn't. You told on yourself… You glory hound."

"Don't worry nobody knows who YOU are." He said back.

"Yeah, well, unlike you, I like it that way."

"No you don't… not always. Hey wait a minute… uh… uh… uh… oh yeah baby… suck it… suck it bitch… uh… uhhhhhhh! Mmmm. Yeah. Let me see your face baby…. Oooo yeah… such a pretty face darlin'."

“You asshole! The last thing on earth I wanted to hear was Kid Rock coming in some waitress’s mouth.”

“Alright, well, somebody’s bangin’ on the fuckin’ door. I gotta go, Man. I’ll see ya back at the palace.”

Chapter Twelve

Booby Cay

I quickly pulled over, and found Beth's cell number in the address book. I hit the dial button and waited for the first ring. And then I started wondering what time it was in Louisiana…

Five pm. The ringing began. It rang six times, then stopped ringing for five seconds, and began again but in a different tone. An operator came on the line and explained I would be charged extra for the overseas call. I agreed.

"Hello?"

"Hey it's me."

"Hi."

"How are things?"

"Fine I guess."

"Are the boys with you?"

"No they're at football practice. It rained all week and coach didn't want to go all week without practicing."

"Oh, ok. Well, uhm, please tell them I called."

"They'll be disappointed they missed you. Are you gonna call again later?"

"Yes. What time's best?"

"About nine o'clock."

"Ok. I'll try back then."

"Ok."

"Ok, bye."

"Bye."

Football practice. Third grade. And I'm missing it.

I sat there in the open cab, summer wind rushing off the water, the salt stinging my face. I did so quietly and still for a few lonely moments, until someone honked as they drove by, waking me from my twilight zone. The Jeep was cranked, but I turned the key anyway. The addition of the starter gears grinding caused my blood to start flowing again to my brain. I pushed in the clutch, moved the stick into first, and spun the rear tires on the sandy shoulder, squealing and chirping as I topped the asphalt.

I drove seven miles before I came to. All of a sudden I looked to the right side of the road and there was a dark green sign that read "Booby Cay". The arrow pointed to a parking lot of part sand, part gravel. I pulled in and parked. I took hold of the map, searching for "Booby Cay." The name struck me as funny. But I didn't recognize it from my previous gander at the A-1 route between Mo' Bay and Port Antonio.

"Shit. There it is. Negril? Shit! How did I end up here? Booby Cay. What the fuck is a cay? And what do boobs have to do with it?"

Curious, I stepped out of the jeep, grabbed a joint and put it behind my ear, and took a Coors Light out of the backseat cooler. I walked down the sandy path toward the ocean, shoulder-high plants and grass blocking my view of the sea. When I got to the beach, there were sun bathers scattered about the sand on their oversized cotton towels, for about three hundred yards in both directions. I noticed then that the walkers were all naked.

I'll be damned! A nude beach!

I took it all in, but only until I noticed people looking at me. I turned then, and walked quickly and excitedly back to the Jeep.

The sun was shining on the sea. The sky was a peaceful baby blue and pink, and water was a mirror image of it. The sun was setting on one side of the world, and the moon rising on the other. I took my cell out of my pocket and hid it under the dash, along with my wallet and key to the Jeep. I walked back to the beach, this time armed with the truth about Booby Cay in my mind. I walked out to a vacant spot on the sand, about twenty-five yards from any one, on any side. I quickly removed my tee shirt, which today read "Joe's Key West" with a likeness of Earnest Hemingway on the front. I laid it down on the sand, slid out of my flip-flops, laid my shorts down next to the tee shirt, and sat upon them. Settling in to my place, and looking just like everyone else for the most part. I watched as the walkers went by, one by one, or two by two… men and women, mostly women, between the ages of eighteen and ninety-three… mostly fifty-somethings. They seemed like ex-hippies, now with shorter hair, or no hair, or even bad toupees. It struck me funny to see a man wearing a hair piece and walking around buck naked. I looked at every man's package as they walked by, which from this distance was not obvious, and decided that I had a larger set than any of these guys.

With that confidence, I got up from my Indian-style sitting position to a crouch, bending at the knees and sticking my butt out, then straightening at the waist and standing upright. In the process I'd assholed the people laying behind me.

"Sorry", I mouthed to them all.

I was soon off, walking first in a perpendicular direction toward the water, then turning left ninety degrees to head southwest. Everyone was naked. I'd just shown my asshole to twenty people, and to be dressed was to feel… different. The lesson was apparent, and I learned quickly.

I was proud of my physique, especially when compared to most of these folks. My height, at six feet one, was taller than most bull riders. I had scars on my back from sharp jagged horns and hooves. My skinny legs were scarred and permanently bruised where blood vessels had been shattered. But a good tan took care of anything too obvious. The tan, though, was what set me apart from most of the walkers. Theirs was an all-over tan, and mine was everywhere but where the shorts had always been. And that part of my body was snow white against the rest.

I saw the triangular shaped back of a braided blonde-haired woman who was sitting waist deep in the tide of clear waves, the salty water splashing on her front, which I was eager to check out. Nice shoulders and a backside that narrowed toward the hips, and when the water washed back to the sea, the sand gave way showing her heart-shaped ass. I'm thinking, Bo Derek in the movie, **Ten**.

I waded nonchalantly into the waves just ten yards or so from her. As I walked in knee deep, I slowly turned around to see her. Big sunglasses. Tan all over. Tits aiming at the sky. Her nipples, covered with what looked like pasties that strippers wear in downtown New Orleans clubs, peeked in and out from the waves. Then in one fell swoop, I turned back toward the open sea, and dove in shallow. When I arose, the water was almost waist deep, my organ and balls swimming freely. I looked at her one more time, and she was smiling directly at me. I waved and smiled back.

"Hi."

"Hello."

"I'm Johnny."

"And I am Beatrice." Her accent was unmistakably French.

"Hi Beatrice. I like your braids. Where are you from?"

"They are called corn rows, yes? Bordeaux. In Franz."

She was French alright. No denying that. Her accent as thick as Brigitte Bardot's.

"So, I'm curious, Beatrice… why the pasties on your nipples?" I pointed to my own chest to signify the question.

"Oh, yes, I use these to keep my nipples pink."

"I see. The sun turns them brown. You don't like that."

"You like pink nipples, yes?" Beatrice peeled each silver glittery round sticker off the tips of her nips.

"Oh, yes, very nice… Good idea."

My second thought was did she shave her armpits. I once had acquaintances with a girl from Paris who didn't. Totally grossed me out. But this one was clean shaven. Even her sex spot was smooth.

"Are you here alone Beatrice?"

"That depends."

"On what?"

"Whether you are a bad man or not." She smiled deliciously.

I was getting a hard on.

"May I sit with you?"

She motioned back to the shallow water rising and falling on the sand.

So there we sat, ass cracks in the sand, in a reclining position in the foot or so of clean clear warm Caribbean Sea, talking… Beatrice in her French accent, and I in my Southern one. The usual interrogation…

"I'm from the states. I work in the rodeo. Do you know rodeo? No? Well, it's a throwback to the cowboy days in America," blah, blah, blah.

"Oh, Cowboys, yes I like cowboys. Are you a cowboy? You do not look like a cowboy."

And so it went. She was an easy win. I knew exactly what to say, when to say it, and when to shut up and listen. That was the key. Getting the girl to talk so I wouldn't have to.

"Are you staying close by?"

"Yes. I am at a villa nearby. We are here until tomorrow morning. We are sailing on our yacht, diving the coral reefs." She pointed to a white ship about four hundred yards off the beach.

"We?"

"My husband."

"I see."

"My husband does not mind if I talk with you, Johnny. He allows me to have friends."

I simply grinned. "Friends?"

"Aren't you my new friend Johnny?"

"Yes I am Beatrice." I swear I could hear seventies porn music in the background. *Impossible.*

Beatrice laughed a feminine chuckle, and asked if I would like to walk the beach.

"My first time on a nude beach", I said quietly.

"Oh… you like?"

"Yeah, I guess. I mean it sure is nice looking at your private parts... you are a very beautiful lady."

Smiling, she wrapped her arm around mine. "You are a very charming man, Johnny... what is your last name?

"Outlaw. I'm Johnny Outlaw."

"Out-Law? Yes. That is your name then?"

"Yes... Outlaw." I pointed to my arm.

"You are cute, Johnny. I like you."

"And you have nice toes, Beatrice." She laughed at the obvious irony... her boobs bouncing up and down as we walked in the sand.

We talked and walked a while, from one end of the public beach to the other, before Beatrice asked me to come back to the villa with her for a fresh water shower and a cocktail. To which I obliged. It was just a couple kilometers up the road, still early evening and I had four more hours to kill.

We went back to the section of beach where Beatrice stowed her towels and clothes. She donned a white tank top and a pair of Victoria Secret boy-shorts that read PINK on the buttocks.

"So ya'll have Victoria Secret in France too, huh?"

"Oh yes, Johnny, it is very popular there."

I loved the way she said my name.

"Small world." I said.

"Yes it is."

As we reached the parking lot, she walked up to her red Honda scooter, and kissed me on the lips.

"Follow me okay."

"Okay. I'm in that Jeep right there."

"Okay. Just about one kilometer that way, okay."

"Okay."

In less than five minutes, we were there. The villa was a mansion, itself built among other mansions, in a neighborhood that rivaled Carmel. Beatrice wondered silently how I would react to such wealth. But I didn't shutter. I, by now, was used to such extravagance.

"Would you like a drink, Johnny?"

"Sure. A beer."

"In there."

"All you got is Red Stripe?"

"Yes, you do not enjoy this?"

"It'll do."

"Where's your husband?"

"He is fishing for the day. He will be here in about one hour… Come."

Holding my hand, and walking upstairs, she escorted me to her boudoir, stripping quickly and turning the shower to hot. Steam poured out of the ceramic tiled shower stall, as Beatrice looked up and into my eyes, running her fingers through my long damp hair, her moist lips open slightly, inviting me. We kissed long and hard and deep. Passion flowed as Beatrice sucked my cock and balls, and then we stepped into the shower together.

This is not love making. This is fucking. Just good old fashioned fuckin', baby. Hot and sweaty and loud. Fucking. In French. I turned her to face the wall in the shower stall, ran my fingers up the inside of her thighs and parted her lips, forcefully penetrating her with my engorged member, pounding her smooth pussy hard and banging her head against the wall as I did so. She moaned, hollered, panted, and screamed my name… "Johnny…. Oh Johnny… Mmmmm, oh yes, Johnny, fuck me Cow-boy…" all in her sweet French accent.

All the while I was wondering if a sound I'd heard was her old man coming home. I have to say, I got off on it.

She came after about fifteen minutes of grinding and hair pulling, biting and choking. She especially liked the choking. Then she went down on me again, and I blew my load all over her face.

Afterward, we washed each other, toweled off, and spoke very little. She looked at me with a quenched expression. And I thought of my exit strategy.

"It's been sure nice to meet you Miss Beatrice."

"And you, Mr. Johnny… hmm Outlaw. I say anytime. Okay."

And that was it. Just forty minutes after my arrival, I was leaving. Beatrice, the twenty-three year old French hot box with braids I met on a nude beach in Jamaica only two hours ago, and fucked her brains out in her husband's villa, would from now on be only a memory… one memory out of many. I would remember her face, but probably not her name.

As I got in Ari's Jeep to drive away, I felt empty inside. That big hole in the middle of my gut was still just as empty now as before. *Same old story. Another so called dream girl, fucking around on her husband. I get the memory, she gets the money, and he gets… a cheating wife who will probably kiss him on the lips when he gets home.*

It was all very depressing actually. And experiences like this made me think twice about marriage to even the best of candidates. I thought about not showing up to pick up Caroline that night. *What is the point? They are all the same.*

I drove down to the beach road again, and pulled over to call my sons.

†

"Hi. It's me. Are the boys still up?"

"I just put them down, but… hold on. They've been waiting for you to call." She carried the phone down the hallway and into the boys' room. "Here's Marshall."

"Hi, Daddy." I could hear the excitement in Marshall's voice. I smiled largely, and my heart pounded.

"Hey, little buddy! I'm sorry to wake you."

"That's ok, I'm not really sleeping."

"I miss you, son."

"I miss you, too, Daddy."

"Mommy tells me you're playing football."

"Yes-sir."

"I think that's great. Do you like it?"

"Yes-sir… Uhm, guess what."

"What?"

"Uhm, yesterday… I mean today… I made a big hit, and the coach was telling me how hard I hit."

"Really! Well I'm not surprised by that at all. Big hits run in the family ya know."

"Yes-sir. I know. And uhm… guess what."

"What?"

"I'm gonna play quarterback."

"You are?"

"Yes Sir!"

"That's awesome Marshall. I'm not surprised. I know how talented and smart you are."

"Yes-sir… I mean, thank you."

"How's school going for you?"

"Gooood. I'm making all A's and one U…"

"What's the U in?"

"Conduct."

"Of course it is." I exclaimed.

"Sir?"

"Nothing. I see… well… a U means Satisfactory comes next, if you work at it."

"Yes-sir."

"That's not too bad."

"Yes-sir."

"Are ya'll getting along alright? You and your brother I mean."

"Yes-sir. Most of the time. He gets on my nerves."

"Well, I'm sure you get on his nerves too. But when that happens, just try to find something else to do."

"Yes-sir."

"Did you get the four wheeler I sent you?"

"Uhm, yeah… Yes-sir. But, the battery needs to be charged up. So I rode Matthew's four wheeler and he got mad at me, and I pushed him down, and he cried and told my mom."

"Hmmm. Well, you know you shouldn't ride Matthew's unless he gives you permission."

"But he won't give me per… permiss…"

"Permission."

"Yeah… Yes-sir."

"Well, then you shouldn't ride it. Maybe you could get Mommy to help you plug your battery in before you go to bed, and keep it charged."

"Yes-sir. But I forget."

"I understand. You'll remember next time."

"Yeah… Yes-sir. Hey, Daddy…"

"Yes-sir."

"I saw you on TV the other day."

"You did."

"Yep. You were riding bulls. But you got bucked off."

"Yeah, well that happens."

"Were you hurt?"

"Naw. I never get hurt. It just looks like it."

"Oh… Did the bull get hurt?"

"Naw. The bull is fine."

"Okay Daddy. (Yawn) Well, I love you."

"I love you, too, sweetheart. I miss you very, very much."

"I miss you very much too Daddy. Are you coming to get us soon?"

"Yes, son, I will. I promise. Just as soon as I can."

"Okay. Here's Matthew. I love you."

"I love you."

"Hello Daddy."

"Hello Matthew. How's my little cowboy doin?"

"Goood."

"Good."

"How do you like first grade?"

"It's good. Guess what?"

"What?"

"Uhm, I have a friend from Mexico."

"You do?"

"Yes-sir."

"That's great. What's his name?"

"Jason."

"Jason? From Mexico?"

"Yes-sir."

"Hmmm….okay."

"And uhm, guess what."

"What?"

"He's comin' over this weekend… I mean next weekend."

"Awesome. Ya'll gonna play nice together?"

"Yes-sir. If Marshall will leave me alone."

"I see. Well, I'm sure he will."

"Yep."

"What do you like to play with Jason?"

"Uhmmmm, well… I like to play cowboys and Indians. But Jason doesn't like to be the Indian, so I have to."

"I see. Well, that makes you a good friend to play with I think."

"Yes-sir… well, what are you doin?"

"What am I doing? Well, I'm sitting on the side of the road talking to you. I don't like to drive and talk at the same time."

"Oh."

"Do you like your new four wheeler?"

"Yes Sir! I like it a lot! But Marshall keeps riding it and using up all the battery."

"Yeah. Well, I talked to your brother about that. He's gonna try to remember to charge his up before he goes to bed each night. I think that will help, don't you?"

"Yes-sir. I guess."

"Well, if it doesn't, you let me know and we'll work it out, okay?"

"Okay Daddy."

"Okay Son."

(Yawn). "Well, I love you Daddy."

"I love you too Son. Very, very much."

"Okay."

"Okay."

"You have sweet dreams tonight okay."

"Yes-sir. I will. You have sweet dreams too, okay Daddy."

"I will now son. I will now. And I will see you both real soon, okay, sweetheart."

"Okay Daddy. Here's mommy."

"Okay."

"Hello."

"Hey."

"Hey."

"So, how's everything with the boys?"

"Pretty good. They both miss you. At practice today, Marshall made a really big hit on the running back, and when he came to me on the sidelines he said, 'I wish Daddy could have seen that.'"

Silence. I was doing all I could to hold back my emotions.

"Their grades are good. Of course they're just getting E's and S's and U's right now. Actually, Marshall just started getting A's instead of E's. But their teachers say they are really smart. Matthew is an angel. Marshall can be a little turd."

"What do you mean?"

"Well, he has a temper, and if things don't go exactly his way, he can get pretty mean. He… the other day he pushed another little boy down because he wouldn't let Marshall have the football during recess. The teacher sent home a note and I'm supposed to call her this week to discuss it."

Silence from me. I felt so… unavailable… so… undependable… so inadequate… so much like my own father had been with me.

"But overall, I'd say they are doing pretty well. They both look for you on TV every night on Versus and CMT. I try not to let them watch those magazine shows you're always on. They worry about you."

"Well, I sure don't want them to worry. I'm doing fine."

"Are you? It doesn't appear that way to me."

Silence again.

She began chastising me. "That's not what it looks like on TV. I saw Entertainment Tonight a couple days ago. Looks like your life is a mess. I hate that the boys will get wind of all that someday. Marshall will want to be just like you."

"Yeah. I worry too."

"So what are you doing about it?"

"First of all, it's never what it seems to be… especially on TV. And second, Ari is working on things. Public relations and all that. I'm putting a book together, and hopefully that'll allow me to retire soon."

"Yeah ok."

Silence at first, then…. "Well, thanks for letting me talk to the boys. You get my check on time?"

"Yes."

"Is it enough?"

"Yes, it's plenty. But money isn't what they need from you right now Johnny. They need their Daddy."

"I know… I know. I really do get it. I'm working on it." My eyes were swelling.

"Whatever."

"Don't do that." I told her.

"Don't do what… fail to believe your bullshit?"

"Goodbye." I said.

She said nothing else, and I hung up.

I just sat there looking at the phone for a minute, thinking about the conversations I just had. Thinking about how low I felt. What a sorry father I was. How selfish I was being, riding bulls for a living wasn't the issue. It was being out on the road all the time, living like a gypsy, my morals in steady decline. What kind of example was I living for my two beautiful children? I put the cell in my pocket, and wiped the tears from my eyes, feeling sick to my stomach.

I swore I'd never be like my father. I was going to make my family the priority in my life. And look at me…. I'm in fucking Jamaica on a dark grey road in the middle of the night… waiting for Ari to handle things for me as usual. I just fucked some married chick from France I don't know anything about. I'm popping pills and drinking too damn much. Smokin' dope. Cussin' all the time. Hangin' out with rock stars… drug dealers on my speed dial. Chasin' whores. Jesus! Is this all there is to it? Everything I thought about in prison… all the things I wanted to do when I got out… and I'm still empty inside

Chapter Thirteen

My Date with a Princess

There were two signs, side by side… one pointing to the right, the other to the left. The yellow sign read "Geejam Resort" in black script. Underneath it, a white sign with gold trim read "Bushbar" in block letters.

She drove further into the jungle canopy. I followed as my curiosity peaked. We parked side by side in a small gravel parking lot, her windows down and moon-roof open. My Jeep's top down and door-less. I looked in the rearview mirror, brushed my hair back with my fingers, and looked away just as quickly.

The two of us met at the rear of her Mini. "So, how'd you like the drive?"

"Oh, it was good. Although I'd hate to have meandered out here alone for fear I'd fail to be found." I smiled at her and she smiled back, and we walked together to the exterior wooden stairs, my hand politely situated on the small of her back, more as a gesture of chivalry than anything.

The place looked like an expensive tree house. The stairs were damp and slick, and mossy. Dim lights showed the way, like a small airstrip on a small private island.

"I keep looking for a tall man and a midget in white suits to pop out and welcome me." We both laughed, although I wasn't sure she was old enough to have ever seen Fantasy Island.

We came to the top of the stairs to a large heavy mahogany door, where I reached over her shoulder to open it, like a large vault that held fortunes and secrets of A-list clientele.

Though it was darker by the door we came in, the thick wooden planks that made the floor were sanded and buffed to a shine. Red leather contemporary sitting sofas and chairs, that reminded me of the ESPN set and Erin Answer, centered squarely around cubed teak coffee tables, on which were perched white lighted candles, all situated near the twenty foot polished mahogany bar, where the bar tender poured an icy blue cocktail into a festive martini glass.

The room was half indoor and half out. The backdrop to the northeast was the majestic Blue Mountain range. The sky was cloudy now, and the aura of light given off by the yellow moon matched the candles on the tables. Jamaica's cove-notched coast fell just below about a mile or so from the ledge of the deck.

"Wow", I said, almost whispering but loud enough for my date to hear.

"You like it?" She whispered back.

"Who wouldn't? Looks like this place was teleported from some stylish lounge in Tokyo, here to the rainforest… I feel underdressed."

"Don't feel that way. Here you're welcome, no matter what you're wearing. Come on. Let's meet some friends of mine. So… you've been to Tokyo?"

"Caroline!" The barkeep said loudly enough for others to hear, and walked out from behind the bar to greet her with a hug and kisses, one on each cheek. All of a sudden, I felt as though Caroline only worked at Hooter's to keep in touch with what the "regular people" were doing.

"Johnny… this is Jason Brown, manager of 'Bushbar' and frequently its bartender."

"Jason."

"And don't forget I can cook girl… Hi, Johnny. Well, welcome to 'Bushbar'. We're glad to have you. Any friend of the Princess is a friend of ours."

I smiled politely, and considered the Princess title for a moment. I wasn't the only one who saw her that way.

"So, where's the boss?"

"You mean bosses, girlfriend, bosses!" Jason was as masculine as any man, but was clearly mocking someone's feminine characteristics.

"Oh yeah, is Steven back?"

"They're in the back, finishing up a recording."

Caroline looked up at me to explain. "Bushbar caters mostly to the Geejam resort guests, complete with a recording studio and a few small but intimate villas on the property as well."

I noticed the music that softly filled the air… sounded like Italian opera. There was a laptop on the bar from which one of the patrons was choosing the next song. It was the modern version of a jukebox.

At that moment two men appeared from a door adjacent to the end just behind the bar, well dressed in tailored slacks and shirts, and Italian loafers. They looked like opposite twins, and reminded me of the movie with Arnold Schwarzenegger and Tony Palma.

"Caroline!" They said in unison and walked swiftly toward her, arms open for hugs and lips perched for cheek kisses.

"Hello guys. What are you up to? I've missed you, Steven. What took you so long to come back?"

"Oh, I wasn't gone that long girl, you just haven't been here lately. And who do we have here?"

"Steven Beaver, Jon Baker… meet Johnny Outlaw."

I shook hands and smiled politely. Although meet and greets were boring to me, especially when I figured we'd never meet again anyway. But I really appreciated this place, its ambiance, its remoteness, and if these were the fellows responsible for seeing it to fruition, then it was worth it.

"Outlaw, hmmm? Oh Caroline, what are you getting yourself into now?"

"What are you a rock star I'm guessing?"

"No, I'm just…"

"Johnny is a famous…", but Caroline was interrupted.

"Bull rider." Came news from the bartender, Jason. "I recognized you as soon as we met."

"Really! A bull rider. Oooo, that sounds so… so… manly!" Steven was smiling ear to ear, happy to have another celeb he could brag about to his guests. He wrapped his arm around mine and smiled. I could feel my face turning red.

"You don't look like a bull rider." said Jon Baker.

Jason chimed in. "That's the mystique, Jon. You know that by now. Say, you know who would just love to meet you… Tom Cruise."

"Yes, you are so right. Tom loves bull riding... watches it on TV all the time." Steven recalled.

"Oh there you go name dropping again! Steven owns the place. Jon Baker here is the general manager of the studios and recordings... founder of Gee Street Records." Caroline grabbed my arm and gently pulled me toward the sofas on the terrace over-looking the jungle canopy.

"Don't pay them any attention. They're just trying to steal you away from me. Jason, fix us a drink will you? Surprise us! See you in a bit boys, I've got to find out more about our Johnny Outlaw before I'll let you have him."

And just as I expected, Caroline... Princess Caroline... was more than anyone else might have thought at Hooter's. She had class. She was a well-bred socialite, somehow familiar with the art and music crowd and all their little eccentricities. Maybe my own past wouldn't be as shocking to her as I'd previously thought. I would know soon enough.

Jason walked over to the sofa where the Princess and I were sitting next to each other. I was feeling underdressed for the rural yet sophisticated ambience of the mahogany, teak and imported walnut alfresco dining deck, outdoor pool table and the open air bar. Somehow, flip-flops and baggy cargo shorts with a faded tee didn't respect the surroundings enough. That is, until I noticed Norah Jones strolling out of the hallway that led to the recording studio.

"See, Johnny. Norah doesn't bother about high fashion. She's barefooted for Christ's sake."

"I thought I recognized her."

Then the bartender said, "We service a very A-list clientele here Johnny. And we try our best to keep them all very happy. Anything you want or need, just ask. We get to know our guests, we won't say what their routines are, but I can say that Norah is one of the coolest celebs here." Jason was a local. Cinnamon skin. Kinky sun-bleached hair. Spoke perfect English. More perfect than most Americans, including me, catching myself more aware of the words and pronunciations coming from my own mouth. He served us each Geejam Blue Martinis, named after the resort the bar catered to, and the Blue Lagoon nearby.

"It's my latest creation… one and a half ounces of blue Curacao, one and a half ounces of Jose Cuervo Gold, and three quarters of an ounce of lime juice. Shaken with ice and served to you with love."

"No rum? Isn't that illegal in Jamaica?" Caroline inquired playfully.

Jason slipped away stealthily, leaving us to sip our drinks and prepare for the inevitable round of questions and answers.

"So…"

"So… you know who I am."

"I know your name. And I know what you do… sort of. But I have yet to find out who you are."

"Bobby told you?"

"Bobby? Oh you mean KID ROCK? Yeah, well, not directly. He told one of the girls, and… she told someone else, and… you know, before you know it everyone's talking about how Kid Rock is in the building. Funny how the girls who didn't think much of him before, all of a sudden want to sleep with him."

"Yeah. That's how it works, I'm afraid."

"Except you… you didn't use your name to get laid tonight. Or were you planning on using that technique later on with me?"

"You flatter yourself, Princess… I don't have to use my fame to get laid." I had a brief flashback of Beatrice in cornrow braids.

Concerned that I pissed her off, I began to explain.

"Truth is, I never really suffered in the getting laid department anyway, even when I wasn't so-called famous… most of the places I travel people don't know who I am… like you for instance. I prefer it that way."

"Is that why you aren't wearing a cowboy hat and boots?"

"I wear what I want, when I want."

She said, "I must say, you don't look like any cowboy I've ever seen."

"You know a lot of cowboys do you?"

"I grew up in Ocala. It's like horse central. Plenty of cowboys there. Starched jeans with creases, long sleeve button downs, George Strait hats. Ropers. Short hair. It was just too boring for me."

"Yeah, well… I used to look like that back in the eighties." Flashing my trademark grin.

"Million dollar smile… so, what, you make your mark with the rebel brand? Gotta be different?"

"That bother you?" I responded.

"No. Not at all. Makes sense to me. You wanna be famous sometimes you gotta be different than everyone else."

I told her, "I don't do it because I want to be famous. I do it because I don't want others to define who I am by the way I dress, or talk… or live."

I sipped my blue concoction and wished it was a Jack Daniels straight, on ice.

Caroline was sitting in the corner of the red leather sixties style sofa, and I next to her, with about twelve inches between us.

"You mind if I sit in this chair, so I can see you when we talk without straining my neck?" I asked.

"Not at all. Oooo, I bet your neck hurts all the time." She said sincerely. "I saw you on YouTube. One of the girls I worked with tonight showed me. I CANNOT believe you do what you do!"

I sat in the low-backed chair and crossed my legs, feeling more comfortable now and able to look into her eyes.

Then, in her wonderfully whispery voice explained, "I'm sorry if I offended you. I don't mean to stereotype."

I was silent, thoughtful for a moment.

"It's alright. I'm a little sensitive in that area I guess. So how'd you know who I was? Bobby, err… Kid, tell you about me?"

"No, I guess the girls kept adding it all up. It appears you are almost as famous as he is. I guess you two run in the same circle back in the states. It wasn't long before Julie was showing me who you were on YouTube. I saw you riding that bull. You must be insane to do something like that."

I smiled. I had no comment on that. I knew one had to be a little insane to strap himself to a two thousand pound wild animal who wanted to kill him.

The Princess continued. "I'm just having a difficult time processing all this. I mean, here I am sitting in an avant-garde establishment with a famous bull rider, in Jamaica, and I met you at Hooter's, where you are hanging out with Kid Rock, one of the biggest rock stars in the world. And you don't seem like that person at all… it's all kind of overwhelming to me."

I replied, "You don't seem overwhelmed. In fact, you seem to take it all very casually."

"And that's the other thing. I've known a few cowboys in my time, or at least they CLAIMED to be cowboys, and you are so much more refined in some ways. You speak well. You aren't dipping snuff every few minutes and spitting on the floor. And yet, you do open doors for women. You say Ma'am. You have good manners… YOU are a walking contradiction," she commented forcefully.

"Kristofferson." I was thinking it, and didn't realize I'd said it aloud.

"I'm sorry?"

"Kris Kristofferson. He's partly truth and partly fiction, a walking contradiction."

She didn't know who the hell I was talking about. I could see it in her eyes. I was used to that when conversing with the young women I dated.

Then she responded. "Well, that's what you seem to me right now."

"Well, then, why are you here with me?"

"I didn't say I didn't like that. I am drawn to you somehow. And I want to know you. I want to know what led you to be here. Why here. Why now. And what do you see in me?"

My drink glass was finally empty, and just like the wind, Jason wisped over to us and asked if he could refresh. To which I declined and asked for a Crown over ice, which seemed a little more higher class than Jack. Jason was eager to please, and asked rhetorically, "Was the blue Martini too much?"

"Just not my style, but good. Very good."

Caroline was still sipping hers, but asked for a glass of red house wine instead.

"You have beautiful hands." I told her as Jason walked away.

Surprised, she said "thank you".

"And beautiful feet." I said.

"Thank you." Her face turned crimson.

"Beautiful hair, beautiful skin. Beautiful smile."

"Okay, don't lay it on too thick."

I leaned toward her and looked into her beautiful sea blue eyes. "I'm just telling you the truth. It's why I asked to see you tonight. I was intrigued as to how such a truly beautiful young woman, with such a dynamic and fun personality, with such sophistication, would be here, in the middle of the ocean on this jungle island."

"And working tables at Hooter's?"

"Yeah."

"Everyone has a story to tell." She replied.

"Yep… everyone has a story to tell." I thought instantly of old Tobias McKlintock.

"So what's yours?" I asked.

Caroline was quiet. An attempt was made by her to change the subject. I didn't mind the idea.

"Let's pick some songs." She nodded toward the bar and the laptop jukebox.

I followed her lead. We approached the Bar-Mac, as it was called, and Caroline began immediately clicking and moving from window to window. I didn't recognize any of the artists… not one. I would have expected to see Bob Marley, or Ziggy, or Scooby.

Jason, the friendly bar-keep, walked by and told us, "Baker and Beaver want us to expand our horizons, to delve into other forms of Jamaican music and even Italy and France. That's what you're listening to now, Italian Nino Rota."

"I know, Jason, I picked it." Caroline was a strong person, I considered. She wasn't the type to put up with any shit.

She was independent. Which doesn't often make for a healthy marriage, I thought. I recalled Granddaddy telling me;

A woman's gotta need a man, and he's got to not take her for granted. That's where I was wrong with your Gran-Gran. I should never have taken her for granted.

Caroline whispered to me, "I don't think we're going to find any of the artists you've mentioned."

"What? No Willie Nelson? No Hank?"

"How about something like… Ravel's Bolero?" She looked at me over her right shoulder, but to unknowing eyes. She clicked.

"Looks like we've got four pieces checked off… let's pick a couple more."

Pieces? What, they don't call 'em songs? They're pieces now? And with that I began scanning the room, the hallway, and the door beyond.

A recording studio back there. Norah Jones.

I inquired of Jason, "So how does one get to record here?"

"One just lays down some cash and doors will open for one."

"How much?"

"Depends. On what your needs and desires are. You play?"

"I sing… well that is I…"

"So you'll want some musicians. You need to talk to Jon. Would you like me to get him for you?"

"No". I said abruptly.

God no. Not while SHE's here. After. After she leaves, I'll talk to Jon.

"Do you sing Johnny? I want to hear." Caroline's eyes lit up.

I looked at her, and in her eyes I see sincerity. She wouldn't laugh. She would hide any disappointment out of politeness. It's what makes her so classy.

"Oh, I try to sing, Princess. But, I'm nothin' anyone would want to listen to. I'm just… expressing myself."

I turned and, gently taking her by the arm, walked her across the rich wooden floor planks and over to the guard rail. Standing side by side, her hand next to mine, we glanced out across the tops of the trees that made the jungle canopy so dense and dark. Over the treetops hid a vast and open sea, reflecting a yellow moon and translucent sky.

"I could never live with a man like you… your lifestyle." This caught me completely by surprise… her honesty was blunt, almost rude. I waited for the rest of it, as she stared forward.

"Women giving you blow jobs in public restrooms. Smelling of pot smoke and stale beer all the time, just because you can. People watch you everywhere you go. So much so, you have to travel incognito to exotic, far-away places just to have some peace in your life. I learned tonight that you have two sons. How can you behave so irresponsibly and be away from them all the time?"

A period of silence followed. I gulped down the glaring contempt that was a slap in my face. Up until that point, I'd been sure this woman would sleep with me tonight. Then, my defense mechanism took over.

I remained calm and spoke in a low tone, where she could hear me, but only her.

"What else did you learn tonight about me? That I'm a man-whore? That I'm an alcoholic drug abuser? An irresponsible gypsy, rock star wanna-be? That I'm not a real athlete because I don't train and lift weights? I'm reckless? I'm just a common punk who got lucky and can't see it?"

Caroline didn't say a word. But her eyes told the story. She looked at me with sorrowful eyes, and then looked away back into the moonlit waves of uncertainty below.

"Don't you think I've heard all that before? I watch TV. I hear people talk. I read the op-eds." I took another drink from my glass, and as Jason the friendly bar-keep approached, he didn't wait for me to ask, he just brought another.

"Well, Miss Caroline… I am all of those things. I entered the psychopathic world of self-pitying, self-adoring rock stars, models, and actors, years ago, and I can't seem to get out. In their world, I am everything they ever wanted to be. To them, I am the real thing. I am a cowboy. Last of the dying breed."

"Well, you do sound like one of them. You've got a lot of self-pity going on yourself." She replied.

"You don't know me. You only think you do. Like so many others."

Her voice became scornful. "You've had all night to tell me who you are. You asked me out. Not the other way around. I'm not one of your groupies… so either you can start telling me who you really are, or we can end this. I'm rather tired."

"If you believe what you heard, why are you here with me?"

Caroline thought carefully for a time.

Looking at me she said, "I don't want to believe what I hear. I know how people can be… the stereotyping. Take me for instance… just because I work at Hooter's people think I'm a slut, or stupid… uneducated." I noticed for the first time that she talked with her hands as much as her mouth. She was quite animated. And her hands were beautiful.

"I've got a college degree and a teaching certificate. People want to believe that guys like you are reckless. The men all want to be more like you. The girls all want to fuck you. Until they've had you. Then they wish they hadn't because you broke their heart.

I'm not one of those… I guess I saw something in you… in your eyes… something worth getting to know… someone gentle and kind, even chivalrous.

Oh, I won't lie, I like the bad boy in you, too. But I'm not willing to take the risk, nor will I believe you if you tell me that I am somehow different than all the other girls… I've heard that one before, and from men who were far less famous than you."

I countered quickly. Now I was looking forward.

"Fame? Fame is relative. Tomorrow I may not be. It's all a very crazy business, this fame. Thing is, you work so hard to achieve it, and when you get it, you want to keep it. And to keep it you have to constantly do crazier and crazier things."

"There are famous people who don't do crazy things, Johnny. People who do what they do, and nothing more."

"Like?"

"Like, I don't know… George Clooney for instance. He's a good actor and handsome, and that's it."

"George Clooney is one of the most liberal activists in Hollywood."

"You don't see him running around with porn stars and drug users. Okay, take Tim Tebow for example. He's the strong one. He doesn't care what the press thinks. He lives his life in a moral and ethical way, and he lets his actions on the field determine how famous and wealthy he's going to be. I don't think he takes himself too seriously. And he certainly doesn't wallow around in his own self-pity."

"Tebow? Jesus. No pun intended. But hell, Tebow ain't human. He's a prophet."

"No he's not. He's just as human as the rest of us… My point is there are lots of famous people who don't give up who they are, to be what they want to be. That's their strength. You need to find yours."

Find my strength? She's right… I'm not brave. I'm just hiding. Does she know Tim Tebow? Probably.

A group of five was walking in to the Bushbar by this time, and the diversion was welcome by us both. All the usual greetings from Jason and Steven and the other Jon… "Hello, haven't seen you in so long", "how have you been", "oh, sit here, I'll create something for you, what would you like".

"Caroline. John. Come here, please, won't you, I've got someone I want you to meet!" Steven shouted.

"Scooby, the lovely Princess Caroline, and her friend, Johnny. Johnny, Princess… this is Scooby."

"Hi."

"How do you do?"

"Hello."

"Nice to meet you."

Caroline looked up at me to explain that Scooby was a local singer and musician from Kingston.

I explained that I and Kid Rock were good friends, and that he had introduced me to some of Scooby's music.

"And how's Bob-bee dese days?" Scooby asked with a thick Jamaican accent.

"Bobby is well, or at least he was last time I talked to him." I smiled down at Caroline.

Scooby is a black man, his skin like brown sugar, with an afro, and wears brown tinted sunglasses at night. He had on a big diving watch, and next to that a wrist band made of woven cotton in the colors of the Jamaican flag… red, yellow and green… earrings in both ears, a navy blue tee shirt, two sizes too big, and starched baggy jeans with large pockets. His chin was covered in a goatee and a large heavy gold chain with a gold medallion hung around his neck. He was shorter than me, around five feet ten inches, and about a hundred and seventy pounds.

"So, Mon, how you know de Keed, huh?"

"We go way back. We're… like brothers."

"Ah. So he is alive den?"

"Ha", Caroline interrupted. "Yes, he's alive. Probably sleeping next to some Hooter's waitress as we speak." She winked at me.

Scooby and his entourage… his muscle bound body guard, and three women, two of whom were Scooby's sisters and one assumable love interest… sat on the red leather sofas, and Scooby asked if Caroline and I would join them all in a round of drinks. We obliged, and the drinking and conversation commenced. The laptop jukebox was playing Frank Sinatra's version of "I Did It My Way".

I, in my cargo shorts and flip flops, was absolutely the most underdressed among the patrons of the club, with the exception of Norah, who I never saw again. And while I was conscious of it, no one else seemed to give it a thought otherwise.

"So, Mr. Johnny, where in de states are you from?"

"Louisiana, originally. But, I've lived in many places."

"And what is it you do for a liveeng, Mon?"

"He's a bull rider", chimed in the Princess.

"A bull rider. Hmmmm, that is very interesting. I would like to know more about dis, Mon. I have seen it only on television. It looks like dey are all crazy, Mon, absolutely craaaa-zy!" Scooby's eyes lit up and his ears perked, he was now leaning across the coffee table toward me, waiting for me to explain.

"Well, there's not much to tell. If you've seen it on TV then you know the gist of it." I said.

"Oh, come on, Mon, you are too modest. Tell us, what makes you do dis crazy ting, Mon? How much do dose bulls weigh?"

"Anywhere from twelve hundred to two thousand pounds."

"Shit, Mon. And you strap yourself to dis beast and ride him? That is fucking crazy Mon. You are crazy!" Scooby gestured with a hip-hop style sideways peace sign and whipped it toward the floor. His entourage was all smiles, and the women with him giggled.

The females in Scooby's group, all very attractive and dressed in nightclub minis and pumps, were growing more and more attentive to the conversation, while Caroline, too, was as curious as the rest.

"How deed you get started doing dis sport? Did you grow up on a cow ranch?"

"No. I grew up in the suburbs, like most folks. I don't know… one day while I was in college, two old friends talked me into it."

"Ahhh… I tink der was a little drinkin' involved, hey Mon! I guess so, Mon. Who the hell wants to get on a fucking bull." The girls all giggled again on cue.

"My guess is you!" said Caroline, pointing at me with her eyes.

I replied, "Yeah, well, I was bored, ya know."

"And den what my friend?"

"Uh, well, anyway, I went with my friends to the rodeo arena, and they dared me to sign up for the bull riding event. I signed up and that night I was the only one to cover my bull for the eight seconds. I won the event and the buckle, and that was it… I was hooked. I figured this is an easy way to make a livin'. I'll go pro and see what happens." I explained more for Caroline's benefit than Scooby's.

"Wow, so how long ago was dat?" asked one of the sisters, who by now was getting kind of turned on, and it wasn't just me who sensed it.

"Long time ago… 1990."

"So, John-nee, what is your last name, and I will look for you on TV?"

"Outlaw."

"Outlaw?"

"Yep."

"Oh, I have heard of you. I saw you on TV already. All de time."

Now, the girls were bubbling over with enthusiasm, their pussies getting wet and their mouths watering. Even Scooby's girlfriend came to life all of a sudden. All eyes were on the Outlaw. This is how it was to be famous.

Caroline found it distasteful, and hoped, secretly, that I would too. She squeezed my hand and said, "I'll be back, I've got to go to the little girl's room."

And as soon as Caroline was out of her sofa seat, Brandi leaned over to me, and asked in her sexiest whisper, "John-nee Out-law, be a dear and sign dis for me?" Brandi put her cinnamon colored fingers to her chest and pulled her top down just enough for me to see her little brown erect nipples and bra-less B-cup breasts.

"Behave yourself, he's with Car-o-line." Scooby gently pulled her back from the shoulders and grinned. "My sister… Crazy bitch", he whispered to me.

Then Brandi said unapologetically, "I've always wanted to fuck a cow-boy." She smiled at me directly, and came across as very pushy. I liked her better when she was quiet and just sitting there giggling.

In an attempt to get past the situation before Caroline came back from the restroom I said to Scooby, "Bobby told me you were from Brooklyn. I see the influence, and, I hear it in your accent."

"Yeah. I was born here in Jamaica. But I moved to Brooklyn when I was a boy."

"Must have been a culture shock." I replied.

"Yeah, it was at first. But der I met people from all over da world… Trinidad, Haiti, Dominica. So, I wasn't alone der, ya know. I fit in, ya know?"

"That's cool… I was trying to remember the name of the album Bobby turned me on to. I think it was Boob-box or something?"

"Boombastic, Mon. Boombastic. Dat song is what launched my career. Did it make you smile?"

"Smile? Yeah I guess so. I remember it was a dance hall meets reggae kind of thing… happy music."

"Yeah Mon! It makes you smile and be happy! It is mad comedic Mon. I am all about being happy!"

Caroline returned and at this time I proclaimed a toast.

"To being happy!"

And everyone but the Princess repeated, "To being happy!"

"So, Johnny, I wonder… would you be able to do me a favor?" Scooby's look turned serious.

"That depends, Scoob, what's up?" The booze was taking effect on my mind and body. I was having mental images of the cartoon characters I'd watched as a kid… Scooby, the blonde headed jock who drove the van, the foxy red head, the cowardly sidekick.

He dropped the island accent. "Have you heard of the Scooby Makes a Difference Foundation?"

I looked at Caroline, who grinned slightly, but "No, I haven't."

"It is a charity organization which raises money for the Bustamante Hospital for Children. It is in Kingston, where I call home."

"I see." I nodded and was thinking I'd give some money, but had no idea at this point if I had any.

Talking as white as any Republican conservative… "Johnny, my charity was formed on impulse, because of what I saw at a hospital one day. I was visiting someone and I saw this little girl with a bullet in her head, and I thought, I have to do something. Ya know? And so, I said 'I'm going to do a concert and give all the money to the hospital'. They said I needed an organization to do this, so we made one. Simple as thot, Mon." He smiled gold capped teeth.

"That's awesome Scoob." I felt ashamed that I had never accomplished anything so ambitious. The bull riding clinic and cowboy suppers were for kids, but really it was more about selling my "Fundamentals" book. And I was aware that Caroline was probably judging me according to my reaction.

"John-nee, you say you are good friends with Bob-by. Like bruthas?" The accent was back and he was talking louder.

"Yeah." I knew I'd regret that "brother" statement.

"John-nee, if I could get Bob-by to play at my concert, it would mean lots of money for de little children. Do you understand?"

"Yeah."

"John-nee, can you get Keed Rock to play at my concert again? He did it two years ago, and it was a smash, Mon!" All the barroom eyes were upon us, even Jason the friendly bar-keep was eavesdropping.

"Well, he's a pretty busy guy. He's going to Europe soon for his own world tour… but I'll ask him."

"Oh, John-nee Out-law, that would be Boombastic, Mon! I will give you my cell number and you can have him call me, ok?"

"Ok." I wondered to myself why Bobby hadn't returned Scooby's calls to this point. If he'd already done something with Scoob in the past, why not now? But then again, Bobby wasn't much on commitments.

Caroline was yawning. The night was growing stale. The newness of the Bushbar was wearing off for me, as well.

"You ready to go honey?"

"Yeah, I think so. I'm really beat. It's been a long day on my feet."

We looked intently at one another, speaking privately. "Are you taking me with you… to your place?"

"Do you need a place to sleep tonight?"

"Sure… well… not exactly. But…"

Caroline's eyes held the answer to my request. The answer was…

"Listen, Johnny… you are an attractive guy, and… in a less responsible time, I would, but… I'm not looking for a one night stand."

"Oh, yeah, sure… I… I understand." I was embarrassed. My cheeks grew flush red, and I couldn't help it.

"I know you're not used to girls telling you no. But I'm not going to have sex with you tonight. I don't want to hurt your feelings. It's just that I could fall in love with you really, really easy, and I don't need that in my life right now."

"Then why did you come out with me?"

"Since when does going on a date mean fucking each other?"

Uh, *forever?*

"Ok. I understand, Princess. Let me walk you to your car."

Bitch! What the fuck do you think I wanted to do tonight? And then you wait until fucking two in the morning to tell me that?

Caroline said goodbye to her friends, and Scooby and his crew. I told Jason I'd be right back.

We got to her shiny silver Mini Cooper and I placed a gentle kiss on her cheek.

We held hands for a minute, and I said, in my deep and soothing low voice, "You're right about me. My life is a mess right now, and you're worth more than that. But I promise I'm not the guy they paint me to be. I'm much more. I am many things. And you are the perfect girl… right girl… wrong time. I want to thank you, sincerely, for the time we shared tonight. And please know I'll be thinking of you when I get back to the states."

"I know… I'll be thinking of you, too… but not because you're famous or wealthy… because you're sweet and kind and generous. If it ever is the right time… call me… you have my number."

Then she glared at me and snarled. "But, if you fuck that Brandi in there you can just forget about calling me ever!"

I smiled knowingly. I knew exactly what she meant by the right time… *When you take yourself off the world stage, and decide to live a more normal life, and you want to have children together and live anonymously somewhere where people don't know who you are… when you're not in bed with the devil.*

And she drove out of sight, her taillights fading into darkness of the Jamaican jungle.

I just stood there. My high was falling. I needed to either crash or get high again. I walked to the Jeep, pulled a fatty out from the glove box, lit it, pulled its crippling smoke repeatedly into my crackling lungs, slowly blowing out through my nostrils, and drank a Coors Light from the backseat ice chest… the last one. Then, I walked upstairs to the Bushbar, and asked Jason the friendly bar-keep for a shot of Crown.

"Hey Jase?" I was talking louder now that Caroline had gone. I have no idea why.

"Yeah, Mon?"

"If I wanted to record a song tonight, would that be possible?"

"Ahhhh, let me see, Mon. I will have to speak with Steven. I'll get him for you."

Steven arrived at the bar just one minute or so later.

"Steven, can you record a song for me?"

"The studio's open. What did you have in mind?"

"It's an old Kristofferson song… 'Loving Her was Easier'. I'll need an acoustic guitar, preferably a Martin Dreadnought?"

Steven was quiet for a moment, looking at me, sizing me up…

"Come, Johnny Outlaw." He clapped his hands together twice. "I'm sure we can come up with something." In a weird way, his mannerisms reminded me of my father's mother, the home econ teacher who encouraged me to write.

The studio was literally right behind the mahogany bar. There was the bar-length mirror, and behind that wall, a twenty-five by fifty foot dim-lit room, paneled with walnut, and seven-foot sound proof tiles made of dark grey foam, like elongated egg crates, spaced every sixteen inches, inlaid into the walls. Candles were lit and in various sizes. There were monitors galore mounted where the walls met the ceiling, one revealing a large picture of the bar on the other side, where Steven or Jon could see the sofas, and the coffee table and even the guard rail out on the deck. Another camera was fixed on the inside of the actual sound proof booth, which was about the size of the inside of a Jeep. The huge mixing board and two laptops took up most of the mahogany desk space, and there were instruments parked along the other walls, and a Pearl drum set was in one corner. There was a trumpet, a clarinet, various woodwinds and brass instruments. This was a state of the art studio, and I was thoroughly surprised and impressed. Adjacent to this room, through a glass door, I could see a black baby grand piano.

"Steven, on second thought, I'm not sure I'm ready for this."

"Oh, come on, Johnny, you're not afraid of this, a bull riding champion? Come, let's sit and talk." *That's exactly what Grandmother would have said.*

I knew the lyrics by heart. I knew the three cords. I just wanted to go into the booth and lay it down, as it was flowing through me at that moment. Steven readied the analog recorder, readied his Mac, turned on the mic, and spoke to me through the headphones.

"Nothing fancy to do here, Johnny. Just you and your guitar. Sing like you feel it, baby. No pressure." He spoke in a low relaxed tone now. It was very reassuring.

I warmed up my guitar playing and my vocals one time, and let it rip.

"I have seen the morn-in' burn-in' gold-en on the mountain in the sky…"

It took just over three minutes to record my first song ever. I paid just under two hundred dollars for the bar tab and a recording.

"Hey, Jason…"

"Yeah, Johnny."

"Next time you see the Princess… you give her this for me?" I handed him the new recording.

Jason looked at me and smiled largely. "Aw, Mon, she will love dis gesture. You done good, Outlaw."

"You haven't heard it." And with that I smiled back, unsure if she would care or not, and walked away.

Chapter Fourteen

The Suzuki Sidekick

Suffering from jet lag, I was as tired and tattered as before I left, looking at myself forcefully in the mirror behind the bottles of liquor in the back of the limo, still contemplating my life and feeling depressed. I gazed out at the twelve lanes of traffic.

I smiled, reminiscing about my departure from Jamaica that morning. I recalled the lump in my throat when I saw Breezy and Jasmin, there to drive the Jeep home from the Ocho Rios Airport. "Breezy. Good morning. I'm surprised to see you here so early." Her eyes were brown, and beige with bloodshot streaks.

"It is early, Mon. Even for me… But… I wanted to see you before you leff Mon."

"You did? About what?" I could see Jasmin sitting in their beat-up white Suzuki Sidekick outside. She wasn't happy. I became nauseous.

Breezy held a small igloo cooler in her left hand, and her right hand was in a fist. "My daughter, she's all I have in dis world. She is every tang to me. She is why I work, why I breade. You know what I mean Johnny Outlaw?" It was the first time Breezy had spoken to me. I didn't even think she knew my name.

"Yes." I replied calmly.

"Jasmin, she told me about what happened last morning. She told me she came to you and trew herself atchew. She wanted you to be her first… lover."

I didn't say a word now. Just stood there in the small terminal, no attendant in sight, the TV on but muted.

"Jasmin tinks you are da lover in her dreams. She is a young foolish girl, easy to take advantage of."

"Breezy, I assure you, I…"

"Please let me finish John-ny… She told me da trute. She know I whip her ass if she lie to Breezy. She say you would not have sex wit her."

She began crying softly. I looked down at the ground, and noticed Breezy was barefooted.

"John-ny de Out-law. You are a good mon. A GOOD MON! And I come here so early in the mornin' to tank you, from deep in my heart." And with that she opened the cooler and handed me one ice cold Coors Light. And in her balled up fist, she held a fatty. "Dis is my best ganja, Mon." She tucked it in behind my right ear, what I considered a very personal gesture.

†

Bumper to bumper traffic… people going to and coming from places they'd rather not be. The BMWs, the Mercedes', the Porches, the mini vans, the Escalades and Suburbans… how many, I wondered, were actually happy in their lives? They work their eight to six jobs, to pay their mortgages and car notes, their fancy clothes and daycare bills. They pay someone else to wash their cars and mow their little yards because they're too tired by the time they get home to do it themselves. They start dreading Mondays on Sunday afternoons. They get their measly two weeks of vacation each year, and charge their trips on credit cards. They die in nursing homes because their kids are too busy doing the same things they did. Their kids play soccer because it's safe and no one has to lose… everyone gets a trophy, no matter who was good at it and who was not. Everyone's looking for less work and more pay, and when they can't get that, they look to the government for handouts. And in either case, you leave this world with nothing.

Why am I here? I sold my soul and for what? Fame? What's that all about? Money? Where's that getting' me? I'm broke anyway. There's always somebody out there tryin' to take it from you.

For all my millions of dollars, I felt empty. For all my admirers, I felt alone. I wondered what a nervous breakdown is like. My hands shook slightly as I reached for the glistening bottle of Gentleman Jack. I poured half a glass, gulped it down, and decided I would know the numbers before leaving Ari's office today.

I wanted to know how much I owed and to whom. I wanted to know how much money I had saved, and what could be sold. I wanted to know what my real chances were in the law suits, and if I was better off settling… but I would make that decision for myself. I would put together a real exit strategy. I wanted out.

The limo was in park, engine running and air conditioner on, on the scorching hot freeway, under the relentless morning sun. The tinted glass divider was up. I pulled my leather bound notebook out of my gear bag, and began to write.

Thoreau said that the mass of men lead lives of quiet desperation. I sit here in the back of my long black limousine, where life is supposed to be grand and fantastic. And yet I am parked in traffic on a hot burning road to nowhere. I am void of feeling. Void of depth. Void of anything my mother would have wished for me to be. And I find the most difficult thing for me to be is simple, yet profound.

Instead I find this world to be shallow, misled, and without purpose. Entertainers and athletes are overvalued… way overvalued. And yet people who have other gifts go unnoticed and are undervalued. A tall man who throws an orange ball into a steel hoop from thirty feet away… they wrap an arena around him and sell tickets for a hundred and seventy-five dollars a seat. He makes millions. And yet, a mother who gives birth to and nourishes our future, struggles to eat… gets no respect when walking down the street.

Ever think about how much a hedge fund manager makes in comparison to a Navy Seal?

There was a time when I wanted everyone to notice me. I wanted everyone to know who I was. Now, I watch others show off, and though I know I need to go out there and do that again, I cannot. It's okay to be wonderful… but on the way to wonderful, one must first be alright. And I am not, nor ever have been… alright.

I've learned much from just regular everyday folks, few of whom ever got the recognition they deserved. They didn't sing in front of thousands of adoring fans, or ride bulls in football arenas, or throw little round balls around. They just lived. We are all accidents at birth. We don't get to choose who our parents were, what color we are, how tall we will be, how strong we're going to get, or how we talk. Nothing. We have no choice in any of those things. One day someone says YOU ARE THIS! *And that's it, you think you're stuck with it. At some point in our lives we have a choice. If we're sane enough at that point, and we apply ourselves, we can overcome what others label us as. A lot of what we do about it is influenced by the people around us. My mother believed in me. And my grandmother believed in me. So I believed in me. Somewhere, though, I gave up doing it on my own, and looked to some other force to get me where I wanted to be… even though it meant trading my soul. I regret that. We all need validation. I no longer want the devil's help. I get the validation I need from my kids… from someone like Caroline, perhaps… and foremost from God Almighty, my energy source. Only He can save me now.*

†

"Miss Rebecca."

"Well, look what the cat dragged in. And how's our Johnny Outlaw today?" She was happy to see me. But still a condescending bitch.

"Don't patronize me today, I'm not in the mood." I countered.

"You look like shit." She said.

"He pay you to talk to me like that?"

"No, he just pays me to make the arrangements." Rebecca punches the button with her left index finger that calls Ari's office. "You know, he's been reallocating my talents to junior associates recently."

"Yeah." *Like I give a shit.*

"Johnny's here."

"Send 'im in."

I glared at Rebecca to let her know things will be different with me from now on. Rebecca stares back with a smirk, and says, "You sure are acting pissy today."

I opened Ari's door, and continued to stare her down as I closed it abruptly to her shit-eating grin.

"John-ny, my boy! How are things this…" Ari looks at his Rolex Presidential… "early afternoon?"

"Been sittin' in fuckin' traffic on the 405 all mornin'. How are you?"

"You mean you've been sitting in the back of a very comfortable limo all morning… it could be worse Johnny. It could be worse."

I waited for Ari to walk back behind his giant black lacquer desk, where he flips open the lid on a new box of cigars. "Try one of these?"

"No thanks." I sat down in the smaller gold covered chair before him.

"You said there was some paperwork?" I said.

"You in a hurry today, Johnny?" Ari asked.

"I'm in a hurry to get down to business."

"I see. Well…" Ari presses gently on the button that summons Rebecca.

"Yes Sir?"

"Bring in the file on Johnny please."

"So, the house in Jamaica suit you okay?"

"It was very nice. And very large. Thank you." I immediately had the mental image of Jasmin running out of the room, her feelings hurt and tears streaming down her cheeks.

"I thought you and Bobby would be comfortable there. Breezy take care of everything for you during your stay?"

"Yes. Everything." I had a vision of Breezy in her bare feet, and her only hormone-driven daughter sitting ashamedly in the ripped passenger seat of a beat-up Suzuki Sidekick.

Rebecca walked in, tight knee length cigarette skirt, black with a white sheer v-neck blouse, ruffles on the sleeves and a black bra. Her hair was shorter this time… just above her shoulders. Still bleached blonde… gold with white highlights.

She walked with purpose, quick, but as if she had a stack of books on her head… and one foot in front of the other, like a runway model. Sexy, and very efficient… prerequisites for the job. She didn't say a word to either of us. Just placed the file on the corner of Ari's desk, smiled harshly in my direction, and walked out, closing the door quietly. Professional in every way.

"Johnny, I've met with the attorneys at Kaufman, Kaufman and Kriel, and I asked them to write up a summary of the cases and where we are on each of them. Becca's made a copy of this for you." He hands me a twenty page memo that reads CONFIDENTIAL in red stamped on the first page. It reminds me of the top secret orders I would often receive in the Air Force.

"Basically, there are four suits out there. Two you can agree to settle for a hundred grand a piece, get 'em outa your hair. That's, uh, the camera guy and the no-show in uh…"

"Kansas." I answered impatiently.

"Yes. That's correct. Kansas. Now, the camera guy will agree not to go through with the assault and battery charges, so that's good. All he wants is money… that's all that motherfucker ever wanted was money."

"That's all any of 'em want." I replied harshly.

"Now, the paternity case. Johnny you're going to have to take a paternity test. That's the best and cheapest way out of this one. You agree."

"I pulled out. Shot jiz on her face. That's what I always do."

"So… yes then?"

I nodded my head to the affirmative.

Ari presses his magic button again. "Becca, Honey, get Johnny an appointment with uh, oh whoever Kaufman wants him to, for his paternity test. Let's get it done today if possible."

"Will do." Rebecca was hating it, and loving it all at the same time. This was my penance for my sins against her.

"Okay. That should put that one to rest once and for all… right? Now, let's see, that leaves us with the wrongful death case."

I got sick to my stomach all of a sudden, like I always did when I thought of that sweet kid. Only now, I wished I'd never met him.

Ari takes a one inch file from the larger six inch file, and opens it. "This one's gonna be tricky, John. It's gonna be ugly. His mother is seeking damages to the tune of fifteen million dollars." He throws the file down on his desk top for emphasis, and swallows hard. He leans back in his big leather chair, swivels to the right, then to the left, then leans back against the wall and places his hands behind his head, clasping his fingers.

I breathe hard and deep but can't catch my breath. My heart beat speeds up. And my heart is pounding in my chest. My face loses color.

"Rebecca, bring us some water, Hun."

"Kaufman, the old man, is handling this one personally... at my request. So far, they've written letters back and forth, but she hasn't budged... Thank you Sweetheart." Rebecca comes in, hands us both glasses of ice cold water, and leaves just as quickly and quietly.

My hands tremble as I drink, and I long for something more... something to numb the pain, to help me escape.

"Johnny, we can fight this. Or..."

"Or we can settle." I said.

"That's correct. We can settle. Or we can go to court. Who knows what she's going to do. Shit, she might settle for half. That's still seven and a half million. That should make her happy."

Ari leans forward in his chair, and pulls up to his desk. A very sober look comes over his face. He brings both hands to his chin and places one fist inside the other.

"John, speaking as someone who's lost a child… nothing can ever replace him. No amount of money in this world will ever make her happy. And we both know… she knows… it wasn't your fault. She's just… angry at God and directing it all at you." Then he continued. "The reason I've been so sensitive about your past, is because if this thing goes to trial it will hurt you tremendously. Ex-cons don't do very well in a court of law, even Civil ones."

I was forced to change my way of thinking. I wasn't the victim here. She was. She lost her baby boy. And though I wasn't directly to blame, I was the one who supposedly taught him how to ride, built the boy up so as to make him think he could be the next world champ, and convinced him "it only hurts for a minute".

"Look, Johnny, I'm here for you. The attorneys are on your side. You've got the best in the business. But it's gonna cost you either way. Let's just see what she'll settle for, and maybe, maybe, we can put this behind us, and you can get on with your life."

"How much money do I have?"

Ari looks at me for a brief moment. His facial expression changes from sober to somber in a flash. His eyes look down once again at the bulging Johnny Outlaw file, and he fingers his way through to the IRS label. Pulls out a manila envelope, opens the clasp, and re-familiarizes himself with its contents.

"You're gonna tell me I have tax issues, when in fact you were supposed to be handling all that. I pay you a very large amount of money to handle that!" I was feeling sicker still. My world was spinning out of control right here in the confines of Ari's over-the-top plush L.A. high rise office. For all its extravagances and cosmopolitan design, nothing could blunt the trauma.

"Now, Johnny, I'm not a tax expert."

"No. But we hire tax experts. That's what you told me."

"That's correct. But sometimes things get… mishandled." He was choosing his words carefully now.

"Mishandled? Mishandled? Like what? What got mishandled, Ari?"

"You remember all that money you made on those Calvin Klein underwear ads?"

"Yeah, I guess. What about it?"

"Those funds were paid to you through some subsidiary company, a third party, for some reason, I won't pretend to understand, but… anyway, the money was never recorded at the accounting firm. There was never any W-2 generated and sent to Bridgeway Accounting Firm. I mean, it was generated, but never was sent to the right people."

"So?"

"So… you made five million dollars and never paid a dime on taxes on that money."

"So who got the W-2?"

"It was sent here, according to the IRS. Why I don't know. The address they have on file was supposed to be the Bridgeway Firm. Why they had a different address for the Calvin Klein thing I don't know."

"It was sent here? Then Rebecca would have gotten it." Now it was beginning to make sense to me.

"Rebecca swears she never saw it, Johnny. And you know she wouldn't lie. She's too damn good at what she does to have just misplaced the thing."

I sat quietly. Thinking of the night I slept with her. Thinking of the next morning, and the look in her eyes when I walked away, never to sleep with her again. I only fucked her because she wanted to. I wasn't even in the mood. I didn't like her feet, and she smelled kind of sour. I had to think of someone else just to get it up. I considered what it must be like to hear about the paternity suits and the one night stands, and the life I lived without her. I knew she loved me… or the thought of me. But I ignored the fact all this time. She knew what she was getting herself into when she did it. She knew…

"So, what, I owe half of that sum… two point five mil, to the government?"

"Yes… and some state taxes as well."

I sat up in the low back chair. I rubbed my chin with my right hand, holding my water glass with the other… still shaking.

"So… two and half mil, plus another mil for state taxes, plus seven and a half mil, if she agrees to it, brings me to… eleven million dollars."

"Don't forget the lawyer fees. And the accounting fees."

"And your fees, Ari, don't forget your fucking fees! And the accounting fees? Fuck them! They should be paying me goddamnit! Who's fuckin' payin' me? Huh? Who pays Johnny Outlaw?"

I was blowing steam, and Ari had seen it before. He knew it was time to shut up and let me drink my water.

I thought as best I could, adding up numbers, millions with all those damn zeroes in my mind, twirling around and around. I wished I'd never seen my first million. That's when everything went crazy in my life. That's when I became the rotten piece of shit I was.

"So how much do I have Ari?"

"After the two settlements we talked about, and taxes and fees, not counting the James Bond case, not counting the properties you can sell…"

"How much Goddamn it!"

"I… I'm still on your side you know. You need friends right now."

Fuck you.

"Just tell me how much. I stood up, slamming my glass onto the desk, and stared Ari straight in the eyes, my cheeks red with blood and lips quivering. "No matter what happens to me, you still get yours."

"Four point six million in bills and liabilities. Subtract that figure from the ten million point six you currently have, and you're left with six million dollars."

"That's not counting the seven point five I hope to settle for! That leaves me with minus one point five, Ari! Minus one point five! Minus one point five? Are you fucking kiddin' me!"

"Now, John, don't get so excited."

"Excited? Excited? I walked in here a multi-millionaire, Ari. A multi-million dollar franchise. Now I'm MINUS ONE POINT FIVE MILLION, ARI!"

"I know that sounds overwhelming. But it's nothing for you to go out and make a couple million. Probably twice that. One endorsement and you're right back in the game."

"You make it sound like riding these fuckin' bulls is easy, Ari. Sittin' behind your fancy desk, with your fancy fuckin' secretary, in your fancy fuckin' office. Fuck you! I'm tired of ridin' bulls goddamnit! I'm too fuckin' old for this shit. They're gonna kill me. You understand… they are gonna fuckin' kill me! And sponsors… who the fuck is gonna take me on now that I'm smokin' a bong on YouTube?"

"You've got the two hundred thou sittin' on the table for your memoirs, Johnny. Don't forget that. And that's just the up-front money. That doesn't count the sales… the percentage of gross."

I sat back down, my legs quivering at the knees and about to buckle. I just wanted time to think… to let all this sink in. Right now I was going to kill someone. Ari. Rebecca.

"Get me a drink!"

Ari finished his water in a gulp, and took the two empty glasses to the credenza on the side wall to pour us both straight Crown. He handed me my drink, and I snatched it from Ari's grasp, spilling only a drop, and drank it down in one fell swoop.

"Gimme another."

Ari looked at me for a moment, as if to disagree with my tone. I looked up at Ari with complete disdain, as if to say you better get me another fucking drink or I'll kill you, you bastard. Ari retrieved the bottle and handed it to me.

"Have your 'Sweetheart' in there type up a summary of all the figures we discussed here today. Right now. I want to leave with that in my hands. I'll be in touch on the sale of the properties. No, to hell with that, just have HER handle it. It's the least she could do. Sell 'em. Sell 'em all. Half price if need be. Liquidate everything. Have the publisher call me directly. I'll work that deal myself."

"If you wish."

"I WISH!"

I walked out abruptly, steaming with anger and frustration, stomping past Rebecca, out the glass doors and into the elevator area. I punched the elevator button and waited. And waited. I watched as the car rolled up from the lobby, one number at a time, stopping at each floor on the way up. I went through the realm of emotions… from hostility, to fear, to hopelessness. I finally laughed at myself. Knowing full well Rebecca was watching me wait. And, I'd failed to wait for the damn summary I just demanded.

As the elevator rolled up to the floor just beneath me, Ari walked out to talk. He put his hand on my shoulder.

"I, I know it all seems like a lot. But I promise you, it's not that bad. It's never that bad." Ari spoke like Moses must have… reassuringly on their way through the Red Sea.

I thought of all that Ari had gone through with the death of his son, Timothy, and his wife's insanity. He never divorced. He visits her every week in Santa Barbara. All of a sudden calm fell over me. My hands stopped shaking. My breath normalized.

"I'm sorry." I said sadly.

"It's alright. Why don't you come back in."

Bing. The elevator opened. Empty.

I stuck my hand in to hold the door open. "I'm tired, Ari. I'm tired and I've got this achin' headache… Can you make time for me in the mornin'?"

"Sure. Be here around nine. We'll get your DNA test done and start closing out some of these suits. You'll feel better."

I nodded, shook Ari's hand, as Ari pulled me close in for a man-hug.

"Get some rest, I'll see you in the morning."

Chapter Fifteen

Shades of Erin

I was settling in for the night, had just called room service for a rib-eye and potatoes au-gratin, and popped the top on my second cold brew, thinking about calling the kiddos, when my cell began vibrating on the lamp table. Normally, I would have let voice mail pick up. It was an L.A. area code.

"Yeah."

Breathing.

"Hello." No immediate answer and I was about to hang up.

"Johnny", she almost whispered.

I didn't say anything. Just waited to hear who it was.

"Johnny? Are you there?"

"Yeah." Drank a gulp of cold Coors, in a bottle.

"Do you know who this is?"

"I don't play games like that."

"This is Erin. Erin Answer."

I was surprised. I fully expected some bimbo might have gotten my number when I was drunk out of my mind. But, Erin?

"Hello Erin."

"Are you busy?"

"No. Not at all. Just settling down after a stressful day." I sat down in the desk chair, wearing only my shorts, and gazed out the high-rise window overlooking Los Angeles. Brown hazy smog as the sun went down.

"I heard you might be in LA this evening."

"Whud you have in mind?" I asked.

"Well… I'm here on business, and I was thinking about the last time we saw each other… I'd really rather it didn't end that way. And I was wondering if maybe we could get together for a beer or something."

I was silent for a few uncomfortable seconds.

"Johnny?" Erin's voice was unusually submissive.

"Yeah, I'm still here... I, uhm..."

"We don't have to go out. I'm not really wanting the attention. Maybe you could come over, or I could come to see you... I'll bring the beer."

"I'm at the Sunset Marquis." I replied. I sure as hell wasn't going to her.

I loved the Marquis for its recording studio. Last time I stayed here I ran into the Red Hot Chili Peppers and partied all night. House of Blues, Viper Room and Roxy were all close by. I tried to book the studio for this night, but Faith Hill was already there.

"Oh, awesome! I'm actually right down the street from you, at the Chateau Marmont. I can be there in thirty minutes... is that alright?"

"Yeah. Yeah, that'd be fine. See you then."

"Ok, bye."

Now what is that all about? Last time I saw her she hated my guts... or I hated hers... Bitch!

I knew why she was coming. She wanted to get fucked. I could see it in her eyes when I opened the door for her, back at the ESPN studios in Connecticut. *Connecticut. What the fuck is up with that?*

I didn't bother showering. She wasn't worth it. My hair was starting to look greasy. And that's exactly how I felt right about then… Greasy. I decided to watch porn to get in the mood. Bondage.

†

A light knock at the door… hesitant and unsure. I waited a moment before answering. I wanted her to stand out there in the hall for a while. I drank a big swallow from a Gentleman Jack bottle, and chased it with cold beer… changed the channel. She knocked again. Heavier. More assertive.

"Hello", I looked at her and memorized the color of her eyes.

Brown.

"Hi, Johnny."

"Come on in. Make yourself at home. Let me take that, I'll put it on ice. How was the drive over?"

Erin put her matching purse on the chrome lamp table by the door. "Short. Easy. Limo a whole two blocks. Sometimes I feel like so many things I do is a waste."

"Yeah, I know what you mean."

"Bad day, huh?" She asked politely.

"Please, kick your shoes off, have a seat." Erin was wearing what I guessed had been the product of anxious moments looking at her travel wardrobe, trying this on, trying on something else, then finally going back to what she'd picked out originally… bold red mini-skirt, with a thin black, lace-back silk blouse… the outline of her erect nipples showing through the fabric… and black stiletto heels. No bra. And diamond stud earrings with a matching bracelet.

"Do you like it? I call it my sexy formal fun look." Her long straight sandy blonde hair swung in the air as she twirled around. Erin was a striking five feet ten inches, and slim at around a hundred and thirty pounds… *long legs.*

Mmmm, I'd say thirty-six, twenty-three, thirty-three. Ass is a bit wide for her hips, but she carries it well. Natural teardrop shaped tits. Nice smile. Kind of a long nose, but, hell, I ain't perfect either.

"You look fabulous, Erin… Can I get you a beer… shot a Jack?"

"Hmmm…. That sounds like what I need right now… yes thank you."

Nice legs. I remember that. Tan and long. She looks damn good for thirty-two.

"So what's been happenin' Erin?"

"Oh, I dunno… nothing… everything. I'm in town for the Jay Leno show tomorrow night. I'm going to begin taping of Dancing with the Stars next month. I got picked by the network to do the Rose Bowl… everything's great. Now, to complicate matters, I just got an offer from FOX… a really nice offer."

"You've got a lot to be thankful for."

It was a two-bedroom villa. Sliding glass doors out to the private fenced patio. Modern contemporary styling. Sixties retro chairs in leather suede. Chrome pedestal tables. Dark grey wall paint in the bedrooms. Kind of a sage green everywhere else. Square backed charcoal leather couch and love seat with dark purple cushions. Recessed spotlights against the art work of desert dunes and one of multicolored thin stripes that reminded me of pants the Partridge family would have worn. The carpet was neutral grey… short-pile shag.

We sat next to one another on the couch, looking up at the flat screen, muted and playing Speed Racer cartoons on Adult Swim. I'd turned off the porn when I heard the knock on the door.

Erin turned, her back to the arm of the couch, and put her pretty naked feet on my thigh. We drank to good times, as if we'd been friends forever.

"Let's drink to the bad times, too, Johnny. Nobody ever drinks to the BAD times."

"Do you have bad times?"

"Ha! That is fucking hilarious, Mr. Johnny Outlaw – The Outlaw. Just fucking hilarious!" She slams the second half of her Coors, and requests another. The ice chest sat on the floor between me and the glass and chrome coffee table.

"Everyone… I mean everyone… thinks I've got it all together. They all think I'm just some good looking bitch who had it easy… Well I didn't have it easy Johnny. I worked for everything I've got. I didn't fuck my way to the top, like everyone is conditioned to think."

"I'm sure you did… work… for everything."

"I've worked hard, Johnny. I mean… my parents were good to me, yes, but, we had our issues at home, like everyone else, ya know."

"I'm sure you did."

She reminded me of the girl on the cheerleading squad who spends all her time trying to live up to the image, only to find out everyone hates her for it. When really, she's a sensitive and caring girl who just wants like hell to be liked. I could relate to that.

"From the time I was in high school, I knew what I wanted to be. Did you?" She asked.

"Did I what?" I replied.

"Did you know what you wanted to be?"

"No. I still don't know what I want to be."

"I did. Cheerleading… Student government… National Honors Society… Bachelors in Telecommunications… all for one goal… to be a sports television broadcaster. My dad was a six-time Emmy award winner… did you know that?"

"No I didn't. That's impressive." I replied.

"Yep. Very impressive. I always wanted to be like him… But ya know what they say… it's a man's world."

"I guess it's all in how you look at it, Erin. You've done well for yourself." She was a light-weight, I could tell. *Two beers and two shots of Jack and she's slurring her words and already coming clean about her childhood. That's why she came. She just needs sympathy. But why me? Why the sexy attire and the fuck me shoes?*

"You mean I've done well for a woman!"

"Aw, don't pull that crap on me. You're sitting on power, Baby. And don't you deny it. I'm so fuckin' sick of women playing THE VICTIM all the damn time." My patience had just run its course.

Erin couldn't hold back the smile. She cracked a laugh. "Haaa. You're so right. It's anybody's world who's willing to do what it takes to get what they want."

"Damn right." I drank to it.

"You're such a good looking man, Outlaw. Outlaw… I love that name on you. I mean, it just doesn't work for anybody, ya know. You can't call Donald Trump an outlaw. You can't call… Bill O'Reilly an outlaw."

We both began to laugh out loud… one of those times where you may not be able to stop giggling if you don't hurry up and think about something else real quick.

"You were a Florida Gator."

"Florida Gator. Yep. Go Gators! I was a Zeta."

"I was a FIJI…. LSU."

"Ohhh, Go Tigers! Yep, and I was a Dazzler."

"You still are honey." The booze was hitting me.

"Awww, aren't you sweet. You really are sweet… I'm sorry about the interview, Johnny."

I didn't say anything, just started rubbing her feet.

"Mmmmmm… don't stop… you know exactly what I need don't you?"

"Actually, I'm not sure I do."

She drank another long swig of Coors, took another shot that I handed her.

"The peephole video ruined my life." She said quietly.

I know I looked surprised. A lump grew in my throat. I found it hard to swallow. I remembered the peephole video. I watched it, before it was seemingly wiped off the planet. It was lame. Not a quality picture. *Hell, it was through a fucking peephole.*

"I know this sounds like a gross exaggeration… but… I truly felt… still feel… like he molested me. And every time someone watches that video, or looks at those pictures, I feel raped of my dignity." She began to tear up, and drew closer to me, bending at the waist and laying her cheek on my shoulder. She wrapped her arm around me.

I can relate to the raping thing. But then again, I'm a man who's not supposed to have issues with being molested by women.

She went on, as if I was her psychiatrist. "I'm not a bimbo reporter like, like Chick Norris, or Ann Lacey. I worked really, really hard to achieve my goals. I want to be taken seriously."

I touched her knee, and kept the other hand on her foot. I wasn't sure what she wanted from me. *This is a very classy girl. Smart… once so confident… hurt… but strong. I should be charging her for this session.*

Still going on, she explained, "If I had given permission… if I had posed for some expose… it would have all been so different. But, I didn't Johnny. I didn't give anyone permission to see me like that… It isn't fair." She began balling at this point… on the verge of uncontrollable. Then, in an instant, she stopped. I reached for the Kleenex box conveniently placed by hotel staff on the bottom shelf of the end table. I'd noticed it there before she came over. I had no idea it would be coming in handy this night.

"I've done all the crying I'm going to do. That scumbag is in jail where he deserves to be. I'm in control of my life. Not him."

The "scumbag" was in a community jail in Seattle, serving a thirty month sentence. Erin's lawyers made sure that any monies generated from books or photos by the man would go directly to her. Furthermore, he would serve more jail time if he exploited her in any way. Erin was still suing Marriot International, Radisson Hotels, and five other entities for negligence and invasion of privacy. She helped enact a tough new anti-stalking law with U.S. senators.

"I suppose you think I'm here so you can console me. Rub my feet, listen to my victim stories."

I shrugged, "I'm not sure why you're here, Erin."

"You ever read Fifty Shades of Grey?"

"No."

"You ever hear about it… about what it's about?"

"Yeah. As I recall it was some rich guy who's really into kink. He offers some virgin a bunch of money to be his slave.

She digs it. And apparently so do a lot of other women. Around twenty million copies sold I believe."

"I'm here because I want you to tie me up and fuck my brains out." Erin was blushing, but never wavered. "I want you to treat me rough, throw me around, slap me if you want, blind fold me, gag me… I want you to hurt me Johnny, but not really hurt me. I want you to hurt me good."

My eyes opened wide in disbelief. My mouth was open. I ceased rubbing her feet. She remained as serious as anyone could be, looking straight into my eyes. She was nervous, but determined.

"I brought the rope. It's in my bag by the door. I was hoping you had a neck tie or something, but from the looks of it…"

I still didn't say anything. *Is this chick flipping out on me? She assumes that I'm into S&M?*

"Power can be very boring, Johnny." Erin pushed herself up and out of the couch position, and stood in front of me, to the side of the ice chest and the coffee table. Her cleavage was showing, her nipples erect, sweat beads forming in between her breasts. I was breathing heavier… my cock beginning to fill with blood. "I submit to you. Take me. Do whatever you want to me… Remember I'm the bitch who asked you about the James Bond accident on national television. Johnny… Outlaw."

Erin, looking intently at me as I still sat there drinking my beer, backed slowly away and walked over to the table where her purse lay. She put her stilettos back on, and threw the shiny new nylon rope at my face.

"I'm a naughty girl. I need to be disciplined by you, PLEASE."

I got up slowly, pulled at my crotch to make room for my growing member, and with the rope in my hands, walked to the bedroom. *I really do hate this bitch.*

The next morning, around ten a.m., Erin awoke to the silence that awaited her. There was no sign of me. Only a note by her bedside, along with a single rose picked from the patio.

Dear Erin,

I treated you badly just to be kind. Hope you feel alright today. See you on the road, somewhere between heaven and hell.

Johnny

Chapter Sixteen

Out of the Ashes

Almost a year since the Jamaica trip, I was relatively broke, but making a comeback. My slate wiped clean by lawsuit settlements and enormous IRS payments, Ari worked diligently at keeping my name in the hearts and minds of the public. I was booked for cameo appearances on Two and a Half Men and How I Met Your Mother, guesting on Saturday Night Live and Jay Leno. The plan, though, was to temper the Outlaw image with good guy events that might re-endear me to my fan base, while also broadening my audience to include country music fans and the adult television audience. I made charitable appearances at St. Jude's and Walter Reed, using my time as a contribution wherever I could. I was off the drugs and booze, and held to a strict work-out regimen, overseen by my personal trainer, Stefan Uzinsky.

Stefan, as part of his eighty-thousand dollar salary, fronted by Ari Pei, was also the cook, or "chef", as he demanded. My diet consisted of around five hundred grams of carbohydrates such as whole grains, vegetables, potatoes and fruit, and an additional eighty grams of proteins like chicken, fish, and low-fat dairy and protein bars.

All this was very difficult for me, who didn't eat anything green, and found whole grains are like cardboard. I basically had survived on whole milk my entire life, and skim was blue water to me. Stefan, whom I referred to as the Hitler of physical trainers, was perfect for the challenge, as there was no way I would have done any of it otherwise. I ate twice the amount of chicken and fish than Stefan previously prescribed, and half as many protein bars. Veggies were limited to carrots, raw and cooked, and fresh green beans, sautéed in real butter or cooked in foil on the grill.

With the two hundred thousand I got as an advance on my memoirs, I purchased two hundred acres in the Ozark Mountains of Arkansas, remote as I could get and still be close enough to Beth to exchange the kids once a week, in Shreveport, halfway between her place in Louisiana and mine, an hour and a half north of Little Rock. All together, we were eight hours apart by automobile.

My new place was far enough away from civilization that I could focus on my new lifestyle. I loved the Ozark mountain region, as it was a quiet and soulful place for me... my own personal sanctuary. Though I'd sometimes complained to Stefan that it wasn't rugged enough as compared to the Rockies, Stefan reminded me that the weather was much more hospitable for training, and far less expensive to live here.

Part of my training had to include riding bulls. There were things about riding real bulls that mechanical bulls just couldn't match. I described to Stefan "the movement and spirit of a wild animal trying to kill you is impossible to mimic." So, using the name John Smith as a joke, I signed up for small time rodeos and bulls-only events in the area, within roughly a hundred mile radius… mostly unsanctioned venues at county fairs. I got my hair cut short, shaved every morning, and wore starched jeans and western shirts with the sleeves rolled down. Even though I still had a closet full of Bolo shirts and Rebel jeans, I opted for old school Wranglers and button downs from the local feed store. I did stick with my favorite hats, beavers handmade in Oakdale, California by Alamosa Hat Works. I claimed "a custom made hat, fit 'special for yer head, is like a good woman… hard to find, and impossible to replace."

It only took a couple of months of living in the country to bring my spirit back to where I was when I lived at Granddaddy's place on Lake Vernon. I was taking time to smell the good air… to see the trees and grasses blowing gently in the breeze… where life was quiet and as it should be. Here, there were more cattle than people.

The acreage hosted a small two room pine wood cabin on concrete blocks, on a ridge overlooking the Bull Run valley, in the shadow of Wright Mountain. The cabin was literally being eaten by termites, and I was making plans to build a house on the ridge further north on the property, where I would have a panoramic view and see clear to Greer's Ferry Lake. It was a mile away, where the Corps of Engineers damned the Little Red back in the sixties, creating more than three hundred miles of pristine mountain shore-line and lake depths reaching more than two hundred and fifty feet.

As a diversion to rigorous training and loneliness, I bought a used pontoon boat at the Sugar Loaf Marina down the road, and spent my afternoons puttering close to the shoreline, jug fishing, writing and playing my guitar.

Stefan chose to rent an apartment in Conway, a college town about forty five minutes south, and commuted each morning and evening for breakfast, training, lunch, more training, and the evening meal. Other than Stefan, and, Joe, the owner of the marina, I was in complete solitude. Stefan bought a new Jeep Black Ops edition, which was a real kick in the ass in this rugged terrain.

It was a terrific place for the boys to live. At the ages of eleven and nine and a half, doing their best to imitate the late Crocodile Hunter, Steve Irwin, they bound with energy… playing cowboys and Indians, fishing in the pond and hunting wild critters, catching snakes of all kinds and even a tarantula or two. Their time spent with their daddy was quality time, and I found it more and more impossible to bring them to their mom's after each of our weeks together that summer.

"Beth, I know I haven't been here for the boys... and I regret that terribly. Believe me I do. And considering all the time you had with them, and the things you'd like to do... I was wondering if... if I might have them for the rest of the summer."

"It's a small house John. And you have your trainer there most of the time."

"Exactly, and good healthy meals, and they really like working out with me. And they love coming to the rodeos on weekends. The land is awesome... you should see 'em runnin' around out there all free and getn' dirty and catchin' bugs..."

"Catchin' snakes and poisonous spiders you mean. And you don't even have a washer and dryer, John."

"That's just small stuff, Beth. We go to town and wash our stuff. Same time we go to Wal-Mart. Besides, I'm buildin' a house soon. We'll have all that we need out there."

"You won't have a house built this summer. But... I know they love being with you. And you do have a lot of catching up to do!"

"Exactly. Beth... I can handle this. It's where I want to be. I need them with me... like they need me. And it'll allow you to take care of yourself… do your thing for a while. Everybody wins."

"I'll call you later when we get home. I'll think about it."

Bitch, don't make me tell your ass off. These are my boys too. Who you think's been payin' your way all these fuckin' years.

"Ok. I'll talk to you later then… Thanks for talkin' it over with me."

Then Beth's attentions were elsewhere. "Come on boys! Boys! What are you doin over there? Get out of the mud puddle. Is that glass in your hand? Put it down. Right now… No, I said put it down… No! Don't break the glass Marshall. Damn it! Get in the car."

"But Mom…"

"Get!"

"See you later." I said.

"See ya… Bye boys. Love you." I continued.

"Bye Daddy. Love you! Love you, Daddy… see ya next week!"

"Yep. See ya soon, boys. Give Dad a big hug… Oh boy that is a big hug! Ok, you too, Matthew… oh boy. Ok, ya'll be good for Mommy now. Call me soon."

"Ok, love you Daddy." They hollered in unison.

God, that hurts. Bye son. Bye little man. I wish you'd tell 'er you don't want to live with her anymore. Tell her you wanna live with yer Daddy.

†

Ari called weekly, getting and giving reports on my progress. Though media coverage of their bad boy star had waned, Ari concluded this was a good and necessary thing.

"We're rebuilding you kid, bigger… better… stronger than before. How you doin' on funds?"

"I don't have a bucket to piss in. Beth's complainin' about money, too."

"Ok, listen, I'm gonna transfer funds to your account today, ok. Don't worry about it. Ten thou do the trick for a while?"

"Yeah, I guess."

"What you need more?"

"No, that's not it… I'm just not likin' this bein' broke all the time. Borrowin' money from you… I don't like it."

"Hey, Johnny, it's my investment in you. Ok? Just like the early days. I'm about to get things goin' up here. You just stay focused. You'll be ridin' the bulls into the ground this coming season, and the money will come. And so will all the other stuff."

"Yeah. I know. Ok."

"Alright, kid. Stay outa trouble. I'll be in touch… you call me if you need anything, huh."

"Yeah, Ok, bye."

"Bye Johnny."

Moments after I hung up with Ari, Bobby called.

"Hey, Man, what's up?" I asked. It was a relief to hear from him, and at the same time… I feared what hanging out with Kid Rock would do to me.

"Whataya say Outlaw! How's the sober life?"

"It's good. How's the life in Sodom and Gomorrah?"

"Same fuckin' thing, Man. Whores layin' all over the fuckin' place. Lines on the table. Fuckin' beer cans everywhere."

"Hmm."

"No, man, I'm fuckin' with ya. I'm just sittin' here up in Michigan, Man… hangin' out in my new house."

"Oh yeah? I didn't know."

"Yeah, well… you inspire me. I bought a nice place in the country. I think you'll like it."

"Y'all got country up there in Michigan?"

"Fuck you, man. Hell yeah we got country. Hell you been here. 'Member the whitetail trip we took up here… my new place is just ten miles from there."

"I'm just fuckin' with ya Man. I'm glad for you and Paul."

"Yeah, well… Paul needs a more stable environment. Hired a housekeeper. She lives here too. Fuckin' mean old bitch… so I can't get in trouble."

"Right on, Man. Now yer thinkin'."

"Yeah, well… you know… I'm getting' too fuckin' old, Man", proclaimed the Kid.

"Naw, we're just getn' smarter." I replied.

"God forbid, Outlaw… God forbid. So… how you likin' your new place in hillbilly junction?"

"I like it."

"Yeah?"

"Yeah… it's… peaceful."

"It's fuckin' boring as hell you mean." Bobby said.

"Naw, not really man. You should come down for a visit. I'll take your ass fishin'."

"Yeahhhhhh…. I will, Man. I will… So they got any herb out there in them there hills?" Bobby was doing his best impression of Jed Clampet from the Beverly Hillbillies. He couldn't pull it off.

"Oh, I'm sure it's around. But I wouldn't exactly know these days."

"No shit. That too, huh? Fuck me, Man. I don't know if I wanna visit a dry hole. You got any beer?"

"It's a dry county." I said.

"OH SHIT… say it ain't so, Outlaw!"

"I'm serious. Dry, like a dead bull's dinger."

"Dry like a what?" Bobby was laughing.

"A dead bull's dinger." I quipped back.

"Oh, Man, I gotta get you outa there before it's too late."

"Whud you have in mind?"

"Welllllll…. As luck would have it… you remember Scooby?" asked Bob.

"Yeah."

“He’s havin’ his big-ass charity event in Kingston this weekend.”

“Oh, yeah?”

“Yeah, and he asked me if you wanted to come along.”

“Hmmmm….”

“He wants you to sing.”

“What? I can’t do that. In front of people… on stage… no fuckin’ way!”

“You can do it, Cowboy. Shit, you can ride bulls and throw your damn hat in the air in front of sixty thousand people.”

“Yeah, but I know how to ride bulls.”

“And you know how to sing.”

“No, I don’t. Not really.”

“Well, you can, but I won’t argue with you. Why don’t you come along for the ride. We’ll have a good time.”

“Yeah… I know we will… I’m in training right now, Man. I’m eatin’ right, not drinkin’, not smokin’… runnin’ every mornin’. Breathin’ clean air. Really gettin’ my head right, ya know.”

“Caroline’s gonna be there.”

I fell silent.

"John, you there?"

"Uh, yeah, I'm here. You say Caroline's gonna be there… how come? How do you know?"

"Scooby told me to tell you that, Man. Apparently, she's the event coordinator for the shindig. My guess is she told Scooby to tell me to tell you."

"Hmmm."

"Yeah, I thought that'd change your fuckin' mind… tell me where the nearest runway's at, and we'll stop by and pick your ass up."

"I don't know, Bobby. I need to think about it. I got a lot goin' on here, Man. My boys are comin' regularly… I just asked Beth if I could have 'em for the summer."

"She give you an answer yet?"

"No, not yet."

"Awright, Man. Call me back tonight."

"Will do. How long you gonna be gone?"

"Be back Sunday afternoon."

"Awright. Call ya later."

"Later."

I would have loved to see Caroline again. In a way, it seemed like fate. But with training, and the boys… the time just wasn't right. I'd learned over the years that making events happen was a lot like putting a round piece of the puzzle in a square hole. As much as I'd like to see her, forcing the matter could be a mistake.

Meanwhile, I was working on my memoirs… another good reason not to go anywhere that weekend. It was taking longer than I'd expected, the publisher was getting impatient, and I really needed to get something going. Having my memoirs published meant the talk show circuit… and that meant tabloid magazines and television… which meant exposure… which meant opportunities… which meant money. None of which was exciting at all to me. Exposure, to me, meant being put on the spot, and possible embarrassment over my past reputation. I'd made up my mind long time ago to embrace the bad boy image, but this was a new era… one I wasn't yet accustomed to.

One thing I did like about writing was being able to express myself. But this had always been a private matter. I kept my leather book to myself. Mostly, it was therapeutic… a private way to go over intimate issues in my mind, spit them out on paper, read them and come to terms. But, now, I was about to go public. And I was writing cautiously. I knew I would have to overcome this dilemma, for it was the private, intimate stuff people wanted to read. And in order to deal with it, I made up my mind to sever from the past, make a clean break of it, start fresh, and this book would be the marking point.

Chapter Seventeen

Black Jets Rule

Kid Rock's jet was painted solid black, gold pin-striping, tastefully done, with a clear coat finish that would make any classic car collector blush. The interior was all camel tan leather, with, of course, a full bar, microwave, warming oven and a bedroom, and still managed to seat four comfortably.

"It's an o-four model Bombardier... just over four thousand hours on it... Fucker 'il do more than five hundred miles an hour, Man. Just got her back from Wichita, Kansas... had 'em go through the whole thing... avionics, life rafts, everything. Before that, I had Chip Foose paint this son-of-a-bitch. Took out four club seats and a table, reconfigured these seats, moved the bar, and put in this bedroom." Bobby was proud of his plane, and lit his cigar.

"Wow. This is very nice, Bob. Very cool. Love the black. Looks like a fuckin' rock star. How much you got in it?"

"I bought it in Santa Barbara for eleven mil. Then I put another fuckin million into it… THEN I have to pay for the two pilots' salaries."

"Damn it Boy! You ain't worth but thirty. You spent a third of your worth on a fuckin plane?"

"Tax deduction. Besides, image is everything Johnny boy. You know that. And, I can always sell her."

"I spend thirty nine hundred dollars an hour to charter the same plane. It's ready whenever I am. AND, I can it write off."

"Yeah, but it ain't black! And yours don't have a bedroom!" Bobby couldn't argue with my logic. And I didn't want to seem unappreciative of the aircraft, so the issue was dropped.

Kid brought a companion on the trip… Pamela Anderson, former Playboy Playmate of the year, actress on the hit series Bay Watch, now in syndication, and recently published author of a fantasy novel loosely based on her three year affair with a famous rock drummer, and father to her two year old son, Tommy Lee. Bobby hadn't informed me about just exactly who his guest would be on the trip, if any. And although I wasn't all that impressed with Pamela, Marshall and Matthew sure were.

"Marshall, stop staring at Miss Pam's cleavage. It's not polite." Bobby said trying to embarrass the boy and get everyone laughing.

"What's cleavage?" Marshall asked innocently.

"That space between her boobs." Acknowledged Matthew.

"Oh, I'm not staring at the space between her boobs, Uncle Bobby. I'm staring at her big Ta-Tas."

"It's okay Marshall, boys have been staring at my Ta-Tas since I was a teenager." Bleach Blonde Bombshell Pamela, in her late thirties, was maturing now, same as the Kid and the Outlaw. But it was different for her. Her looks was what she built her career on. Not her acting skills, or her writing abilities. She couldn't sing, and the closest she'd ever been to a bull was back in Texas, when she wasn't a vegetarian. She was still a gorgeous woman to look at. Her feet and toenails were perfect. The arches in her tanned feet were as sexy as the arch in her back. She was wearing a backless pink blouse that hung delicately on her constantly erect nipples, and short black shorts that barely covered her still-firm ass cheeks. The only signs of her age could be found in her hands and around her eyes. *It sucks get'n old, dudn't it baby.*

"So, Pam, how have you been?" I could tell she'd recently added collagen to her lips, and probably had Botox injections. *What women do for us men.*

"I'm good, Johnny, and you?" She replied smiling gleaming whites.

"I'm hangin' in there… how's your son?" I asked politely.

"Scout is fine. Thank you for asking. He's running and climbing on everything. You know, being a boy. Thank God Bobby's been around to play with him." I looked at Bobby quickly, and then fixed my eyes back on Pam's. I had seen some article on Yahoo recently about Pam and Kid Rock being seen together at some Easter egg hunt in Carmel.

"Your boys are sooo cute! And so well behaved. Yes Ma'am. No Ma'am. They're going to be real lady killers when they get older."

"God… I hope not." I replied seriously.

"Johnny wants his boys to live normal quiet lives… preferably far away in the hills, away from all the obscenities of the modern world." Chimed in Bobby with his cigar clinched between his teeth.

"Well, good luck with that. I moved back home to Texas when Scout was born, you know, to put some normalcy back in my life… for my sake. But to no avail. They'll find you."

I kept my thoughts to myself. *If you really didn't want 'em to find you, you could make it harder for 'em.*

The fifteen hundred mile flight from Clinton, Arkansas' rural municipal airport to Kingston, cruising at forty thousand feet and at five hundred miles per hour, would take just a few minutes over three hours. Once the small talk ran its course, the boys went to sleep on the carpeted floor, Bobby and Pam recessed to the bedroom to update their status in the mile-high club, and I sat alone looking out the window at all the man-made squares below, or atop the fluffy white clouds that occasionally came between them, and eventually down into the deep blue gulf.

It had already been nine months since the Princess and I had met. There had been no attempt by either party to contact the other, as far as I knew. And yet, here I was coming all this way, getting myself into who knows what, just for the chance that she might be interested in seeing me again. *What if she's already seeing someone else? What if she looked into my past and didn't like what she saw? Wait, though… Bobby said she told Scooby to ask me to come. Or is that bullshit?*

The black jet circled Kingston waiting for clearance. The boys were waking and starting to stir about the cabin, bouncing from window to window, each one trying to out-comment the other.

"Look at THAT cloud!"

"No, come look at THIS cloud!"

"Mine looks like a DRAGON!"

"Mine… Mine looks like a really hot babe layin' on the beach with her Ta-Tas stickin out."

"Marshall! Dude! Like that's soo not appropriate." I looked away to erase the smile and the comment that caught me by surprise. I knew I should give my sons a lecture on respecting women and so on, but my nervous gut wouldn't let me.

I was pouring Matthew Sprite over ice when Marshall commented on "all the people down there". I looked out my window and saw what looked like thousands of islanders at a giant party at the fairgrounds near the beach. The stage was a massive steel structure with a wooden floor and rows of lights hanging from their webbed racks… clearly visible from fifteen hundred feet. The size of the event startled me and inside I began to quiver. This wasn't like other times when I rode along as part of Kid's entourage, drinking, smoking, singing along to Bobby's warm-up songs. This was an event in which I would be taking part, live on stage in front of thousands of people, all paying attention to me, and only me, for at least four minutes, if I could remember the words. *Words to what?* I hadn't even decided that yet. *I'll just have to back out. Probably a dozen acts. I won't matter. One song. Who cares. The last thing I need to do is get up there and make a fool of myself in front of Caroline.*

The jet landed abruptly but without incident, and quickly taxied into the parking lot of other rock and roll airplanes. "Two more black ones." Marshall observed.

Bobby and Pamela were dressed and drinking cocktails. Bobby heard Marshall's observance of the like-colored craft, and hissed.

"They ain't been Foosed like this baby has." He lights his half-smoked Cuban cigar. "You seen the gold and silver leaf on my tail back here? Huh? I'll have to show ya when we get outa here." Bobby… Kid Rock, the Bad Ass Rock Star from the suburbs of Detroit… is about to step once again onto a stage where rabid fans expect him to be high, drunk and rowdy as hell, yelling into the microphone over POUNDING drums, a thundering bass, and raucous guitar, while simultaneously running the length of the stage, all eighty feet of it, jumping up and down, doing the splits in mid-air, and stopping to gulp from a bottle of Jack Daniels that sits on a stool nearby. And he is as calm as anyone could ever be.

"How do you remain so, so calm?" I asked him.

"Damn boy, are you shakin?" He replied.

"Hell, I guess. I'm st, stutterin, and my hands are shakin. I got butterflies."

"Good. That's good my friend. That's the way it should feel." Bobby sat next to me and toasts his glass to mine. I was now on my fifth hi-ball.

"I used to get nervous. Adrenaline rush, ya know. But, shit man, I've done some awesome fuckin' shows. In some awesome fuckin' places. After a while, it's hard to get up for it… which is why I got so heavy into the coke, Man. You just keep lookin' for that feelin'… that feelin' you got right now. So, enjoy it my friend. Enjoy! And then… quit. Run away and hide somewhere. Before it goes sour. On your own terms. Like Elvis or Jim Morrison, only without really bein' dead." Bobby smiled, and at once, looked out my window and began his metamorphosis into Kid Rock.

The plane halted, the engines whined to a stop, the pilots exited the cockpit, asking about the flight, and met the passengers as they disembarked, and assuring us that they and the plane would be ready to go in exactly twenty-four hours. Kid was forced to go back to being Uncle Bobby long enough to show Marshall and Matthew the Foose work on the tail.

"Come on Man, I got a damn show to do."

"Well, Uncle Bobby, you said you WANTED to show me the Foose gold and silver lease."

"Huh? Not Lease. LEAF! Gold and silver Leaf!" Even as he spoke this way, everyone knew he was kidding, as he smiled and struggled to handle his cocktail glass and his cigar, AND fix his fedora at the same time.

"Pam, Honey, how come you're not helping me?"

"Oh, Bob, you know whenever I do offer to help you, you shun me away. Here let me hold that!" Pamela reached down and grabbed a handful of Bobby's boulders. Bobby yelled out something starting with Argh… threw his glass in the air which came crashing down on the debris free tarmac. The cigar fell to the pavement, and instantly Marshall and Matthew raced to pick it up. A gust of wind blew his fedora off his head, twenty or so feet where it lodged against one of the rubber tires on someone else's plane. Pam and I laughed uncontrollably, until all three of us were sitting on our asses in the middle of the hot tarmac, one more jet having just landed and heading our way.

According to the program, no doubt put together by Caroline, Kid Rock was to take the stage at nine pm. It was now only five-thirty in the evening, Jamaican time, to which Pamela responded, "You brought me along so I could take care of your ass, but you're not about to get fallin' down drunk and wantin' me to carry you! I'll leave your ass!" The more she drank the more you could hear her Texas twang.

Hotel reservations were made by Scooby's staff, and a Jamaican driver of a newer model white Lincoln limousine was stationed at the airport to take us there. Marshall continued finding ways to look at Pamela's ta-tas, and Matthew marveled aloud at all the black people.

Bobby told Scooby he'd call him upon our arrival. "Hey. Uneventful so far. (Pam backhands him in the stomach.) Yeah. On our way there now. Ok. Ok. Yes. Will do. Bye."

"Stage is already set up. Band's already had sound check." Bobby informed us.

"When will you do YOUR sound check?" I asked.

"Someone else does that for me… in cases like this anyway… So… Johnny Outlaw. We need to pick a song and go over it a couple times…"

"Couple times? Couple times? A few times. Lots of times. I'm not get'n up there with you, Man."

"Johnny. You know you can do this. It's no different than if we were at my house. You've been in front of crowds before."

"Yeah, but I knew what I was doing in front of THOSE crowds."

"Dude, you're in fucking Jamaica! Ok! Jamaica. Now where else could be better to try out your new thing. It's the perfect place… you're gonna transition from bad ass cowboy bull ridin' dude to bad ass singing cowboy bull ridin' dude. Not a big stretch. Besides, these people are gonna be so liquored up and stoned out of their minds… they'll love you!"

"He's right, Johnny, I've heard you in the Sanctuary, and I think you sing good." Pam was being sweet.

"No offense, but ya'll love me. Ya'll are gonna say that. But these folks here, they don't know me. They'll boo me off the stage and I'll never recover. I can't take that chance."

"Bullshit, you're just worried about what Caroline's gonna think."

†

On our way across town from the Presidentiale Hotel to the fairgrounds, our little group learned from the limo driver that the free concert was a three day affair, which began yesterday, complete with craft booths, vendors selling all kinds of homemade clothing, blankets, bandanas, island crafts… knock off Rolexes. Not only was the festival necessary to keep the children's hospital going, but it was an economic boon for the city, and for the whole island.

"Las night, uhhhhh….las night de uhhhh, Lew-da-kris?" The driver, who said "call me BooGoo", was at least sixty years old, and looked as though he'd grown up wild on the beaches and someone taught him to drive and slapped a suit on his back. He reminded me of an Aborigine from the Outback. His voice was young, which made me wonder if maybe he just looked old.

I looked at Bobby, who looked at Pam, and we all three agreed in unison the driver must be referring to Ludacris the rapper.

"Ludacris? Hip Hop singer?"

"Mon is won craaa-zy son-of-de-bitch Mon!"

The boys were already inquiring about his short sun faded dreadlocks. "Can I touch your hair", asked Matthew as they drove away from the hotel.

"Why?" The driver looked annoyed.

"He was doin' dis song, called uhhhhhh…. Get Bock, Get bock, Bock de fuck up mudafucka!"

Bobby looked at Pam and said "Back Up", referring to the song's real title.

"Yeah, so what happened?" asked Pamela.

"Fuck-eeng riot Mon. The people go craaa-zy Mon."

"No shit?" replied Kid.

"How bad is it?" I asked.

"Uhhhh, they is working on de stage today." Replied BooGoo.

"Great. Now Ludacris caused a fucking riot… what am I gonna do to top that?" said Kid.

"We don't need any fuckin riots, Man. I thought this was a family thing. Scooby can't be pleased." I countered.

BooGoo's cell phone was ringing. Loudly. For the third time.

"Hey, BooGoo, I think your phone is ringing." Pam informed the driver.

"Oh yeah, Mon. Tanks. It is new to me."

BooGoo worked the cell out of his right pants pocket, pressing more and more on the accelerator pedal as he dug deeper, causing Pam to clear her throat.

"Judging by all the business class jets, I'd guess there's gonna be some pretty big acts here… a lot bigger deal than I thought." I was growing more nervous by the second.

"What the fuck did you think those jets were doing here?" asked Kid rhetorically.

"We need to keep get'n fucked up." I was nervous about seeing Caroline. I'd already resigned in my mind to playing or singing tonight.

The limo bar was out of Crown, Jack, and now the Jim Beam was almost dry.

"BooGoo." I said.

"Yeah Mon."

The boys were jet lagged, and yawning excessively. Marshall found his way to Pamela's side, and pretended to sleep with his head under her left arm and against her bra-less breast. Matthew was stretched out on the seat next to me.

I, sitting in the seat adjacent to the driver, facing the rear of the Lincoln, leaned back to get closer to BooGoo's ear. "Who's gonna hook us up with some ganja?"

BooGoo was silent. I sat and waited for an answer, and wondered if BooGoo might be anti-herb.

"I have it, Mon. But, I do not wan to give to you wit chidren looking."

"Good BooGoo. Good Man. Be there soon?"

Just then we saw the entrance to the fairgrounds coming up. Signs in bright yellow with bold green type, on both sides of the blacktop, told the story. One large banner hung above the entrance that read;

WELCOME TO THE 2ND ANNUAL

SUNSHINE FESTIVAL

Benefitting the Scooby Make a Difference Foundation

and the Bustamante Hospital for Children

The limo was waived through and around the pedestrian gates by security guards in police-type uniforms and neon green safety vests. We drove to the area behind the enormous stage, and the black netting material that made the huge backdrop… eighteen wheelers carrying stage equipment, speakers, and musical instruments, and countless catering vans, ice delivery trucks, two more white limos on standby, and Scooby's own tour busses.

"Damn! This is get'n excitin'!" I proclaimed with enthusiasm.

"Yep. Pam what time is it?" asked Kid.

She looked at her iPhone. "Seven… you have two more hours."

"Don't forget we lost an hour comin' down here." He said to her.

"I didn't forget… and neither did my phone." Pam replied, seeming annoyed.

The car parked next to Scooby's rig, where Bobby and Pam proceeded to knock on the door and yell Scooby's name. I was rousting the kids and helping BooGoo with the garment bag and guitar case that was Kid Rock's, and the frayed duffle that was mine. On it was embroidered PRCA NFR CHAMPION 1999. BooGoo shook hands with me, slipping me a couple of monster joints. "Scooby will have more weed, Mon."

Scooby's sister, Brandi, opened the bus door and welcomed Kid Rock and his guests. Scooby had been taking a nap, and was now in his bathroom brushing his teeth. He had a new gold cap, Brandi, explained, and he liked to keep it shiny.

Much to my liking, Marshall and Matthew were sleepy, and had curled up into balls in the front two seats of the bus. I covered each of them with blankets. Scooby came out of his hiding place and gave Kid a bear hug, thanking him for making the trip, kissing Pamela on the cheek while holding her hands and telling her he had seen almost every one of her Bay Watch episodes.

I remembered the sister, and her tit that she asked me to autograph. I politely asked for the bathroom and just as I shut the door I heard a knock at the other one.

"Hi", came the sweet voice of Princess Caroline.

"Wut up, Girl", came Scooby's voice.

I could hear Caroline stepping in and greeting Bobby and meeting Pam. I quickly turned on the faucet and began washing my face, running my fingers through my hair, putting Visine in my eyes, and rinsing with the Scope that was beside the sink.

I stepped out of the bathroom without pissing, for fear it would look like I had been taking a shit for being in there so long.

"Well, Hello there Princess." I kept my voice low and deep… calm, cool and collected. *Love those shorts on you. Awesome legs. Got your jogging shoes on… and a ball cap… didn't know your hair was curly… not a lot of make-up… you've been busy.*

"Hi, Johnny." She smiled her Farrah Fawcett smile, and the room glowed. My heart pounded immediately, and my breath became short.

She called me Johnny. Not John. She might not have even said my name at all. But she did… she called me Johnny.

"It's been a while." *God, your eyes are even more beautiful than I remembered.*

"Yes, it has… so these are your sons I presume?" Caroline was carrying an orange plastic clip board with an ink pen attached to it with a twelve inch cord. "They are so cute. Look like little cowboys, just like I pictured them." She whispered as she hovered over each one at a time, commenting on their features. "Oh he looks just like his daddy."

"Acts like 'im too", grunted Bobby. "I understand you had a riot on your hands last night."

"Oh it wasn't that bad. Was it Scooby?"

"It could have been worse. I should have known better dan to get Ludacris here. Too crazy for our little fest-ee-val." Scooby could talk Brooklyn black, Jamaican islander, or West Coast white, seemingly at will. I recalled in my mind the night we first met at the GeeJam Bar. One minute Scooby was talking like a Hip Hop artist, but when it came down to business, or talking with Caroline and I, he was quite white. Today, he sounded that way.

"Fortunately, we decided not to put any folding chairs out this year. All people had were beach blankets and empty ice chests to throw." said Scooby.

"And a few empty liquor bottles… Don't remind me Mon, I just want to forget about it. Did the engineers decide on the screen or not?" Scooby was looking directly at Caroline.

"Yes. They decided that the wind gusts have subsided, and they're going to leave it up. The slits in the screen are supposed to help let the wind pass through." It was a warm, rainy day so far, but the forecast was for low eighties and clearing skies by night. The wind was steady at about five, with gusts up to thirty.

Scooby shook his head in relief and beckoned to his sister, who had been practically unnoticed in the rear of the bus, to walk with him and Caroline as they covered the checklist and made certain all was going as planned.

"Do you have an extra schedule on you?" I asked, hoping my name was inadvertently left off the list.

"You can have mine. I'll get another one from the booking agent." Caroline handed the print-out to me, and while I did my best to touch my fingers to hers, I came up short.

"Hell, I thought Scooby was the booking agent!" Bobby chimed in with a roar.

"You're on just before Toots and the Maytals." Said Caroline.

"Shit!" Said Bobby as he took a swig of Scooby's Gentleman Jack.

I asked, "What? Shit what?" I had never heard of Toots and the Maytals.

Bobby answered, "Toots and the Maytals are very big, especially here in Jamaica. They go back to the sixties, Man. Used to hang out with Otis Redding and Marvin Gay, shit like that. Hell, they won best reggae at the AMAs last year."

I was growing more humbled by the minute.

Then Caroline chimed in. "They're going to perform "Let Down", "Beautiful Woman" and "Johnny Cool Man". Then you come out and sing… right after they do Johnny Cool man… I thought that would be an excellent way to introduce you."

"Johnny decided he dudn't wanna sing after all." Bobby had given up trying to talk me into it, and decided to play hardball.

I was silent, looking out the front window of the tour bus at the grippers and stage hands scurrying about, waiting to see what Caroline would say.

"Well, there will be a lot of disappointed fans who wanted to see you perform. Why don't you do 'Loving Her Was Easier'? I think you do that one perfectly well."

I looked around at Caroline with a grin. *She smiled at me. She got the song I recorded for her. And she liked it. Good boy Jason.*

I began reading the list of performers aloud to Bobby and Pam and the boys. "Robert Plant? He was here yesterday?"

"Yes. He did this really unique version of a bluegrass song called "Bron-Y-Aur Stomp". She spelled it rather than try to pronounce it.

"Ini Kamoze?" I asked rhetorically.

"You ever hear 'Jailhouse'?" Bobby replied.

"Can't say as I have… Wow, The Script is playing tomorrow. They're doin 'Nothing' and 'Hall of Fame'. Damn! Tom Petty and the Heartbreakers are gonna be here tomorrow? Jimmy Buffet and the Reefers! And Scooby closes it all out tomorrow night. Holy shit. I should be out there in the field layin' on a blanket and watchin'."

"It 'tis a good show, huh, Mon?" Scooby was a proud and able promoter, now speaking in his Jamaican dialect.

"Ludacris Friday night. Kid Rock Saturday night. Jimmy Buffet Sunday and Scooby Sunday night… Sounds like a fuckin' party to me, Scoob!" I was giddy like a schoolboy.

As Scooby and his sister, along with Caroline, exited the bus, Bobby commented that he could hear sound check.

"That's Toots and the Maytals warming up now", said Caroline walking away, "Johnny you better start practicing. Bobby, will sound check in thirty minutes be okay with you?"

"Thirty, forty, somethin' like that." Kid never really paid attention to schedules and start times. Once in Baton Rouge, he made the audience wait an hour, while he got drunk and high on coke in his dressing room. "I've got to FEEEEL it, ya know. I can't just go out there and rock the house without feelin' it. They wouldn't want that." Just before the crowd went into riot mode, Kid Rock came bustin' out with "Cowboy", and the energy was freaking amazing. The crowd forgave him immediately.

The band's instruments had been shipped in two days ago, and the crew had already set up what they had and plugged in to the speakers and monitors and FOH (Front of the House) mixer that the audio crew was providing. The Maytals set up in front of KR's Band, and their stuff would be rolled away during the intermission between sets. I didn't have, or require, anything other than my own Martin Dreadnaught and what KR would provide.

"Bobby, can we please just sit in here for a few minutes, play a couple songs, let me warm up? I'm not sure I can remember the words."

"Light us up one of those torpedoes BooGoo gave you. Pamela, honey, you mind takin' these boys for a little walk to look around?"

I chimed in appreciatively, "Yeah, Pam, that would be so cool of you."

"Sure. I need to walk around anyway. Hey boys, you ready to check it all out?" Pam still had it. Even with her age catching up to her looks, she was one of the sexiest women I'd ever seen when she was being… maternal.

The boys were super excited, and after Pam checked herself in the mirror and applied lip gloss, they were off.

We found the cold bottles of Red Stripe in Scooby's fridge, slammed a couple shots of Jack, smoked a joint, and Bobby started playing his Martin.

I chose "Weary Kind" and "Dinosaur", in which I'd changed the lyrics to include a stab at Lady Gaga.

"Johnny… you sound good, Man. You're gonna do fine. Now, I don't think we need anything more than a couple of acoustics on 'Dinosaur', that'll make it easy for both of us. So, let's have the band concentrate on 'Weary Kind'. I'll get Trip and Boner in here to listen to your demo real quick, just so they can remember how to play it."

"Sounds good, I guess." By now, I knew Bobby's band was incredibly talented and skilled in their respective crafts. Any of his guys could listen to a song and within a couple minutes have written down key, chord progressions, notes… they could interpret the song and play it like a studio recording.

Bob put his hand on my shoulder and gave more advice. "Dude, get fucked up, but not too fucked up. Just look out over everyone's heads. Sing to your lady, Man. Sing to the Princess. When we get to Dinosaur, you just sing your heart out. Let the FOH man handle the fucked up pitch or whatever. That's what he gets paid to do. Okay? The sound engineers, the grips, the spotlight guy, the lighting designer… are all here to help YOU sound better and look better. So just relax and… have fun."

I continued to sing the lyrics to myself, for fear I'd forget the words. But the booze and the ganja were taking effect, and the music being played on the sound system outside, Jimmy Clift, was chilling me even more.

†

After our set was finished… "Whew! Hell-yeah! Now that was a party!" I hollered.

"You were terrific baby. Give me a kiss…. Mmmmm I want you sooo bad right now." Pam said to Kid. She acted and talked as if no one else was in the bus. *No class.*

"You were terrific, too." Caroline whispered her compliment into my ear, grabbing my arm with one hand and gently squeezing her approval.

I was grateful for Bobby's help, and the adrenaline was still running rapidly through my veins. "Man, Dude… I am so thankful to you. You made all this possible for me. There is no freakin' way I could have gotten up there without you sitting on that stool next to me. Thanks Bro." We punched each other's knuckles, and smiled.

"Nothin to it Outlaw. You did it! Not me."

"Whoever told you you couldn't sing was from another world." Caroline had become a Johnny Outlaw fan.

"Thank you, Darlin'." I returned the kiss.

Then Pam chimed in again. "Applause was pretty flat at first, when ya'll first walked out there… I was kinda worried."

"I don't think anyone really knew what was about to happen. They didn't recognize Johnny the Cowboy in his flip flops and no cowboy hat. It was like they thought you all were stage workers for a minute." Caroline stated. She had been standing back stage with Marshall and Matthew, off to the side and behind the large speakers, all during my performance.

"You were great dad." Marshall affirmed.

"Yeah, Daddy, you were great." Matthew reaffirmed.

"Thanks guys. That means a lot to me."

I continued. "But, I don't think most of these folks even know who I was. They just knew I was with Kid Rock."

"Hey, Man, by the time we got to 'Dinosaur', it didn't matter." KR smiled. But he looked exhausted. His hair was ringing wet with sweat. His eyes bloodshot.

"Kid, when you walked off stage with me, and then the drums started, and the digital preamble to 'Cowboy' kicked in... Man, people started getting up off their asses and started storming the stage."

Matthew proclaimed rather loudly, "Yeah, and Uncle Bobby when you ran out there and started screaming I thought I was going to go deaf."

"Can you hear me now? Can you hear me now Matthew? Huh?" Kid Rock, Black Bob, was transitioning now back into Bobby... Uncle Bobby.

Caroline said, "Well, it was a great show guys. But work's not done for me. I've got to make sure the clean-up is going as planned and the porta-potties get serviced tonight."

"Princess? Will I see you tonight?" I asked hurriedly.

"Oh, I hope so. But it's already ten thirty, and it'll be late by the time I'm done."

"I'd be happy to come with you, give you a hand." I said.

"You know I'd love that… but it would only cause a distraction." Caroline reached for my hand. "Your boys are wonderful. I'm glad you brought them with you."

"I wanted you to meet 'em. And them to meet you."

"Well, I hope they liked me as much as I liked them." The Farrah smile again. *God, your killing me.*

"Oh, I'm sure they do… Marshall… Matthew… come hug Miss Caroline's neck. She's gotta go do more of her work." *She's the one. She's the one in my dreams. I know she is.*

Caroline said her goodbyes to Bobby and Pamela. Scooby was just getting to the tour bus when the door opened and Caroline stepped to the ground.

"Prinnn-cessss!", Scooby was smiling his gold capped teeth. "You are doing a terrific job. Boombastic baby!"

"Thanks Scooby. I'm glad you approve. See you early tomorrow."

"Okay, so around noon then?"

I had also come out of the bus by now, shook Scooby's hand and appreciated his compliments.

Caroline insisted to Scooby, "Oh, it'll have to be a little earlier than that… around ten or so. Will you be in your bus?"

"No, I'll be going to the hotel tonight, but I'll be here in the morning in time to welcome our guests."

"Good. You know Jimmy Buffett should be flying in on his Albatross around ten or ten thirty. I understand we should expect a fly-over."

"Ok. Ten it will be. See you then." And with that Scooby stepped in his bus to call BooGoo for a ride home.

"Caroline Goodbody. Princess of my heart." I spoke low, and looked in her sea blue eyes.

"Johnny Outlaw, the Outlaw in my dreams." She spoke softly.

"I don't want to fly outa here in the morning knowing I didn't get to see you privately."

"I know, me too. I've really been looking forward to seeing you here. It's the reason I volunteered for this job… to make sure you were on the schedule… to get you here, so I could see you again."

"Then don't let the night end. Let me walk with you. I can help with the porta-potties. "

"Oh, John. You're so sweet. I see where the boys get their good lucks AND CHARM…. Tell you what… I'll try to wrap things up by midnight, and we can sit and talk for a little while, okay?"

Midnight? "Okay. Sure. I'll just hang out in the bus with the boys and I'll be waiting." I had had a long day as well. I was jet-lagged, yawning constantly, and would otherwise pass out at my hotel room.

"Still got my number?"

"Absolutely." I replied.

"Really? Why haven't you used it?" she asked.

"I was waiting for the right time."

"It's been almost a year."

"I know."

"You too busy to call?"

"Yeah… just working on being a better person."

Caroline gazed into my eyes, holding both my hands in hers, and said, "I see that." I could tell she wanted me to kiss her. I leaned down to her petite five foot three inch frame, first kissing her softly on her nose, then slowly moving my lips to hers… a quick but deliberate lip kiss, then another… and slowly I parted her lips with mine and our tongues met for the first time, slow dancing in figure eights and swirling in soft circles… we embraced one another for a couple of minutes, losing ourselves in each other and leaving the world behind.

When the kiss was over, we stood there, ten feet from Scooby's tour bus, in the green light given off from behind the stage, holding on to one another, relieved our first embrace was one to remember.

It was corny, and I knew it, but I said it anyway. "You know, deBergerack, the ugly Prince, said that 'Love enters the heart through the lips.'

She brushed my cheek with the back of her fingers, and whispered, "I'll see you in about an hour."

"I'll be here."

Caroline walked slowly away, looking back at me every couple of steps, smiling her Farrah Faucett smile, and eventually getting on her two way radio and requesting a security guard to pick her up in his golf cart.

It was about then that Bobby and Pamela and the boys came out and inquired, "You ready lover boy?"

Smiling from ear to ear, I replied, "I'm gonna wait here in the bus 'til she gets done."

"I see," Bobby responded, "how bout we take the curtain climbers with us back to the hotel. We'll put 'em to bed in your room."

"Uhm, I dunno. They can stay with me in the bus."

Pam chimed in. "Now, Johnny, do you honestly want those boys in the bus when she comes back?"

I considered it. "Yes. I do. And I think Caroline does too… So, go on now, have a good time. Be loud, be crazy, Mon! Ya'll get kicked out of the Presidentiale, ya'll just come on back here and sleep in the bus."

The hour passed slowly for me. I talked with Marshall and Matthew about the time they'd had, the things they saw, the music they heard. We wrestled around, me throwing the kids from one seat to another, tickling them and enjoying their laughter, until they were plumb tuckered out, and put them to bed in Scooby's bedroom.

"But we don't have any jammies, Daddy."

"That's okay," assured Marshall, "we're big boys now."

I was living the role of father that I'd instinctively run away from for so long. "Boys, I'm sure glad ya'll are here with me. I always miss you when I'm on the road."

Marshall rubbed his eyes, and Matthew yawned.

"I love you, Daddy."

"I love you, Daddy."

"And I love you, Marshall. I love you, Matthew." I kissed them on their foreheads as they smiled sleepy smiles, and bid them good night.

†

At midnight exactly, a gentle knock came to the door. I had already showered and was wearing only a clean pair of shorts I had tucked away in my duffle. Out of old-fashioned courtesy to the Princess, I grabbed for a clean tee shirt as well. I was still pulling it over my head when I opened the door.

"My, my… you have a very sexy core." She smiled with approval, and I held out my hand to help her up the steps.

"Sorry, I intended to be dressed when you got here." I was whispering slightly.

"Boys still with you?"

"Yes."

"Good, I would feel awful if you made them go with Bobby and Pam on my account."

"Bobby's a good man, and a good friend. I wouldn't have any concerns… I just miss 'em too much. I like knowing they're here with me, ya know."

"Good. I like that in you." She replied.

"So, how was it? Get everything ready for tomorrow's fest-ee-val?"

"I've done my part." She looked exhausted, yet wholesome and naturally pretty. Caroline excused herself to the bathroom, where she did away with the Sunshine Festival ball cap she'd worn all day, let down her hair from the pony-tail, washed her face, and talked to me as she re-did her eyes with fresh mascara and eye liner, and applied frosty pink lip gloss.

"It is soo humid these past two days. My hair is naturally curly, and this weather just wants to friz it out."

"Curly? Your hair's as straight as anybody's I ever saw."

"I do that with a hair iron."

"Don't you like it curly? Most girls would die for curly hair. Isn't that why they get perms?"

Caroline stepped out of the bathroom, walked through the kitchen area, and I motioned to her to sit next to me.

"Would you like a glass of red wine? I found some here. It's an Argentine Malbec… 'juicy fruit notes with aroma of violet."

"You speak like a wine connoisseur." She said.

"Ha, no I just read the label on the back. All I know is its red."

"Let's try it."

We sat on the same side of the black leather sofa on the roll out side of the bus, which created a kind of living room space. The lights were dim, the XM radio on the mood music station, and Caroline rested comfortably next to me, nestled under my left arm which itself clung to the upper couch cushion. I put my feet on the coffee table, and Caroline crossed hers.

"Are you driving home tonight? It's getting foggy out there."

"Oh, I'm not living here on the island anymore. I went back to Jacksonville recently."

"Oh. I see. I didn't even think about that. Sooo, you're just here for the weekend. You fly in commercial?"

"Scooby flew me here on his jet. It's a nice Gulf Stream. Very classy way to travel."

"Yes, I agree. I don't know how I'll ever fly commercial again."

"Pam mentioned you'd be going home in the morning?" Caroline inquired.

"Yeah. I guess. The boys have to get back. And I have my training to get back to."

"You look well. You've been working hard and it shows. So, are you going to start riding again?"

"Yeah, well, actually, I already have. I bought a place out in the country… way out in the country…"

"Oh really? I didn't know that? So, you're not in Carmel anymore?"

"Naw. No reason to. I sold my properties and most of my toys. Just trying to get right, manage my own life a little better."

"Marshall told me they were going to start living with you full time soon."

"Well, I hope so. Beth agreed to let me have them for the summer, but now that's coming to an end, and she hasn't made her decision about whether she's going to Europe with this Army officer she met. She wants to, but she's worried about what her family and friends would think about a woman who could leave her kids."

"What would you think?" Caroline asked.

"Well, she's raised them from the time they were newborns. She gave birth to them, postponed… even altered her dreams, if she ever had any… I think it's time for her to do what makes her happy. It's time for the boys to be with their dad. It's time for their dad to cowboy up."

"Oh, I do hope that works out for you… and them. They need you. And YOU NEED THEM."

"I know. They're everything I've done right in this world… maybe the only thing." I, in quiet tears, gulped down the emotions that were rising in my chest.

We sipped our wine from the crystal glasses I found in the cabinet, talking of childhood memories, good and bad, and mostly about Caroline's upbringing. She assured me that her parents were educated and worldly people who would not be concerned about our twenty-five year age difference, as much as my reputation. She had an older brother who could lift twice his own body weight.

"You'll like my mom and my brother will think you hung the moon when I tell him who you are. My dad, not so much."

"I can understand why your dad would be concerned."

"He's very protective. Sometimes too protective. I care what they think, and I respect their opinions, but I'm still going to do what I think is right for me. I think they'll respect my decisions, too. After all, they raised me, so they trust my instincts like I do."

"Good point." I admired her spirit.

"I thought they would have a cow when I told them I quit teaching to take a job as a television news anchor."

"You did what?"

"Yeah."

"You're a tv news babe? What station? Where?"

"WAFL In Jacksonville."

"How did that happen?"

"Well, after I saw you last year, my manager at Hooters asked if I'd compete in the Hooters International Swimsuit Pageant and represent his location. I'd already competed and won the local contest, so I was eligible."

"Well, I am absolutely thrilled for you. How'd it turn out?"

"There are eighteen thousand Hooters girls world-wide, competing in these local contests, trying to earn a spot among the one hundred girls chosen to compete for the International pageant. I never, ever thought of myself parading out in front of everyone like that. But, out of the hundred girls chosen to compete, I finished third... And I actually won the Viewer's Choice Award, which is dearest to my heart."

"Wow." I was speechless. Of course she did. I was ashamed for not expecting news such as this. Certainly, I wasn't the only person in the world to think Princess Caroline was fantastic.

I kissed Caroline again, this time harder and longer than before. My hand on her shoulder now, I pulled her into me until I could feel her heart beating against mine. I slowly placed my freehand on her breasts, and began massaging her as we kissed. She moaned quietly with wanting pleasure, our breathing getting heavier and heavier.

"Sleep here with me tonight." I posed the suggestion only between tonguing her mouth and biting her neck.

"It's not the right time."

I kept kissing, feeling, sucking and nibbling, all while wondering to myself what she meant by "not the right time".

"I want to. Believe me. But... not here... not on a bus. Not with the boys so close they can hear me screaming your name."

My cock was rock hard, and protruded in my loose fitting khaki shorts like a gourd.

"I'm sorry Johnny, I don't mean to tease you. It's just that... "

I kept kissing... nibbling... feeling.

"Mmmm.... I'm trying.... Oh God you are so good... but I just don't want this to be our first time. I've been working for about eighteen hours straight. I look a mess. I need a shower. And I've got a really long day again tomorrow… that starts in about six hours."

With that explanation, I cooled off slowly, taking another sip of wine, slightly embarrassed about the bulge in my pants. *What's the deal? This playin' hard to get thing is get'n old. Are you on the rag? Is there something wrong with you? Something amiss about your female parts? Some disease you can't tell me about? Still broken up from your last romance? What?*

"So, will we see each other again?" She could hear the aggravation in my voice.

"I don't really know, Johnny. I guess that's up to you."

Again… thoughtful silence. We could hear Matthew snoring, and Marshall telling him to rollover. We both smiled at one another. *I think this woman would be an excellent mom.*

"Ya know… I've had a few concussions in my career. Aaaand… I get these headaches. Which I try to remedy with pain killers, or pot, or alcohol…"

"Looks to me like you're mixing all of those things."

"Yeah, that's true enough. Bobby calls it a cocktail… First you pop a Xanax, then you smoke a doobie, then you start drinking. An hour later your headache's gone…"

"Along with sensory perception."

"Yeah. It alters the world a bit. But, the more you do it the more normal it becomes."

"I think that's so sad."

"Hey, it's better than not being able to function at all... besides, I'm really a nice guy. I'm not a mean drunk or anything like that."

"John, I'm not too concerned about your drug habits. You seem very normal to me. I think you're just self-medicating because you found what works and what the doctors can prescribe doesn't. But eventually, your concussions, your broken limbs, your crushed vertebrae... along with the prescription drugs, the illicit drugs, the pot, the booze... it's the lifestyle that's gonna kill you. Whether it's a stupid, crazy bull, or a car wreck at a hundred and twenty miles an hour... or whatever foolish thing you adrenaline junkies do. I don't want to watch all that."

"That's who I am. Life is so boring to me without adventure."

"Like moving to the Ozarks and becoming a rancher? Or being a father to your children? Writing your book? Aren't those adventures, too?"

I thought for a moment... "Yeah, sumpm like that." I smiled gently at Caroline, squeezed her hand softly, and looked into my wine glass.

Maybe I WAS there. Maybe I had made the turn towards

responsibility. And maybe… maybe I WAS ready to grow up… to hell with fortune and fame and all that goes with it. Although the show tonight really set me back in my progress.

My real fear, which was nearly impossible for me to face, was that of living and dying alone. I knew that the only way I could be faithful to any woman, would be to live in a far-away place where the temptations were few and far between. At the same time, I would have to have lots of land to play on, and toys to play with… motocross bikes, four wheelers, side-by sides, a swimming pool, a lake to fish and ride jet skis in… In other words, I could have no reason to leave my side of the fence for another, greener pasture.

But how to make a living in such a rural setting? And without ever leaving the area? By this time I had only three skills… growing chickens, riding bulls, and calling in airstrikes on unsuspecting enemies. The bull-riding was nearing it's end. And I had enough killing. So that left chickens. I couldn't help but laugh at the irony. I tried to picture it…

World Champion Bull Rider, Johnny Outlaw, war hero, womanizing renaissance man, now raising chickens for a living.

I remembered my oath to always do the opposite of what my father would do in most cases. This philosophy had carried me, and would carry me, to success.

So what would my father do?

He was selfish… greedy. Only cared about himself. He let the women and the lifestyle he led take priority over his own wife and child. So, the answer was now obvious. I would retire from rodeo, pay Beth for custody of the boys, ask Caroline to marry me, maybe have a child together, live and work from our own farm, and shut the world out of our lives.

Problem was, Caroline was waiting around for me to make things happen. She was a career woman, with her eyes set on big things. One day, small time WAFL, next… FOX News, or The Weather Channel. And THAT, wasn't part of my plan.

DP Fletcher

Chapter Eighteen

The Rolling Stone Interview

It was the magazine's eleven hundred sixty-eighth issue. On the cover was Taylor Swift, looking like a college freshman who just got drunk for the first time and fucked some frat-boy to death. Her mascara is smudged, and she is otherwise without make-up. She is referred to here as The Heartbreak Kid. It was a very sexy photo of the in-between, I thought, and was stoked that my name was on the cover.

One of the headlines reads **Johnny Outlaw's Wild Days**, which was clearly a gimmick, as the whole story was centered on what a domesticated and reformed outlaw I'd been lately. Inside, on pages fifty-eight through sixty-one, was the transcript of the interview by Austin Scaggs, with a few old photos thrown in.

The first picture you see is of me, the year before I met Caroline, standing next to Kid Rock backstage at one of his concerts. Bobby has a joint in his hand. Smoke surrounds us in the black and white photo. Our eyelids are half shut.

On the opposite page, a color photograph of a very together and wholesome looking family… me, Caroline holding baby Madeline, and my two college-bound sons, Marshall and Matthew. They are bigger than I am. The Princess is wearing a stunning classy brown angora dress with a conservative neckline, faux snake-skin pumps, diamond stud earrings, and a two-carat diamond solitaire on her left hand. I am in old faded Levi's and a tan sport coat with tussled hair. We are all smiling and laughing. It's my favorite picture of all time.

The printed version of the interview begins with a brief bio, beginning with my bull riding accolades, progressing through to my singing/songwriting years, and finally to the place I'm at today… farmer, businessman, writer, husband and father… not necessarily in that order.

> If I didn't know better, I'd think John Toller, a.k.a. Johnny Outlaw, was an ordinary guy. But I do know better.
>
> We are sitting in white rocking chairs on the front porch of his plantation style home deep in the beautiful Ozark Mountains, somewhere in northernmost Arkansas. I

have never been here, and quite frankly, I am surprised at its majesty, as we sit drinking sweet iced tea on a hilltop overlooking a bowl-shaped valley. John told me I'd be surprised.

John is what Caroline calls him. But when she walks away he insists I call him Johnny.

At forty-seven, Johnny looks ten years younger. I know because I'm thirty-seven, and he looks younger than I do. The Outlaw looks different now. Still tall and thin, he now wears a long beard with his shoulder length hair, and a bandana takes the place of his cowboy hat. His son, Matthew, says he looks a lot like Jesus. From the pictures I grew up with, I'd have to agree.

We have been conversing for about forty-five minutes. In this time, I met his beautiful wife, Caroline, who, by John's admission, is the prefect mate, mother and home-maker. Caroline walked away from a promising career as a Fox News correspondent and conservative talk show host to be here, and shows no signs of remorse. She insists she's not missing anything she can't get online or by airplane.

Their two sons, by John's previous marriage, Marshall and Matthew, are tall, handsome, and athletic. Marshall, the spitting image of his father, is quiet yet polite. He is preparing for his acceptance into the Reserve Officer

Training Corps at the University of Arkansas. He wants to fly jets.

Matthew is the Brad Pitt kind of good-looking. He is taller than his dad, and has sandy-brown hair. A high-school senior, he is following in his brother's footsteps in football as a linebacker. He has a 3.9 GPA, and is a high school all-American candidate. He, too, plans on an ROTC scholarship, and would like to try-out for Para-rescue.

Baby Madeline is two and a half. She is a perfect baby, full of boundless energy and personality. White blonde hair makes you wonder if she is adopted, until Caroline explains that John and Matthew both had blonde hair at that age. Madeline already knows the alphabet.

You've accomplished so many things. Your memoirs, *Everyone Has a Story to Tell*, recently hitting the New York Times best seller list, reveal an interesting transformation.

My short time in prison, as a young man, convinced me that life is fragile and often short-lived. It gave me a perspective that I only had one shot to make my mark on this world. Though fate played a part in what I became, much of my success had to do with the anger that fueled me… it propelled me forward. In other words, I used all that angst and frustration, I learned to harness it, and use it up like jet fuel whenever I was gunning for a championship, or a sponsorship, or a spokesperson deal, or a book deal… whatever.

The transformation, as you call it, happened when I decided that being angry all the time wasn't how I wanted to live. Ya know? Let's face it, ah, being angry is expensive. It costs you money… and it costs you relationships.

So, the real challenge for me was to find a new source of fuel.

What is your new source of fuel?

Look around you. I am surrounded by people who love one another. We're all happy. We are blessed with good health. We make a good income. We desire nothing more than what we have. It's this that took the place of the insanity that plagues an outlaw's life.

In your book, you talk about your friendship with Kid Rock. He's still out there doing the rock star thing, and you're out here… farming. Do you ever miss life on the road?

(Johnny laughs.) Well, first of all, he's not out there replaying the Destroy Your Liver Tour. Kid flies home to his farm between shows. So…

Besides, we may look tame around here, but we still get out from time to time.

Do I miss it? Yeah, sure, sometimes. I miss the attention. I miss the craziness. The spontaneity. But, whenever I start feeling that way, I grab the ol' lady and we hit the road on my Harley.

I heard you've been laying off the marching powder and weed, is that true?

Damn boy! I wasn't ever in to coke. That's Kid on that one. Weed… now that's my thing. It keeps my adrenaline addiction under control. Naw, I don't do any of that shit like I used to. These days, I'm drinkin' with my buddies and, I'm like such a lightweight. Back when we were runnin' hard, the drugs kind of balanced out the alcohol I guess. Back then we could run for days. Now, I'm in bed by ten o fuckin' clock.

Would you like to plug your apparel business?

Well, yeah. Thanks. You know Caroline and I started an online apparel business called Outlaw Moto Concepts. We design and market t-shirts with biker themes. And we've gotten into selling koozies and hats, jackets, shit like that. It's fun. We get to travel to the motorcycle rallies and sell stuff and meet new people. It's something we get to do together.

Aaaand, on that same website… OutlawMoto.biz, you can purchase my book and musical CD as well. So… yeah, thanks for letting me say that.

You've got a wonderful family. You served your country, with distinction I might add. You've been world bull riding champion multiple times. You've written, played and recorded your own music. You've played on stage in front of thousands of people. You've appeared on numerous tv shows. You're a published author, on the Best Seller's list. You operate this large farming enterprise. You have an online apparel business. What's your next big project?

I don't know, quite honestly. My family, of course, will continue to be my priority in life. Farming is kind of a never-ending thing. And I really do enjoy it. Other than maybe writing again, I don't see any big things in our future, other than watching our kids grow into good American citizens.

I expect the interview requests to slow considerably as I grow more boring with age. But, then again, Caroline is okay with that. And what the Princess wants the Princess gets.

If you've learned only one lesson in life, what is it?

Don't let anybody tell you that you can't do whatever it is that you want to accomplish. If you want to do something great, then work hard and do your best. At the same time, keep your family at the forefront. You can't sacrifice them to get what you want and expect happiness.

About the Author

D.P. Fletcher earned his bachelor's degree in English and History from Louisiana State University. He served with distinction in the United Sates Air Force, attached to the Army First Special Forces Group at Ft. Lewis, Washington. He is a veteran of the Gulf War, the Bosnian War, and two African campaigns.

His father, Nolan Toller, is one of the founding fathers of the Louisiana State Penitentiary at Angola Annual Convict Rodeo, one of the longest running and most successful of its kind. Fletcher, by coincidence, rose through the ranks of professional rodeo, specializing in the bull riding event, winning several championships along the way. His first book, Fletcher's Fundamentals of Bull Riding, sold more than thirty thousand copies before being taken out of publication.

Later, he joined the corporate world of executive management, rising to the position of Human Resources Director for the largest poultry company in America.

Currently, he owns and operates a successful, family run farm and ranch operation in the Ozarks of Arkansas, and writes in his spare time. With the completion of his first novel, Vicariously Me, he is currently working on a book of short stories.

Additionally, Fletcher has just completed his first musical studio album with his band, called Johnny Sometimes.

His greatest accomplishment is his family. He is married to the former Miss Stephanie Hayter of Ocala, Florida. Together they are raising three children ranging in ages from three to eighteen… Wyatt, Rex and Madeline.

Words From the Author

I was born into a normal baby-boomer family. My father was constantly searching for himself. He wasn't part of the great generation that fought World War Two, and he sure as hell didn't want to fight in Vietnam. His favorite movie was Easy Rider, with Peter Fonda and Dennis Hopper. Harleys on an open road, free of responsibilities and government establishment bullshit. My mother wanted equal rights and liberation from male oppression. At the same time, she wanted a loyal, conservative husband, like her father was, and five kids. She ended up divorced with one kid, and had to work two jobs sometimes, while my father ran whores and motorcycles. See, told you… normal stuff.

Fortunately, there were other people and influences in my life that taught me about God, Country, Family… in that order. I learned that there are consequences to my actions. Sometimes big and everlasting consequences.

Through life's lessons, I have learned much about what is important.

I've learned that a man without a moral compass is void of spiritual direction and destined for unhappiness.

I've learned to accept my weaknesses, face them head on, and avoid situations I am not strong enough to handle.

I've learned that next to God, family is most important. They are the ones I will take care of, and they will take care of me.

I've learned that the United States of America is the greatest nation on earth, and it's our constitution that makes it so. I can and will fight to defend it, and the freedoms we enjoy because of it.

Made in the USA
Middletown, DE
08 December 2022

17359782R00229